THE DYING MAN

The body that lay twisted on the hard stone paving slabs seemed unrecognizable as the vicar. Wearing ordinary gray trousers and a V-neck pullover, out of his church uniform he was no longer a representative of a higher power, but just a person, vulnerable and so pathetically human. Hearing Simon letting out a long shaky breath beside her, Alex absorbed the details, her eyes and brain working together against her need not to know, not to see.

"Still alive…he's still alive." Simon stared as the vicar's eyelids fluttered open. Alex fell to the ground, kneeling in the man's blood, her heart pounding in her chest with hope. Reverend Baker coughed; a weak, wet sound that sent a shiver up Alex's spine, and spots of blood appeared on his teeth as he opened his mouth, his breath raw and sweetly rotten.

"Shhh. Don't try and speak. Don't try and speak." Her own eyes were blurring with tears, but she could see that the vicar's were so full of pain he couldn't even focus. When he whispered, he sent his words somewhere between her and Simon, as if a ghost had joined them that only he could see.

"Melanie Parr…."

Other *Leisure* books by Sarah Pinborough:

BREEDING GROUND
THE RECKONING
THE HIDDEN

THE TAKEN

SARAH PINBOROUGH

LEISURE BOOKS NEW YORK CITY

This one is going out for the girls:
For Liz who's living it large in the States, and for Sam
who's hotting up the beaches in Dubai. Live your dreams,
ladies, and thanks for being such fab friends.

Also for Jan and Peggy, for quietly supporting my writing.
It doesn't go unnoticed!

A LEISURE BOOK®

April 2007

Published by

Dorchester Publishing Co., Inc.
200 Madison Avenue
New York, NY 10016

ISBN-10: 0-8439-5896-0
ISBN-13: 978-0-8439-5896-6

The name "Leisure Books" and the stylized "L" with design are trademarks of Dorchester Publishing Co., Inc.

Printed in the United States of America.

Visit us on the web at www.dorchesterpub.com.

We may be dead and we may be gone
But we will be, we will be, we will be, right by your side
Until the day you die.

This is no easy ride.

—The Smiths

THE TAKEN

CHAPTER ONE

The air hung invisibly heavy, dragging downward from the sky, its weight almost humming with the tension of an approaching breaking point. There was a storm brewing, the kind that hadn't come to this sleepy part of Somerset for years, or so it seemed to Mary as she wheeled the last barrowful of mowed grass to the compost heap, or "compost mountain," as she liked to call it, glad that at sixty she was still able to do these things for herself without a twinge or an ache. She smiled. Well, maybe just one or two nagging aches that set in a little later, but never too painful to dull her warm glow of satisfaction; in a weird way, maybe they even heightened it slightly.

Despite the discomfort caused by sweat that clung to her like a second skin unwilling to be shed, Mary's spirits were high. After getting Paul's party decorations up, Alexandra would be making them both a cool gin and tonic, waiting for her aunt to come in and be amazed at what could be done with a few streamers and balloons if you had that special creative touch, and maybe her smile would light up a little like it used to in the days before Ian left. Twenty-seven was too young to be carrying that much pain around with you like lead on your back, and Mary feared the strain was beginning to show. Her niece had lost weight over the last few months, and it seemed at times that Alex had become a reserved shadow of her former self, all that beauty and brightness bound up inside, afraid to be released. Maybe Paul coming would do her some good; maybe she'd open up to him.

Pushing the low-hanging leafy branches aside, Mary wheeled the barrow forward into the hidden space that Paul had called "Pooh Corner" when he'd been little—a long time ago now, her bouncing boy was forty today—preparing her shoulders and thighs for the sudden push up the side of the heap of fresh grass to dump her load over the back.

Out of the corner of her eye, in that space where on clear winter mornings the light came pushing through the far side of the trees like one of those crazy laser shows, she could make out the worn shapes of the headstones in the graveyard on the other side of her land. Sometimes the peaceful sight of them would make her stop and think about the nature of time, and how it sped past so quickly, the questions bubbling in her brain. Where had those years gone between when Paul was ten and now, and would he bury her there amongst family and strangers when her race came to its inevitable end?

Yes, sometimes it would make her stop and think. But not this time. This time her eyes froze like the rest of her, confused for a moment, vision fixed on the pile of grass. No, not the grass at all, but what was on top of it, what hadn't been there ten minutes before when she'd emptied the lawnmower last, and what shouldn't, *couldn't* possibly be there. Her shaking arms released the metal barrow, which banged heavily into her knee as it dropped, and deep in her mind she knew there'd be a nasty black bruise blooming there the next day, but right then, right in that silent moment of stopped time, she couldn't feel a thing as the past raced forward to meet the silent, twisted present.

The small red sandal sat on the bed of sweet-smelling cuttings, polished and shining, untarnished by mud or blades of murdered grass, as if deposited from above, a gift from the angels. Staring at the shoe that had been out of fashion for thirty years, Mary felt her breath catch in her throat. So time was moving, not stopped at all, but pouring out slowly like glue, savoring itself, allowing Mary the possibility of seeing everything, every color in the trees, the leaves and the thousands of different shades in the leather. Who could have put it there? Who would have? No one. Not after all this time. Needing to touch it, needing to feel its reality, its dead flesh next to her skin, she reached slowly forward, her hand shakily stretching out into the tunnel of her vision.

The giggle slashed the silence and Mary spun round, a whimper escaping her. Branches rustled, first to her left, and then moving back behind her, back to the other side of the compost heap, where the long, tired limbs of the trees almost touched the ground of the graveyard, no hedge required to define the boundary. Slowly turning, her feet shuffling over the dead wood, Mary's eyes widened. *It can't be. It just can't be.*

3

At the bottom of the crippled tree in front of her, in the gap between branches and the hallowed ground, she could see the lower half of a small girl, dressed in a perfectly pleated green kilt, the upper torso hidden from view.

The scalpel of memory sliced into her brain, sharp and painful. The giggle came again as Mary's eyes dragged themselves down, past the pink skin of young almost-chubby knees, to the high white socks, and then downward, knowing what she was going to see, one foot shoeless, the other strapped up in a perfectly polished red sandal. Standing and staring at this surreal snapshot, something stirred inside Mary, a coiled snake waiting to strike, and if her frozen face could have moved, she would have frowned. The terrible familiarity of the clothes and the shoes itched inside Mary and she could almost taste the child's name in her mouth before she whispered it.

"Melanie Parr."

The giggle came again from somewhere out of sight, and Mary moved to take a step backward, to get help, help for or from what she didn't know. The voice that came through the branches lilted childishly.

"I lost my shoe, Mary. Have you got it? Have you got my shoe? I'm cold without it. You've made me cold, Mary." The reproach in the voice was clear, the sentiment jarring with the young giggle.

Shrieking, Mary stumbled over a branch behind her and fell forcefully to the dry ground, the shudder that spread through her bones making her bite down on her tongue, her mouth filling with the taste of metal as she bled.

"I've come back, can't you see?" The quiet voice

barely carried in the heavy air, but Mary flinched as she listened. "I've come back home. The Catcher Man brought me home."

As the giggles got louder and harsher, too harsh for a ten-year-old, *a forty-year-old ten-year-old*, Mary knew that if she didn't get away right then she never would, she'd go crazy, really never-come-back-down crazy, and squeezing her eyes shut, she dragged herself backward until she was out of the wall of branches and in the fresh air of her garden, pulling herself to her numbed, heavy feet and running like she hadn't in years, letting the scream trapped inside her out, giving it free rein in the humid air, knowing that no matter how hard she yelled, it would never be able to take all of the madness with it.

Chapter Two

The party decorations hung bright around the farm-house lounge, their cheerfulness all out of place, and Alex wished she'd thought to rip them down before Mary's son Paul had got there. Not that she'd really had a moment to. By the time she'd checked the gardens for herself and called the doctor for Mary, it was clear that her aunt needed her by her side. Dr. Jones had left an hour before, leaving her only minutes to ring around and hastily cancel guests before her cousin's car pulled up the graveled drive, Paul and his friend Simon climbing out of the MG clutching bottles of champagne and wearing beaming grins that didn't fade until they were close enough to read Alex's taut expression.

Still, she thought, as her eyes rested on the unspun glitter ball hanging from the central oak beam, she should have pulled them down. This wasn't the kind of birthday welcome Paul had been expecting, but, hey, when does life ever deliver what you expect?

Cursing herself for the bitterness in the thought, she

picked up the decanter, poured out three large brandies, and sighed. Hopefully Aunt Mary would be sleeping by now. She'd looked like she might be when Alex had poked her head inside the door a few minutes before, and the doctor had given her a shot of something that must have been pretty strong because her Aunt had calmed down pretty much the instant the needle came out of her arm. He'd left some sleeping pills just in case, but didn't think Mary would need them. Not that night anyway.

Alex hadn't liked the way he'd suggested that maybe she should try them herself. As if sleeping pills could help her. Well, maybe they could, but she hadn't liked the expression on his face when he'd suggested it. Too much kindness. Too much pity. She'd pretty much booted him out the door after that. *Frozen him out* would have been more like it. She smiled a little. There was still some spirit left inside her after all.

Turning her mind back to the present, she handed the two men a glass each and took a sip from her own, enjoying the burn. Paul's face was full of worry, the lines etched into his skin making him seem older than his FORTY TODAY badge declared he was. She met his gaze as she spoke.

"There was nothing there. I went and looked for myself straight away. I searched the whole garden and the orchard—I even checked the barns. Nothing." She shrugged. "I guess a child could have run away quickly, but I'm sure I'd have seen her if she'd been there."

Alex felt awkward talking about this in front of a stranger, but glancing at the tall man next to her cousin, it seemed as if Simon's concerned expression was pretty genuine. And this couldn't be too comfortable for him, either.

Paul sat down on the sofa by the unlit fireplace and stared into its lifeless heart. "Did you call the police?"

"And say what? No. It would have to be a local girl to play a trick like that, and nearly all the kids around here are either teenagers or toddlers. It's not as if the village has got the largest population in the country. We're not exactly on the beaten track out here. I don't think Watterrow is even featured on maps outside of Somerset."

She perched on the wing of the armchair and nodded at Simon to take the other sofa seat. Noticing how blue his direct gaze was behind his glasses, Alex thought that in another lifetime she might have been tempted to pay him a little more attention. Handsome, but not too handsome. Charming in an unaffected way. Despite his almost boyish face, she figured he was maybe only a couple of years younger than Paul. Thirty-six, thirty-seven? Yeah, who am I she trying to kid? she thought. In another lifetime, she'd have been upstairs in the bathroom frantically reaching for her lipstick. The wistful thought was bittersweet and she pushed it away, suddenly rebelliously pleased that she hadn't had time to change into her party dress and do her hair. The romance days were over; she couldn't escape that and it was easier for her just not to be noticed. She didn't want his attention.

"Anyway, it was weirder than that. I mean, she was hysterical, but I think she knew the girl. She was screaming a name. I couldn't catch it because she was pretty incoherent, but I'm sure she was trying to tell me a name." She paused and shrugged. "I just wish I could understand why it upset her so much. A shoe and a girl, and that's if there was anything out there at all. I don't get it. I just don't get it."

A shadow passed across Paul's face. "How's she been? Has she been all right otherwise?"

Alex could see the fear in her cousin—the fear people carry with them for their elderly loved ones. Although the way she figured it, the fear was more for themselves than for any mother or father—fear of dealing with the loss, of having to watch the suffering, of being forced to face the inevitable future that comes cold, bleak, and inconsequential, stealing away our tomorrows with the blink of a random eye, with no "get out of jail free" card, no matter how special you think you are. Seeing all that in Paul's expression, Paul, who had lost his painful childhood shyness to become a chubby, confident, successful newsman with the world at his feet, made Alex's insides ache. She had a feeling she'd somehow got older than Paul in the last few months.

"She's been fine. Look, let's not blow this out of all proportion. Sometimes people just think they see things that aren't there. She'd been out in this sticky heat all afternoon gardening and she was really excited about you coming home. On top of that, she didn't have her glasses on. Your eyes and brain can play funny tricks on you from time to time. There doesn't always have to be a reason."

"She's right, mate."

Alex looked up and felt a vague disappointment that Simon didn't glance at her while he spoke, his slight London accent dancing in step with the depth of his tone.

"I know what it's like when I don't wear mine." He

nodded out the window. "Especially in this kind of weather. The whole world is different. Everything looks strange." He smiled a cheeky, innocent grin. "You'd laugh at some of the things I've thought I'd seen, only to find out the monster is just a sweater I'd chucked behind the sofa or something."

Paul stared at his friend for a second, his serious expression unreadable. He shook his head before he spoke, almost with disappointment. "Let me get this straight. You're a hard-hitting foreign correspondent, and you still believe in monsters behind the sofa? And you're trying to make me feel better? Now I've got two people to worry about. Fantastic."

Simon threw his head back and laughed, a throaty open sound, and Alex found herself joining in, not able to do anything but, and within seconds the three of them were giggling like kids, maybe more than the joke deserved, but enjoying the breaking of the somber tension. Her own breath hitching as she laughed, she watched Paul snorting into his brandy and felt so happy to see him again, the warmth bubbling up inside her. It was good to see him, despite the afternoon's events, despite *everything,* and it was good to feel good.

A big part of her had been dreading the weekend, the energy of it all, the pretending to be fine, but now that it had arrived, now that Paul was there, she was glad she hadn't taken the decorations down. Glad she'd made the effort. Paul was the closest thing to a big brother that she had, and she loved him and Mary more than anyone in the world. Pushing herself off the armchair, she grabbed him around the neck and kissed him, hoping he wouldn't notice the tears finding life in her eyes.

"Happy fortieth, Paul. Happy birthday."

CHAPTER THREE

The ravenous thunder prophesied the damage seconds before lightning flashed bright and ripped through the dark countryside sky. Alex hastily swallowed a couple of large pills with a gulp of red wine and pushed the packet back into the depths of her jeans pocket before leaving the kitchen and joining the two men gazing out of the patio doors at Mother Nature's fireworks. Mary was still sleeping, but the three of them had fried themselves steaks and eaten them with mushrooms and heaps of salad, before slicing open Paul's chocolate cake. Alex had sent the other two away to the lounge while she loaded the dishwasher, and it was seconds afterward that the storm had arrived over the village, the men turning out the lights to fully see the dazzling show above their heads.

Despite the exhaustion that filled her thin frame and the pain that was creeping back, niggling at her insides, the pills a reminder of its unwanted presence, she stood breathless for a second, her eyes no doubt glowing in wonder like those of Paul and Simon beside her. For a few moments they had been transported back to their childhoods, a time when pleasure and fascination could be found in the simplest things. Light exploded ahead of her, stabbing downward into the dark fields that surrounded them, and she hoped that old Tucker had brought his animals in. Nothing should have to face such angry beauty, no sheep or cow, however doomed to slaughter, should be out there on a night like this, shivering and helpless and full of fear. Not on a night like this. This was a night when *anything* could happen. Anything at all. The world was off-kilter, this time not just for her, but for everyone. She could feel it crawling on her skin.

Behind the noise of the battle that raged above them was the steady thrum of the rain hitting the glass and the ground outside, a noise more like that of the harsh hammering of hailstones than the normal gentle patter. Despite the warmth inside the old house, Alex shivered. The world had gone wild outside, unrecognizable from the sedate, gentle and ordered country of yesterday. For some reason, when she spoke, her words came out in a whisper.

"I can't remember ever seeing it like this. If it goes on too long, the river will flood like it did in '89." She smiled up at her cousin. "Do you remember, Paul? Everyone the other side of The Rock was trapped. The road was completely submerged. You piggybacked me through the water. I thought it was wonderful."

Paul's teeth shone in the gloom as he grinned. "Yes, I remember. You were only about ten. Skinny little thing with that awful fringe. I think I'd just finished University.

Must have been when I'd got that job on the terrible local rag."

"Does the river flood often?" The ice tinkled in the glass as Simon sipped his whisky, and feeling him looking at her rather than her cousin, Alex fought the pleasant tingle that threatened to overrun her body. She shook her head.

"No, not really. A little bit most years, but not like that. I don't think it ever broke its banks like that before or since." She smiled up at him. "Until tonight, maybe."

"There was one other time."

The papery voice behind them was so unexpected that Alex almost dropped her wine.

"When Paul was ten. The day before his birthday, in fact. Thirty years ago. The river came alive that time. Nothing could stop it. Nothing. The whole village was cut off for days."

"Jesus shit, Mum."

Almost giggling at the childlike tone in Paul's voice, Alex turned. The sight of her aunt stopped the laughter dead, aborted it in her throat. Mary had aged twenty years or more since going outside to mow the lawns that afternoon. That energetic, smiling woman, defiant of the restrictions of age, had gone, and Alex felt with a cold certainty that sent a wave of nausea through her that she was gone for good. In her place stood a stranger: a fragile, elderly woman clad only in a sleeveless cotton nightie, the flesh of her upper arms hanging loosely from her bones, the skin on her face sagging downward as if having given up the fight to stay lifted and young. Her eyes seemed too wide as she gazed out past the living and into the night.

"Are you okay, Mary?"

Not getting any reply, Alex glanced up at Paul, but he didn't move, so she reached for his hand, as much for her own comfort as for his. Simon had gone to the other side of the room to where the light switches were, but as he reached for them Mary's shrill voice stopped his hand.

"No! No lights!"

Simon looked over at Paul and then Alex, who shrugged at him. If Mary didn't want light, then that was fine. No lights. Looking at her barely recognizable aunt she ached inside—a long, tired, cold ache that filled the hollow inside her. There wasn't much more she could take. There wasn't much more left in her to give herself, let alone Mary. It made her feel bad, but it was the truth and there was nothing she could do about it. What the hell had happened today? What had Mary seen out there?

At least she was calm and coherent, something Alex hadn't really expected. Taking a seat on the sofa, she pulled Paul down beside her and glanced around for Simon, who had vanished. Where had he gone? She smiled humorlessly inside. Probably got back in that flash little car and shot off at a hundred miles an hour, storm or no storm, and she wouldn't blame him for it. They probably seemed like a bunch of crazies to him. And he didn't even know the half of it. Yeah, that was it. He'd gone back to London. Back to sanity.

When he came back into the room carrying a tray with a mug and a plate on it a tear pricked the back of her eye and she rubbed at it angrily. There were too many tears these days and no point in them.

"There you go." Simon's voice was gentle as he set the tea and sandwich down on the small table next to

Mary's chair before withdrawing quietly back to his seat a little away from Alex and Paul, as if aware of his intrusion in this mad family reunion.

Watching his broad frame sinking into the shadows, a dark outline in the gray, Alex found herself wondering about this quiet man whom Paul obviously held in high enough regard to bring home. Her cousin never brought colleagues back to the farm; it was his sanctuary against London and all its harshness, and Alex sometimes thought that as much as he obviously loved journalism, Paul had no love for journalists and their inherent ruthless arrogance. Yes, there must be something about this man, something special, for Paul to have felt okay about inviting him along for his birthday. She let out a short sigh. He wouldn't be so eager to do that again. Not after today.

Mary shifted slightly in the armchair, one hand rising slowly to her hair, absently fiddling with a loose strand, ignoring the food and drink beside her. "Yes," she said calmly, her head tilting slightly as her soft words cracked through the silence. "Yes, thirty years ago the river rose and burst its banks, washing them away to nothing, just like it's probably doing tonight out there in the dark." She seemed to be speaking more to herself than anyone else. "Funny how I could have forgotten the weather that day. I should have thought of it. I should have felt it this morning." Pausing, she let out a small unsettling sound, somewhere between a sigh and a giggle that sent a shiver down Alex's spine. "Today had the same smell as that day. Sweet and heavy. How did I forget?" Her hand had left her hair, but still hovered, forgotten. "The little girl in the garden was Melanie Parr."

The change in direction confused Alex slightly, but

Paul's hand twitched violently in hers before he withdrew it, making her look up at him. The name meant nothing to her, but it obviously did to Paul. He drained his glass before speaking, spitting the words out like chunks of ice.

"Don't be ridiculous. It couldn't have been." Although her son was glaring at her, Mary was oblivious, gazing out into the night, a small, scared smile on her face. "Melanie Parr . . . That child could have been anyone, if there was a girl there at all." Paul's voice lowered to a mutter. "You're sounding like a crazy person."

Alex looked from cousin to aunt, her curiosity rising despite herself, hating the feeling that she was suddenly as much an outsider as Simon. What had got into Paul, anyway? He never spoke to Mary like that, never. Why do it now when she'd had such a terrible day? She reached for his arm. "Who's Melanie Parr?"

"She was in my class at school." He wasn't looking at her, and Alex frowned slightly as she heard a hint of his long forgotten stutter behind his words. How could the mention of one name shake his confidence like that?

"It was a long time ago. I barely remember what she looked like. I'd forgotten about her."

Watching him gazing into the bottom of his glass, Alex rejected his words. She didn't believe him, and that realization felt as if the breath had been punched from her lungs. Her cousin had never lied to her, but she knew with the insight granted to those with nowhere left to hide that he was lying to her now. Paul closed her off; her gaze was drawn back to her aunt. Mary was nodding at nothing in particular, as if someplace where only she was, everything was making sense. One finger teased her bottom lip as she spoke.

"She was a beautiful little girl. So perfect to look at. Of course, things that look so right invariably aren't. They can't be. Something is normally broken inside." She looked up at Alex directly this time, her eyes almost *too* full of clarity. "Like your mother. So gifted, so talented." Her gaze drifted to the grand piano that had been an ornamental relic since its owner had wasted away in the cottage at the other end of the village twenty-three years ago.

"And yet so *unmeant* to be."

Unmeant to be. Alex felt the fear of reality biting at her stomach and pushed it back, down into the very pit of herself, where it had lived and grown each day for months. She felt Simon's blue eyes fighting through the enveloping gloom to reach her, but didn't acknowledge him. Pity would be plentiful soon enough; she didn't want or need any extra now. Her mother was just a vague, elusive memory. A phantom. Mary and Paul, they were who'd raised her, all she'd ever had until Ian had come along and they'd dared to have dreams of a family of their own. Well, Ian had turned out to be a spineless bastard and the dreams had been sucked away from her like dust thrown against the wind. Yeah, Mary and Paul—they were all that mattered. There had never really been any space for the ghost of her mother, and certainly not now. She had been gone too long. So much dirt under the ground just a few hundred feet away in the old churchyard.

Paul got up and refilled his glass, his movement awkward and stiff, as if all his muscles were taut. "She wasn't like Aunt Alicia. N-n-n-not like her at all."

Shaking her head, Mary stared at her son's back.

"Maybe not, but she was damaged all the same." Her eyes misted over, drawn back to the night outside. "She went missing on the day of that storm thirty years ago. No one ever found her. She disappeared as if she'd never existed. Most people decided she must have fallen into the river and drowned, but no one ever knew for sure. No body, no solution." Her breath seemed labored for a second. "All they found was one of her shoes. A red sandal. On the steep bank on the edge of the woods. It was amazing it wasn't washed away."

Alex's heart contracted. "Poor thing. No one should have to die alone and afraid. Especially a child." Her voice was barely above a whisper as she imagined the icy water beating the small girl into unconsciousness before sucking her into its fluid depths, any small cries for help lost in the rage around her. "She must have been terrified."

"Yes, she must." Mary nodded, but even through the shadows the satisfied, smug expression that seemed so contrary to the words was visible on her haggard face. "Yes, she must." For a long moment she said nothing more, the silence filled only with the rattle of nature at the windows, invisible greedy fingers seeking out any gap in the defenses of their fragile stronghold of brick and thatch.

"It was her I saw in the garden today. Melanie Parr. She's come back."

Paul spun round, taking angry strides toward his mother's shrunken figure, one shaking hand pointing at her. "No! That's not possible. She's dead." He grabbed Mary's shoulders. "She died thirty years ago. Jesus Christ, Mum!"

Only one step behind him, Simon gently but firmly pulled Paul back to the sofa. "Take it easy, mate. Take it easy." Despite his apparent calm, Alex knew that her cousin's friend must have been shocked at his outburst. He had to be. She was. She'd never seen him act like that.

He's scared. Scared half to death. She watched Paul let out a deep trembling breath. *Yeah, that's scared to death. That's something I can recognize. Why should he be so afraid? He should be calming his mother down, not adding to the hysteria.*

Mary, however, seemed unaware of her son's protests as her eyes narrowed thoughtfully. "I should have known it was her. The minute I saw that shoe. I should have known. She said the Catcher Man brought her back." Her smile was edged with a frown.

Sitting on the edge of the settee, Simon leaned forward, the fingers of his large hands linking together. "Who's the Catcher Man?"

Despite himself, Alex could see he was getting drawn into the story. He was, after all, a journalist. Stories were their life's blood, and when he'd spoken this time, like the professional he was, he'd stolen the question from her lips.

"The Catcher Man doesn't exist," Paul said. "A long time ago he was a pagan figure that women who were having difficulty getting pregnant would go out in the rain and do various rituals to in order to conceive. But over the centuries his myth changed until he became something parents used to control their kids. Like a bogeyman. Don't wander off or the Catcher Man will get you. He steals lost children and then they're never found. That kind of thing. Silly stuff to make you behave." Paul just sounded tired now, as if his small outburst had drained his reserves.

Slightly confused, Alex scanned the memories of her childhood. "I don't remember that one."

"You wouldn't, dear. After Melanie Parr disappeared no one wanted to tell it anymore. The threat had become real, you see. It appeared as if the Catcher Man had come to life. That's what the children thought and they were scared enough after that. We didn't need the story anymore. We didn't have the stomach for it."

Paul placed his empty glass on the coffee table in front of him. "Anyway, none of this matters. Whatever or whoever it was you saw in the garden, it wasn't Melanie Parr. She's been gone for thirty years. Dead and gone, more than likely."

Alex glared at Paul, annoyed and confused by this sudden stranger beside her, before speaking softly herself.

"He's right, you know, Mary. It couldn't have been that little girl. There are no such things as ghosts." She swallowed hard, her mouth dry. "The dead are gone. You know that."

Her aunt's laugh drifted pity across to her. "Are they, Alex? Are they really? The ghosts live inside us; that's what I think. The dead never really leave us in peace." Her voice floated away, as if disembodied. "Sometimes, they feel so close I'm not sure where they end and we begin."

Alex shivered despite herself, and she was sure that next to her, Paul did the same.

"I don't think this sitting around in the dark is doing any of us any good." Simon had stood up and made his way to the far wall, flicking on the switches and filling the room with the relief of light. This time Mary didn't protest, but blinked, confused. Simon retook his seat and leaned forward.

"Listen, Mary. Alex and Paul are right. There are no such things as ghosts. But people do play tricks. Stupid tricks." He held his gaze steady, and Alex could see that he was calming her aunt with just his easy manner and gentle honesty. "Would anyone in the village want to play a trick on you? Do any of the children know about Melanie Parr's disappearance? Is there any way they could have found out about it recently? Kids can find all the wrong things funny sometimes."

"No. No one knows. No one could know. No one talked about it. Not *after*. It was easier to forget it ever happened." Mary smiled at some private joke squirming inside her. "We forgot it ever happened."

Moving to the chair, Alex sat on the arm and took her aunt's cold hand and slowly rubbed some warmth into to it. "It'll all seem better in the morning. Once this storm has passed. It's too easy to be afraid in the dark." She knew the truth in those words only too well. Since sleep had started deserting her, she and the night had formed an uneasy truce, but despite their growing familiarity, she often felt terror gnawing at her in those silent hours spent listening to time ticking by. Feeling the chill in her heart and her aunt's hand, staring out at storm, she knew that some things didn't get better in daylight. They just hid themselves well.

CHAPTER FOUR

It wasn't long after that conversation that they'd all headed off to bed, leaving the storm to continue without its audience. The atmosphere amongst them had changed after the conversation about the missing girl, and Alex was too tired to either deal with or think about Paul's sudden black mood. Whatever had happened with that Melanie Parr all those years ago had obviously affected him more than he was willing to let on, but if he didn't want to talk about it then that was up to him. She was sure they'd all feel better in the morning. Swallowing two more tablets of morphine, she crawled beneath her duvet. Well, all of them but her, that was. There would be no feeling better for her. Maybe an occasional "feeling better than yesterday," or "better than last week," but there was no *getting better* in her future. It was a downward slope ahead; the doctor had been particularly clear on that point. For the millionth time of the day, she bit back the panic and the tears and the self-pity until they settled down in the pit of her gut, not quite gone, but manageable.

You're still here now, girl. That's all that matters. One day at a time.

The duvet was cool as she pulled it under her chin, although the air in the room was muggy. Normally she would sleep with the window open, enjoying the feel of any breeze, especially on the warm summer nights. It was funny the simple things that she had learned to value, to appreciate for the first time after a lifetime of barely being aware of their existence, and a gentle breeze on a hot night was one of those things.

The air felt funny and she could smell the dampness in it, but it wasn't the normal clean damp of the country; it tasted almost dirty as she breathed it through her mouth. But then, maybe that was just the morphine, another one of its weird side effects. Sometimes, more and more as the days passed, she would get strange sensations in her skin, as if maybe a cat had brushed against her leg or someone was gently squeezing her arm, but there would be nothing there. Nothing but just another sign that her body was breaking down. Every day it seemed there was something new to deal with and soon she wasn't going to be able to hide it from people, especially Mary. She wasn't looking forward to that. That switch from being normal to being *other* in everyone else's eyes. Someone to be treated differently. Someone dying. As if it were never going to happen to them. But then, she'd never really contemplated it happening to her until it did. Life was like that. A motherfucker that kicked you in the face when you least expected it. Swearing was another thing that she'd learned to appreciate. The sheer rebelliousness of it helped with the fear.

Unmeant to be. That's what Mary had said about her mother. Was that the legacy that Alicia had passed through her blood to Alex? The doctor had said that the cancer hadn't been hereditary, but who really knew. Maybe it was all just in the blood, little genetic time bombs waiting to go off when you least expect it. It had happened to her mother and now it was happening to her. The morphine and sedative were taking hold and for the first time in a long time, as she drifted into her restless sleep, she allowed her mind to wonder about the dead woman buried in the churchyard so very close, and just as she passed into unconsciousness Alex thought she could see her in a faded memory laughing over her bed. Or on reflection, maybe she was crying. There wasn't enough time to decide which before the blackness overwhelmed her.

"Don't you remember me? I couldn't move my legs. Look how they move now!"

Alex woke up with a start, her breath caught in her throat, her eyes immediately glancing around in the gloom for whatever had disturbed her. What was that? What had woken her so suddenly? Her hair sticking to her scalp with sweat, she pushed it out of her face as she sought out the glowing hands of the clock beside her bed. Three o'clock in the morning. *Fuck.* Her breathing slowing, she lay back down on the pillow, waiting for her internal disquiet to ease.

It must have been another dream. As if she weren't getting enough of those these days. Another side effect of the drugs were the nightmares. They normally involved people trying to bury her when she was dead, pushing her back into a coffin and whispering, *"Relax, your time is up,*" and her screaming back at them that she was fine, she was still there, right up until they nailed the lid down and she would wake up, stifling a scream. Yeah, morphine couldn't kill all your pain; that was for sure.

The air still felt heavy and her mouth felt furry. Pushing herself up on her elbow, she took a sip from the water that had warmed in the glass by the bed. It was odd that she didn't remember the dream, though. Shaking some of her sleepiness away, she waited for her body to calm down. It wasn't real. Whatever had woken her wasn't real, just her ridiculous drug-fueled imagination. Still, she thought, lying back down, maybe not remembering was a blessing sometimes. There was only so much terror a girl could take. She could hear the rain still beating hard at the window, aggressively tossed at the glass by the wind. Maybe that was what had woken her. Or maybe Paul or Simon had got up to use the bathroom. The thought of the house full of other people was a comforting one, and she shut her eyes to try and get at least another two or three hours sleep.

The giggle came from the other side of the room, a little girl's laugh, and this time Alex sat bolt upright. *What the fuck was that?* Her heart began to pick up the pace again and her head darted to the noise as the lilting laugh came again, this time from her wardrobe. And then a few moments later from *outside* the window. Her spine rigidly straight, it felt as if she couldn't breathe, let alone move, but Alex could feel sweat forming on the palms of her hands as she gripped her duvet, ears straining. It was the drugs; that's what it was. It had to be. The morphine playing tricks on her.

For a few long seconds there was only the steady

beat of the water on the window and her heart pounding; then lightning flashed angrily outside, illuminating the emptiness of the room. *It's just the morphine, see. No more chuckles coming from the wardrobe. Get a grip on yourself.* She fought back the urge to giggle herself, but then came the second flash of lightning, lighting up the room again, forming a halo around the little boy that stood at the end of her bed, one finger over his lips.

The small yelp her terrified body allowed to escape was drowned out by the roar of thunder, and with the next bright sheet of light that broke the sky, the boy was beside her, his finger covering her own lips. Squeezing her eyes shut, Alex screamed inside. *It's just the morphine, it's just the morphine, but Jesus, his finger is so small and cold and damp, just like he'd been playing out in the rain. It feels so real. It all feels so real.*

The sensation on her lips didn't change, and she forced her eyes open. *It can't hurt you. It's not real. If you scream you'll wake the others up. You'll wake Mary up. She doesn't need this. Not now. Not after today. And if the others come, you may have to explain. Explain the pills and the reason behind the pills. And this isn't real. It can't be.*

Still, when she saw the boy beside her, his face wet with rainwater, glancing fearfully over to the window, she had to bite the inside of her mouth to stop the sound from escaping. How could her imagination make something up like this? All this detail? The child was no more than ten, but his dark bowl haircut was like his clothes, all out of place, like something from the seventies. Even in the gloom she could make out the bright reds and yellows on his knitted tank top that sat over a wide collared shirt, patches of dried mud up the sleeves. Her mind felt hot. *How come if his hands and face are wet, the mud is dry? Why did my head make that up? How can that be? How can any of this be?*

Taking his finger back from her lips, the boy covered his ears with his fists and whispered. "She's hurting him. She's making him cry." His voice sounded congested, as if he needed his adenoids taken out but no one had ever gotten around to it. "I don't like it when she makes them cry. She's going to make him jump."

It's the morphine, kiddo. It's taking you on a trip. That's all it is. That's all it can be. Staring at him, she whispered back the only question she could think to ask. "Who are you?"

The answer was barely audible. "I don't remember. He keeps us in the storm." Glancing again at the window, at the weather on the other side of it, he leaned forward to get closer to her, and she realized he smelled the same as the air did earlier that night. Dirty and damp. "They don't know you can hear them. They don't know you're in between. Like us."

Staring at him, his words weird and meaningless, Alex could see how wide and scared his eyes were, and despite her own fear she almost wanted to touch him to see whether that garishly old-fashioned shirt felt as rough as she imagined it would.

But then the lightning flashed again and he was gone. The room was empty. She sat frozen, listening to the clock ticking out the seconds of her life for a full five minutes before she crept out of bed and over to the light switch and flicked it on. Warm yellow light filled the room, bringing with it normalcy and sanity. Leaning back against the bedroom door, Alex stared at the furnishings and empty spaces that she knew so well and finally let out her breath. God, that was weird. Too weird. Nightmares were one thing, but hallucinations? Those she could live without. Maybe the next night she'd halve the dose and see if it was any better.

Berating herself for the small edge of fear that came with the action, she flicked the switch again, sending the room back into darkness, and then jumped back into bed, curling up on her side under the duvet. Half-expecting to hear more giggling, she was relieved to just have the company of the sounds of the rain. Tiredness washed over her as her body relaxed.

See? Just the morphine. Nothing more.

Allowing her eyes to shut, she drifted off to sleep, twitching slightly as her lips moved silently, unconsciously reciting the Lord's Prayer.

CHAPTER FIVE

"Our father who art in heaven. Hallowed by thy name. Thy kingdom come . . . Thy will be done . . ."

Reverend Barker is crying as he climbs the stairs of the old church up to the bell tower, which overlooks the village that has been his home for more than thirty years. The words come out in a spray of spit that mixes with the wet air around him. "On earth as it is in heaven." The village. His first parish. His last parish. His purgatory for a quarter of a century.

His feet slip on the old stone stairs and he falls heavily on one knee, the pain jarring up his body and forcing him to moan aloud. He has been unsure about what is real and unreal in the madness of the last few hours, but the sharp heat in his leg as he drags himself back to his feet is true, as is the feel of the rough wall under his fingertips, and he dimly accepts what is happening. The devil has come for him. And with that acceptance he realizes that he's been waiting for it to happen for many years.

Outside, the gray of dawn is starting to break despite the thick clouds and heavy rain and as he reaches the top he can hear laughter from downstairs, and the sound of one shoe tapping against the stone as she comes up after him. "Don't you remember me? I couldn't move my legs. Look how they move now!"

Her giggle is young and full of malice and glee and empty emotions that she shouldn't know at that age. That no one should know. Listening to her approach, he doesn't even realize he's still reciting the Lord's Prayer, and even if he did he wouldn't expect it to bring him comfort or any hope of salvation. The Lord has abandoned him. He'd abandoned him a long time ago. He'd seen what they'd done, and for the past thirty years Reverend Barker has known he'd been speaking sermons in a soulless church that his disgusted God has vacated.

Still, climbing onto the small raised wall and clinging to the side, he feels a wave of self-pity rush through him.

"I didn't know what else to do! I was very young! I didn't know what else to do! Forgive me!" Whether he's speaking to her or his God he's unsure. Whichever can give him the opportunity of salvation.

Looking down, he is sure that in the gloom he can see children peering out from behind the gravestones. A few are smiling up at him, unpleasant smiles, their teeth and eyes glinting sharply in the pale light, but others are hiding their faces or covering their ears. He doesn't know which group terrifies him most. Rain stings his eyes. It is madness, of course. All madness. It has to be. The madness of guilt catching up with him. Below, a boy in a baseball cap, sitting cross-legged on a tomb so old that the name has worn away long ago, waves and winks, his finger curling, signaling for the vicar to come.

THE TAKEN

"There is always a choice, Reverend. Everyone always gets a choice." Her voice is young and playful, yet so very vile. The devil's voice. Squeezing his eyes shut, he presses his face into the granite. He doesn't look at her. He doesn't need to. He knows she'll have one shoe on and one shoe off, her knee-high white socks pulled neatly up to her knees under her tartan skirt. Her blond hair will be perfect and her eyes clear and innocently blue. Just as she was then. Just as she always will be. For ever and ever, amen.

"Now, your choice . . . ," she purrs almost seductively, the tone jarringly wrong in a child, "is do you want to jump, or do you want me to push you?" She giggles again. "You see? Everyone has a choice. Even you."

Tears are running down his face, and keeping his eyes closed, not wanting the last thing he sees to be her or any of the children-things below, he forces his shaking fingers to loosen their grip and lets himself fall forward.

"Thy will be done . . ." The words are lost in the rain as he hits the ground, snapping his spine. And then there is silence.

CHAPTER SIX

Dawn was breaking when Alex opened her eyes, still tired but knowing that sleep had gone again for another day. It didn't stop her lying there for another ten minutes and trying to drift off, but as it did every morning, the panic eventually took hold, *Dying. I'm dying. Really dying,* and the only way she could deal with it was to get up and do something. But shit, she was exhausted.

Swinging her legs over the side of the bed, she grabbed her dressing gown from the back of the door and crept down to the kitchen. Coffee. That's what she needed. And maybe some toast. Something to shake away the unsettled feeling that had been left behind by the weird dream or whatever it was she'd had in the night. The memory of the whole surreal experience hadn't faded like dreams normally do, and she could still almost feel that cold finger on her lips.

Sighing, she waited for the kettle to come to a boil on the old stove and then poured herself a very strong coffee laden with sugar. She'd be buzzing for hours on that amount of caffeine, but at least she'd feel awake. Leaning against the warmth of the oven, for comfort more than a need for the heat, she gazed aimlessly out into the gloomy day. The rain was still coming down hard, and it didn't look like it was likely to stop, but the wind seemed to be dropping. For a while at least. Not that she really minded the rain. There was something special about summer storms. Something outside of normal that she'd always loved. Yes, she loved the hot, clear days best, but if she couldn't have those, then storms would do.

At six A.M. she'd eaten some toast, emptied the dishwasher from the previous night, and was about to go upstairs and shower when Simon wandered into the kitchen, dressed but disheveled and waving his mobile phone in the air at about shoulder height.

Alex smiled. "You're dreaming if you think you'll get a signal on that thing out here."

Glancing up, obviously surprised to see her there, Simon almost dropped the tiny handset, and this time she couldn't help a laugh. "Sorry I startled you. I'm an early riser. Do you want a coffee?"

"Yes, thanks. I'm not very good at lying in myself. Too many nights spent in hotel rooms around the world and having to report at god-awful times in the mornings." His own smile was slightly sheepish as he sat down, but Alex found she liked it. She also liked the way his hair was still ruffled from sleep and blond stubble was starting to come through on his chin. Great, she thought, absently finger-combing her own long dark mane into some semblance of tidiness, just the complication I need. An attractive reminder of everything that couldn't be.

Glancing at the phone he'd tossed down on the table, she couldn't help but wonder who he'd needed to call at this time in the morning. Probably a girl-friend. In fact, definitely a girlfriend. Somehow, the idea of him being a taken man made her feel better. And anyway, after seeing her first thing in the morning, he wouldn't exactly be finding her very sexy. She was well aware of the bags under her eyes and the tired-ness that clung to her skin, and the pajamas she'd cho-sen to wear were hardly adding to her sophisticated image.

As she poured the water into his mug and slid it over to him, the checked trousers and top felt all too obvi-ously awful. But then style hadn't really been at the top of her list of considerations recently. Biting her lip, she was angry at herself. Why the hell did she care, anyway? What would be the point of him finding her as attrac-tive as she did him? It would all just end in more pain for her, which she could live without on top of every-thing else. *Live* without. Live without or die without.

He added a sugar to the mug. "Is the signal bad round here then?"

"Well, the phone companies will tell you differently, but you can barely get a signal in the village on a clear blue-skied day." She nodded toward the window. "But in this, you've got no chance."

"Christ, how great is that. Obviously all us London-ers would go into complete mental meltdown at the thought of no mobile phones, but there is something appealing about a life that quiet."

Grinning, she put two slices into the toaster for him and drawled in her strongest Somerset accent, "Well, we may be slightly backward down here, but we do have landlines. There's one over on the wall by the fridge if you want to use it." She raised an eyebrow. "Cordless and everything."

"Thanks." He smiled again. "And sorry if it sounded like I was accusing you of still burning witches down here."

"Ah, but we do. Although only on Tuesdays."

"Well, that's a relief." He held the handset to his head for a moment or two, then quizzically clicked the receiver button down. "I think you may have spoken a little too soon about the phones. It seems as if this one isn't working." Swapping the phone for the plate of toast, Alex held it to her own ear. He was right. There was no dial tone; just emptiness.

"I guess the storm must have brought the lines down." She clicked the button again, just to double check. "It was pretty fierce out there last night." Checking her watch, she saw it was coming up for half-past six. "Look, why don't you eat your breakfast, and then at seven we'll wander down to the shop. Alice is always open by then and we can try her phone. It may be just the lines up this end of town that are gone."

"Sounds like a good plan. It'd be nice to take a look around, as well. Driving up yesterday I could see how beautiful this part of the world is. I bet even in this weather the village is pretty stunning."

"Oh, yes," she grinned, placing her plate and mug in the sink and heading upstairs for the shower. "We're full of country charm down here."

"I can see that." He retorted to her retreating figure,

and Alex allowed herself a brief moment of happiness at the mild flirting. Maybe the pajamas weren't that bad after all.

She quickly showered and pulled on her jeans, a white T-shirt, and a sweater before scraping her still-wet hair back into a ponytail. There was no point in drying it, because the minute she stepped outside it would be soaked again. For a second she glanced at her unused makeup bag, then grabbed it and shoved it into the top drawer of her dressing table, out of sight. There was no point in it. He'd made one flirtatious remark, and all her resolve had dissolved as if she was a giggly schoolgirl without a care in the world. Yanking her socks on, she dragged her oldest sneakers out from the bottom of the closet. And that definitely wasn't how it was. Another two months or so and then it was seriously downhill for her. And there was no point in trying to forget it. As if she ever bloody could.

By the time she got back downstairs, Paul was shuffling round the kitchen, still sleepy, but pulling eggs, bacon and sausages out of the fridge while sipping coffee. Simon's hair was neatened and glasses back on, the stubble had disappeared, and Alex threw him one of Paul's big coats from behind the door.

"That should fit you. It'll keep the rain out better than the jacket you brought with you."

Simon glanced at Paul's thickening waistline. "Yep, there should be plenty of space in there for me. Especially with the way he's been watching his figure recently."

Paul raised an eyebrow. "Very funny. Nothing wrong with having a bit of padding. A lot of women like it, you know. And anyway, this breakfast isn't just for me. I thought Mum could probably do with something to eat. She didn't have anything last night."

"How is she?" The thought of Mary's experience in the garden reminded Alex of her own weird dream. Although hers was probably triggered by what Mary had said, she still felt unsettled by it.

"I popped my head in when I woke up, but she's still sleeping. I'll take her up a tray when it's done. Hopefully she'll be feeling better after a good night's rest."

"I'm sure of it," Alex said, not entirely convinced she felt it. Remembering how frail and fragile Mary had been when she'd come into the lounge the previous evening, it would be hard to imagine that she'd be back to normal overnight. Whether what she saw and heard in the garden was real or imagined, it had shaken her Aunt to the core. "Is there anything we need from the shop? If we're going down there anyway, I may as well get it now."

"Nope, we've got a fridge full of party food to eat our way through. Hopefully her phone line will be working." He tossed a lump of butter into the frying pan on the stove. "Not that I can see ours being down for long. Even out here in the deepest darkest countryside, the world won't leave you alone forever."

Alex grinned at Simon. "So I've explained. Okay, Paul, we'll see you when we get back." Kissing her cousin on the cheek, she pulled open the back door and stepped out into the rain, Simon following her.

Even before they'd reached the end of the gravel drive, the water had found its way inside her clothes, running in rivulets down from her chin and in through the gaps around her sweater and T-shirt. Although the wind had dropped, it was still blowing hard enough to push the rain through the material of her jeans, making her legs itch slightly. Glancing at Simon, she could see that his tan chinos were also darkening.

"Maybe we shouldn't have bothered showering before we came out. I'm soaking already! Looks like you are too."

Simon nodded, his eyes squinting slightly. "Yeah, but at least it's not cold. I quite like summer rain."

Alex stared at him for a second before turning left to head down into the village. Great. He liked summer rain. Another thing they had in common. Looking down the steep uneven road, she watched the streams of water running down it, forming mini rivers in the battered concrete. "I hope you're shoes have got a good grip on them. If you fall over in this, then I fear you may be making your first trip into Watterow sliding on your ass."

"Thanks for that. I'll concentrate on staying upright."

"Good plan."

Focusing in the main on their feet, they walked down the steep hill, side by side, in a strangely comfortable silence. After passing the overgrown churchyard there were no other houses until they reached the outskirts of the tiny village about a quarter of a mile away, and it seemed to Alex as she looked down that the houses there were hidden in a haze of dropped clouds, only the occasional wall or chimney of dark gray stone standing out clearly against the lighter gray that surrounded them. The mist came halfway up the hill before it ran out of steam, beaten into submission by the constant heavy rain.

Maybe it was because of the dull light struggling to make it daytime, or maybe it was because of the sheer volume of water that had fallen, but the green of the leaves and fields around them sung out brightly, a thousand shades hitting the eye at the same time like a symphony of color. Paul and Simon could keep their big cities, Alex decided, sucking in the warm, wet air. Even in this gloom the countryside was more attractive than any concrete jungle could ever be. Looking over to the man next to her, she could see that he too was moved by the strange, dangerous beauty of the day.

Out in the farms dotted around the village, people would have been up and working for at least a couple of hours by now, but in the houses around them the residents would only just be stirring, and the cobbled streets were empty and silent as they trudged past the wooden sign welcoming them to Watterrow. On the other side of the village there was a newer one, black lettering on white metal, the kind seen all over Britain, another hint at the shrinking nature of the world, but this one had been in place for at least a hundred years. And it would be there long after Alex was gone. That much was for sure. She ran her fingers over its rough surface as she passed, just as she had since she was a child. There was a kind of comfort in the action that she couldn't quantify and didn't try to.

As they were swallowed up by the blanket of mist, the houses around them became clearer; walking through the main street, she could see lights coming on as people slowly woke up to the new day.

The shop was out toward the other side of the village and Alex quietly pointed out the interesting quirks of the town as they passed them. Buildings that had been there for hundreds of years ranging from the local pub, The Rock Inn, to the old schoolhouse, which was now the closest thing they had to a library. In the small square they saw the site of the original maypole, although there were rumors and legends, all joking aside, that it also had a more sinister history. It had been a place of trials and judgment when visiting magistrates or knights would pass through, and people would wreak their revenge on neighbors who'd done them wrong. If the records were to be believed, then plenty of locals had been hung and burnt there, suspected witches included.

She wasn't sure if he found the town and its history as engaging as she did, but he nodded and asked the occasional question.

"Hey, look at that."

This time it was Simon that was pointing something out to her, and Alex followed his gaze. It stopped at the corner of one of the narrow side streets that petered out at the edge of the bank of woods.

"Isn't that a bit odd?"

She stared. "Yes. Yes, it is."

There were two children standing in the rain face-to-face on the road, and as she and Simon got closer she could hear they were singing, or at least reciting something. The one whose back was to them was a girl, wearing a black tunic dress and thick tights over her thin frame, and the boy facing her had glasses on, as wet as Simon's were. Alex didn't recognize either of them, which was strange because she was pretty sure she knew all the kids in the village, at least by sight.

"What the hell are they doing out at this time in the morning? And not wearing coats?"

Simon shrugged. "God knows. My experience of children and parenting is pretty limited. Maybe they've snuck out."

As Alex and Simon came up level with them, the words and they way the children were standing began to make sense. Neither child broke the rhythm as they turned their heads and smiled at the two adults.

"Patty cake, patty cake, baker's man,
Bake me a cake as fast as you can. . . ."

They clapped their hands together in patterns that are lost from memory as childhood passes, and as she walked by them, Alex found their smiles a little uncomfortable. Too confident. Not like children should be.

"Roll it and pat it
And mark it with B
And put in the oven for baby and me. . . ."

The girl looked no more than fourteen and the boy was a couple of years behind her. His jeans and sweater didn't match with her more formal clothes either. Their voices jarred as they recited the nursery rhyme, her accent Liverpudlian but his more Yorkshire, the abrasiveness of each clashing with the other. So they weren't local. Maybe they were staying at The Rock or the caravan park a couple of miles away. Either way, Alex was pretty sure they shouldn't be out so early.

She paused and Simon stopped beside her as she called back to them. "Hey, kids. Do your parents know you're out playing? Don't you think you should go home and get some coats on?" She tried her best disarming smile, despite feeling suddenly awkward. Maybe it was the way the children were looking at each other and smiling as if there were a joke being played on her, and not a nice one at that. "You don't want to waste your holiday catching the flu, do you?"

The little boy stared at them for a moment, his rain-splashed glasses making his eyes look blurry, and as both children broke off the game and rhyme in perfect synchronicity, he took a battered red New York Yankees baseball cap out of his back pocket and pulled it onto his head. The girl gave them one more smile and then took the boy's hand.

Alex expected them to turn around and head back to The Rock, but they didn't, instead breaking into a run up the side street that led nowhere but the woods. Beside her, she felt Simon's jacket brush close to her own.

"Do you think we should go after them?"

She shrugged. "I don't think so. She was old enough to look after him." Raising an eyebrow, she glanced up at the tall man. "And they weren't exactly friendly. My aunt would have crucified me for being so rude to adults when I was a child." She tried to make a joke to break the weirdness of the moment. "Kids these days, eh?" But once again she'd been reminded of her strange experience in the night.

He nodded, but he was still staring after the children that had already disappeared into the woods, and Alex knew he was only half-listening. "You okay?"

Simon didn't speak for a moment, chewing his bottom lip, and then he met Alex's gaze. "Yes. Yes, I'm fine. It's just that there was something familiar about that boy, and I can't put my finger on it. I can't possibly know him, but I feel like I do." He stared off into the distance again for a minute and then shook himself. "But I guess he might just have had one of those faces."

A thought came to Alex. "I wonder if it was one of those kids that played the trick on Mary yesterday." Almost as soon as she'd vocalized it, she dismissed the idea. How the hell would they have known about

Melanie Parr? Or the Catcher Man? Still, it was more credible than Mary thinking the little girl's ghost had come back.

Continuing on their way, the silence that had been so comfortable now seemed deafening, the rain like a shroud, and Alex was relieved when they climbed the short steep hill up to the store.

"Here we are."

Alice Moore's store was an all-in-one that served as the local post office and as a grocery shop with all the basic essentials. Despite her advancing age and generally nervous disposition, she had a good head for business, and over the past few years she'd increased her stock to ensure that everyone in the village's pennies came into her till. Along one wall at the back was her DVD rental selection, and she'd also leased a Basic Baker, which cooked hot rolls, baguettes, and pies. The smell when you walked in was enough to make you leave with a bagful of food that you weren't exactly sure you needed in the first place.

Alice was just turning over the sign to open as they stepped up, and she smiled at them through the glass before pulling the door open.

"My, you're up early, Alex."

Alex smiled to herself as Alice's eyes ran up and down Simon. Alice may have been talking to her, but her attention was definitely focused on the stranger beside her. The shop didn't yet have the smell of baked bread that would fill it by nine, but Alice herself was perfectly made up, her hair set neatly in those curls that women of the sixties preferred and stuck to as they'd aged. Her eyes flitted from Simon to Alex and back again, the question hovering obviously in the air.

"Hi Alice." Alex kissed her on the cheek. She may as well put the old woman out of her misery, if only to make Simon feel more comfortable. "This is Simon, a friend of Paul's. He came down with him for Paul's birthday."

Smiling, the older woman shook his hand. "Welcome to Watterrow." Her brow furrowed. "And how's Mary this morning, Alex? Has her head cleared?"

Alex nodded, her stomach twisting slightly with the lie. Alice Moore was an old friend of her aunt's and had been on the list of guests invited to Paul's canceled birthday. A migraine had been the only excuse she'd been able to think of in the aftermath of Mary's panic attack when she'd had to ring round and cancel—it wasn't as if what had happened was anyone else's business. People were people wherever you went in the world, and underneath all the country charm, which big city dwellers like Simon were so entranced by, were all the personality traits that could be found everywhere else: pettiness, jealousy, the need to gossip.

But with country people, along with these traits came an ingrained toughness that was the result of living so close to nature. Country people dealt with things. Country people took care of their own business, and yes, that strength could work for you, but if someone chose to be cruel, well, they could do it better than most. She'd had her share of snipes in the pub and sharp, knowing looks when Ian left, not that anyone in town, apart from Dr. Jones, knew the cause of the split, but that didn't stop them passing judgments.

"She was still asleep when we left." Simon answered Alice smoothly. "I'm sure she'll be right as rain when we get back."

"Well, that's all right then. As long as she's okay." Alice smiled. "Now, what can I get you two so early in the morning?"

"It's the phone line at the house," Alex said. 'It's not working; I think the storm must have done some damage somewhere. We just wondered if yours was still on and if Simon could use it to make a call."

"I'll pay you for it, of course," Simon added. "I just need to check into my answer service. I'm a freelance journalist and that's often the way clients get hold of me."

Alex bit back her grin. So he wasn't trying to call a girlfriend. Not that it meant that he definitely didn't have one, but she obviously wasn't top on his list of priorities. *And whether he has a girlfriend or not shouldn't be on the top of yours.* Making the point to herself, she took a step away from him.

Alice had scurried behind the counter and she lifted her own phone to her ear, pulling away the clip-on earring when she did so, the way actresses used to do in Hollywood films of the fifties. Alex had always found it strange that Alice took so much care in her appearance, but had never been married. Mary said that Alice had never really had an interest in going down that route, but between her warm heart and her precise, well turned-out looks, Alex had often wondered why. Still, you never could tell what went on in other peoples' lives. Alice must have had her reasons, and those were nobody's business but her own.

Tutting, Alice replaced the receiver. "Nothing, I'm afraid. It seems that mine's down too." She sighed and looked around her. "That's a pain. They'd better get it back on soon."

"Why? Are you expecting a call?" Alex didn't think

Alice had ever lived outside Watterrow, so she couldn't see her social circle expanding much beyond its confines.

"No, no dear. It's this place. In the old days it wouldn't matter too much, but now just about everything relies on the phone working. The cash machine over there, and the chip and pin thing the bank persuaded me to install, they both need the phone running." She paused and looked out into the gloom. "Still, I should imagine that in this weather trade won't exactly be too brisk." She peered a little harder. "I actually think the rain is getting heavier again. Well, I'll be . . ." Her face clouded over. "I wonder if the river will burst its banks."

Through the shop window, Alex watched the trees begin to sway. Alice was right. The storm was picking up again. "I should imagine it probably already is. The water has been coming down solidly for about twelve hours." She paused, and the next words came out quietly. "Aunt Mary said she could only remember one other time when the storms were this bad—about thirty years ago and the whole village ended up cut off." She glanced at Alice, whose hands had fluttered to the crucifix at her neck, fingering it absently. "She said a little girl went missing in it. Melanie Parr? Do you remember it?"

Alice's smile was tight. Maybe a little too tight, Alex thought. "Vaguely. I didn't have children, so I didn't know her very well. And it was all a very long time ago."

The small glass panes of the door had steamed up where Simon gazed through them. "Surely if it's likely that the village will get cut off, shouldn't we be evacuating or something?"

Despite still fiddling with her cross and the collar of her blouse, Alice's smile was genuine. "That's not the way we do things out here. There's nothing so important in the towns that we can't live without them for a few days. And anyway, even if we did leave, where would we go?"

Simon grinned at her. "I guess you have a point." He turned to Alex. "And I think we should head back before this weather gets any worse."

Zipping their coats back up, right to the top this time, they stepped outside and left Alice staring quietly out at the angry weather.

CHAPTER SEVEN

Hearing movement upstairs, along with the latest effervescent tune from Girls Aloud bursting into life on the bathroom radio, Kay Chambers put another two slices of bread in the toaster before buttering her own. Phil wasn't back from his conference in London for another two days, so it was just her and Laura in the house, which was nice occasionally. It would be even nicer in a couple of years when Laura would be a teenager and hopefully want to lie in bed for half the day during the holidays. At last Kay herself might get to sleep late, the bed all hers. Those days would be bliss, she decided, biting into her breakfast. Or better still, she might even get to go along with Phil and have a few days in the capitol. It had been years since she'd been to London, and as much as she loved being a country girl, the buzz of the big city was great every now and then. Although now that the big four-oh was looming, she might not have the energy to keep up. Forty. Just where the hell did the years go to?

Smiling, she heard the bathroom door opening upstairs and Laura trudging down the stairs. Kay had a feeling that her daughter had been lying in bed awake since before seven waiting for her mother to get up, probably already eager to ring her friends and sort out their plans for the day. Over her head came a thud from the spare room as if something had fallen heavily to the floor, but Kay didn't even look up. Everything in the house creaked and moaned with movement and sometimes it did it just because it felt like it. But then, the house was a hell of a lot older than her or anyone else in Watterrow, so she figured it had the right to a little ache or pain every now and then.

"Morning, honey, there's some toast on for you. And tea in the pot if you want it."

"Thanks, Mum." Laura, already in her jeans and T-shirt, ready for the day ahead, bounced to the fridge and pulled out the jam, spreading it liberally and messily over the hot bread. "Can I call Jenny and Jimmy and see what they're doing today?"

Kay smiled. "After your breakfast. It's only half seven, they can wait another ten minutes or so." She didn't worry about Laura ringing her friends so early. Dave Granville worked over at Tucker's farm so he'd have been up since around four, and with five children, the oldest being the twins, Jenny and Jimmy, who were eleven like Laura, it was unlikely that Emma would be in bed much beyond six. And anyway, sweet as the Granvilles were, Dave and Emma had an old fashioned country marriage. Kay would bet that Emma got up at four and made Dave a full English breakfast before sending him off to the farm, just as her mum had done for her dad before her. Thinking of those five kids and early mornings made Kay realize how lucky she was with her very loving husband and one child, who in the main was pretty much as good as you could expect a girl to be.

Looking out the window, the trees in the garden were bending slightly. She'd thought that the storm had peaked in the night, but maybe not. Watching the gloom and the rain hammering at the glass, she shivered in the warmth of her kitchen, a bad taste forming in her mouth. A dark memory flashed in her head, but she pushed it away before she even became aware of its existence.

"What are your plans for today? I don't think the weather's looking good for playing outside too much."

Laura shrugged, swallowing half a slice of toast in one mouthful, leaving Kay to wonder why her daughter wasn't the size of a house. "Don't know yet."

"Well, if you do go out, make sure you wear your coat. And don't go into the woods or down by the river."

Laura rolled her eyes. "Yes, Mum. I know."

Kay kissed her on the top of her head, enjoying its warm smell. "I know you know, but it doesn't stop me worrying about you."

The good thing about country children is that they were hardy but full of common sense. Yes, they probably would play in the rain, and be all the more healthy for it, but they wouldn't be stupid enough to go down to the overflowing river or up the steep wooded banks to the old tin mines. Not in this weather. They'd all seen what happened to sheep and cows that went astray, and it rarely had a happy ending. Her face was still pressed into her daughter's hair. Her baby smell was gone, but Kay reckoned if it came down to it, she would still be able to recognize Laura by scent alone.

"If you get lost the Catcher Man will get you and then where will you be?" The words tumbled out in a whisper, and Laura wriggled out of her mother's suddenly too-tight grasp and twisted round, confused.

"The Catcher Man? Who's he?"

Kay stepped backwards, shocked by her own words. Where the hell had that come from? She tried to smile, but the expression wouldn't fit on her face. "Oh, forget it. It was something your gran used to say to me a long time ago when I'd go out into the woods. I don't even know why I said it." The palms of her hands felt clammy, and she ran them through her hair.

Laura grinned. "Cool. The Catcher Man. I like it."

Upstairs there was another bang, and this time it did get Kay's attention. "Did you leave a window open upstairs?"

"In this weather? No. Why?" Laura pulled out two more pieces of bread from the bag and put them in the toaster.

"I just wondered what that banging was up there."

Tilting her head quizzically, Laura listened for a moment. "I can't hear anything." She grinned. "It must be your age. Nearly forty . . ."

"Oh, you're so funny, young lady. You'll be forty one day and then it won't seem so very old. Trust me on that one."

Her tone was light, but inside she still felt a little unsettled. Why the hell had she mentioned the Catcher Man? It wasn't even anything she'd thought about for years. Not since . . . well, not for a very long time. She gazed back out of the window. It was the storm, that's what it was. The storm and Paul's fortieth birthday—not that they'd even had the party to celebrate. It had been a storm like this hitting the village when Melanie had gone missing all those years ago. That must have been what made her think of it. She shivered again, her arms folding across her chest. She hadn't been sad about Melanie disappearing. Shocked maybe, but not sad. But she'd often wished she'd known what happened to her. There was a dark space in her head around that day, something the eleven-year-old inside her had locked away, a suspicion or a doubt that she'd never really wanted to face up to.

Watching the wind getting stronger outside, she wondered if she should take the time to examine that dark space and dig up the memories, but decided against it. The storm would pass. And that was all that was unsettling her. The storm. There was no point in raking over the past. Her own mother was dead and couldn't give her any answers, and she wasn't even sure she wanted any.

Yes, she thought, her heart warming as she watched her own child pacing innocently around the kitchen. The storm would pass.

CHAPTER EIGHT

The weather was definitely getting worse, and as they headed back to the house, Alex had to lean forward slightly into the wind to keep her balance.

"Thanks for not saying anything about what happened to Mary yesterday. Alice is a lovely woman and has a heart of gold, but villages are full of gossip and old women are the worst for it. She'd tell one customer and before you know it, they'd have Mary all ready to be hauled away to the funny farm."

Simon shrugged. "Don't mention it. Hey, I'm a journalist. I know all about how stories spread. Anyway, she just had a turn. It's no big deal. She'll be right as rain when we get back."

Nodding, Alex stayed silent. Simon might believe that, but then he didn't know what right as rain actually was for Mary. He might think that the fragile woman that came downstairs the previous evening was her being normal. Maybe if he'd seen her just a few hours earlier, he'd have realized just how much she had changed over the course of the day.

She brushed her hand over the old wooden sign as they reached the base of the hill, feeling the dampness soaking into the dead tree, and sighed. Life was such a fragile thing and everyone took it so much for granted. Always wanting things, but always waiting for tomorrow or for a better time. She wanted to shake the world and scream, *There is no better time. There is only now*. But what was the point? No one really got it until it was too late. Maybe that was just the way it was meant to be.

Water trickled down her nose and as they curved around the wall of the old churchyard, she lifted her head to sniff it out of the way, stopping in her tracks. Up ahead, twenty or so yards away, a little boy stood by the tiny side gate to the church, one finger up to his lips.

No, no no. It couldn't be. She was awake. Wide awake. And she'd only taken one tablet of morphine at breakfast. Just one.

The boy stared at her, unmoving, and her eyes wide, Alex could see the bright colors of his knitted tank top, and the mud patches on his sleeves. It was the boy from her dream. *Oh man. And I was worried that Mary was going crazy* . . . Her breath hitched in her chest and somewhere outside the bubble that seemed to be around her she could see that Simon had stopped and was watching her. He may have even been speaking; she wasn't sure.

The boy took his finger away from his mouth and pointed to his left. To the church. His mouth moved and she could make out the shape of the words even though she couldn't hear them.

I told you. Look. See.

The rain was hitting her face, but under it the skin on her cheeks was burning hot. *This can't be. This just can't be.* She needed to speak to Dr. Jones about this. As much as she hated his sympathy and pity, she definitely needed to talk to him about this. Feeling things that weren't there was one thing, but *seeing* them was quite another.

"Are you okay?" Simon's hand touched her arm and she jumped, breaking eye contact with the boy and turning to the man beside her. "You're shaking."

She stared at him for a second. "The boy over there . . ." Looking back to the church gate all she could see were the overhanging strands of ivy and water running from the branches of the oak tree. No strange boy. He was gone.

"What boy? The one we saw on the way to the shop?"

"No. No, not him. A different one." *Where did all these children come from, anyway?* "Didn't you see him? Up there by the church gate. He was pointing at something."

Staring at Simon, all she saw in his face was confusion. "No. I didn't see anyone." He shrugged and looked around at the empty road and fields. "But then I was concentrating on where I was putting my feet, so I guess if there was a kid there, they could have run away."

Alex thought about the lightning last night. One minute he was there beside her bed, and with the next flash, gone. Maybe it was best to keep that story to herself for the time being. Otherwise Simon would think they were a family of lunatics.

"Maybe he ran into the churchyard. It's the only place he could have gone without us seeing it. Let's take a look."

Silent, Alex nodded, glad that Simon had suggested it. After the words the boy had mouthed to her, she definitely wanted to look, just to reassure herself that everything at the church was normal. *Yes, that would be good. Everything normal, and the madness just inside my head. Great. Very reassuring. Cancer and insanity. How much can a girl hope for in life?*

Keeping their heads up, they walked quickly to the gate and peered over it. "I can't see anything. But then there's an awful lot of trees blocking my sight."

A few inches below, Alex was finding it equally difficult to see, and she clicked open the gate. It moved stiffly, as if it hadn't been used in a while, and Alex didn't find that at all surprising. *Because he didn't run away, did he? He just disappeared. That's what figments of the imagination do—vanish like a puff of smoke.*

Crouching to duck under a branch, something caught her eye. "Simon, look. The church door is open. Why would Reverend Barker be in the church at this time in the morning?" Ahead she could see the wood swinging backward and forward with the growing wind. "And why would he leave the door open in this weather?"

"There's only one way to find out. Come on, let's go and take a look." He smiled at her. "At least it'll get us out of the rain for a couple of minutes."

Fighting past the last of the grasping limbs of the trees, they emerged on the lawn, which covered the sides and front of the quiet fourteenth-century chapel. Both their trots slowed to walks. The door banging in the wind sounded like an untamed heartbeat, or a death knell; the two were one and the same thing— markers of precious time being lost. Alex shivered. This didn't seem right. It didn't seem right at all.

Simon jumped up the worn steps and held the solid wood open, letting the yellow, dim light from inside reach out to them. Watching him waiting for her, Alex bit back the urge to turn and run back to the farmhouse and stepped hesitantly through the archway, before Simon shut the door quietly behind them. Atheist that she was, she had still always felt some serenity, some inner peace in this church. But not now. All she was feeling now was unease. Whatever sense of sanctuary that had existed here was gone.

"Reverend? Reverend Barker? Are you in here?" Stepping forward down the aisle, her feet echoed as she glanced down the rows of pews. Simon followed her, peering under the benches for any sign of the boy or the vicar. Alex wasn't quite sure what they were looking for, but the two of them moved slowly side by side, she searching the shadows and light to the left, and he to the right. After the constant noise of nature's angry rage outside, the quiet of the church was eerie. Every drip of water that slid from their clothes or hair to the floor seemed to chime out their presence. She sniffed and the sound came back at her from every corner, taunting her. Despite the gloom that seemed to eat at the cold stone walls and alcoves, the lights directly above Alex and Simon seemed almost too bright, like spotlights scrutinizing their every breath as they walked side by side in a parody of a wedding march.

"Look." Alex's heart thumped in her ears as she whispered, drawing Simon's attention toward the altar. He nodded silently, and as she got closer she wondered why she hadn't noticed it as soon as they came into the church. The beautiful gold and red tapestry that normally covered the aged surface had been thrown carelessly to the stone floor, and beside it a dark, oozing patch spread out where a large vase of flowers had been knocked over, some of the buds now dying on the steps by their feet. All that was left on the large space was a candlestick, the candle burnt right down. But something had been written on the altar. Scrawled in hot wax, which had now set.

"What the hell does that mean?" Simon sounded confused, and for the first time, Alex heard uncertainty in his voice. She stared down at the abused altar.

Look how they
move now

The words stared back at her, her throat tightening. She'd heard those words somewhere, she knew she had. When?

I couldn't move my legs. Look how they move now!

"What did you say, Alex?" Simon was staring at her, and she dragged her eyes away from the altar.

"I didn't say anything."

"Yes, you did. You muttered something about your legs. And then said 'Look how they move now.' Do these words mean something to you?"

Alex stared at the words. Did they mean something to her? Should they? Fear bit at her insides. This writing was real, not just something in her head brought on by the medication. Just what was going on? She looked up at Simon, and felt tears suddenly threatening to spill. "I don't know. I don't know if they mean anything to me or not. They just seem familiar." The confines of the church were making her feel claustrophobic. "Let's go and check outside. See if there's been any more damage. Maybe the kids that are staying at the caravan park or wherever broke in and vandalized the place."

Once outside, Simon led the way around the side of the church, Alex using his back to shield her from the wind. She was glad they weren't walking side by side, because it gave her a few minutes to try and pull herself together. Maybe there was something odd going on, but at least there was now physical evidence rather than just her overactive imagination. Maybe there even was a little boy. Maybe he had hidden in the house last night and really had been in her bedroom. She hadn't checked under her bed after turning the light on, so maybe he'd hidden under there and snuck back out when she'd gone to sleep.

The more she thought about it, the more she liked it. It was thin and flimsy, but in daylight it certainly seemed plausible. Although she didn't know why anyone would want to hide in her room to scare her. And his finger was cold and wet, the small voice of reason in her head whispered quietly. Not like someone that had been hiding in the warm all afternoon, but I guess you don't want to think about that right now, do you?

They turned the corner and ahead of them the old graveyard opened up. Toward the other side of it was the border with Mary's garden, through which she'd seen or heard whatever it was that made her so upset the previous day, and between them and that were rows of deteriorating gravestones and tombs. About halfway back, amongst a neater line of modern stones, was her mother's; in the not too distant future, Alex would fill the space beside her. Her stomach tightened slightly. Each day, a day closer.

"Oh God."

Simon's voice was loud and deep, and he stopped so suddenly that Alex almost walked into the back of him, having to swerve to his side, stumbling over her feet. Steadying herself, she stared down at what had stopped him and for a moment, for a long, blissful moment, she didn't understand what she was seeing.

The body that lay twisted on the hard stone paving slabs was nearly unrecognizable; it was the vicar. He wore ordinary gray trousers and a V-neck pullover; out of his church uniform he was no longer a representative of a higher power, but just a person, vulnerable and so pathetically human. Hearing Simon letting out a long shaky breath beside her, Alex absorbed the details, her eyes and brain working together against her need not to know, not to *see*.

Reverend Barker's hands had gone slightly blue, no, more like bluish-purple, where they had been exposed to the elements, the liquid that filled his veins congealing in the extremities of his fingertips, bloating them with pressure from within, maybe from the smashed bones that must be the cause of the sickening shape of his legs and arms. Beneath the thinning hair on his scalp, blood as red as communion wine gathered and then dispersed outward, filling the cracks between the slabs of stone and running through them, using them as canals for escape, disappearing into the dirt.

Although Alex's rational mind told her this was Reverend Barker ruined on the ground, she couldn't come to terms with the reality of it. His dignity and quiet serenity had been stripped away, leaving only a humiliated husk of a human being. Looking upward, Alex could see the bell tower directly above where he lay.

She's hurting him. She's making him cry. She's going to make him jump.

"Oh Jesus. Oh Jesus . . ."

It took a moment to realize that the disjointed voice she could hear was her own, and when Simon touched her arm she yelped, pulling away.

"It's me, Alex. It's just me." He held her arms for a moment, focusing his eyes on hers. "Stay with me, Alex. We're okay. We're *okay.*"

Breathing deeply, the air feeling shaky around her, Alex nodded. Simon held her gaze for another few seconds, then moved her so she was leaning against the wall before he crouched by the body, touching the man's scrawny neck where his head was twisted sideways, one cheek pressed into the coldness beneath.

"Still alive . . . he's still alive." Simon stared as the vicar's eyelids fluttered open. Alex fell to the ground, kneeling in the man's blood, her heart pounding in her chest with hope. Reverend Barker coughed; a weak, wet sound that sent a shiver up Alex's spine, and spots of blood appeared on his teeth as he opened his mouth, his breath raw and rotten.

"Shhh. Don't try to speak. Don't try to speak . . . ." Her own eyes were blurring with tears, but she could see that the vicar's were so full of pain that he couldn't even focus. When he whispered, he sent his words somewhere between her and Simon, as if a ghost had joined them that only he could see.

"Melanie Parr." He spat the words out accompanied by a spray of blood and saliva. Alex's heart froze, but this time the dying man's gaze met hers, and for a moment there was clarity within the glare of pain. She could see his jaw and throat working, desperately trying to communicate, those two words obviously not enough. Not nearly enough. A clicking sound came from his chest and he shut his eyes for a second, concentrating on the effort of speech.

The sound came out in a rattle of air. "Our . . . sin . . . warn them . . ."

He stared at Alex, the frustration at her confusion obvious as he tried to move his head forward, needing to be closer, needing to make them understand something. Alex and Simon both leaned forward, Alex trying not to recoil from the warm smells erupting from Reverend Barker, the death that was shrouding him.

". . . Warn them . . . ." His lower body had started to convulse slightly, but still he pushed out the words before the shaking overtook him. "Come . . . for . . . us."

This time the cough raped his being, sending warm blood into Alex's hair as he angrily expelled his last breaths. She shrieked, burying her face in Simon's shoulder, his arms wrapping round her, pulling her in. The awful choking hack stopped almost as suddenly as it had begun, but Simon held on to her, rocking slightly backward and forward, whispering soothing sounds, his hand holding onto her crimson hair as they sat in silence.

Eventually, she lifted her face. "Is he dead?" She didn't want to look. She didn't want to look back at the mess of the corpse beside them.

Simon nodded. "He's gone."

"I need . . . I really need . . ." The heat had returned to her face, and looking down at her hands, her red hands, she saw how they were shaking. Her whole body was shaking. Bile began to burn her chest as spots of blackness ate into her vision. She had to get away. She had to get away immediately. Pulling herself to her feet, she clutched at the wall behind her, numb feet clumsily lurching back the way they had come, toward the lawn, to where she wouldn't be able to see him, not able to get her there quick enough, fighting the scream that seemed to be filling her brain.

Doubling over in the open space, she let it go, her stomach emptying itself, the steak, the flesh of the previous night's dinner not welcome inside her anymore. She heaved and heaved until there was no longer even any liquid left to relinquish. Tipping her head backward, she let the heavy rain run through her hair and over her face and sighed, letting her skin cool. Somewhere down in the mess at her feet were her painkillers and medication, probably only half-absorbed. Should she take some more? Would she be able to hold them down? And what the fuck would she start seeing if she did? Maybe a bit of pain wasn't such a bad thing.

Turning around, she tilted her head up into the rain, enjoying its attack on her face, the way it stung her skin. She ran her hands through her hair as if she was in the shower, imagining the water running first red, then pink, and then clear as she rinsed away the blood and tears that covered her. Her muscles ached from throwing up and her limbs felt heavy. God, she was tired. But then she was always so goddamn tired these days.

Opening her eyes, she saw Simon standing beside her. He didn't seem bothered by the weather anymore either, ignoring the way it buffeted him.

"I've covered him up with the cloth from inside the

church. It's the best we can do for now. Maybe he jumped or just fell by accident, but with that vandalism to the altar it's probably best we don't move him. Not until the police get here, anyway. The best thing we can do is get back to the house and see if the phones are back on."

Alex nodded. "Just give me a minute. I'll be fine in a minute." Despite the relief of the cleansing cold and rain, she didn't think she had it in her to move. It was all too much to deal with—Melanie Parr, the boy from her dream and the things he said. How could any of it make sense? And on top of all that she could feel the pain deep in the core of her abdomen throbbing into life, her cancer reminding her of what she really had to fear. Not ghosts in the night.

Simon put his arm around her. "It's the shock. It's okay. It's shock."

Anger flashed inside her, white and hot and she pulled away from him. *What the hell does he know, the patronizing bastard? What the hell does he know about me?* This had nothing to do with the shock, and everything to do with the shitty hand life had dealt. Her rage gave her energy and she pushed herself away from him and stood upright.

"Like you said, we need to try and get help. Let's go." She wondered if her bitter tone carried over the sound of the rain as she turned and headed back to the road, ignoring his offer of an arm. She hoped it did. She didn't care whether he liked her or not, and as soon as he realized that, the better it would be for both of them. There was no more time for romance, and as soon as she got that through her own thick skull the better.

CHAPTER NINE

Kneeling on her bed to pull the curtains open, Laura figured it wasn't all bad. Yes, it was raining, but it wasn't cold. And surely once the storm passed, the sun would blaze down for at least a week and then there'd be plenty of time for exploring and dam-building and treasure hunting in the countryside. Not that they'd be staying inside all day today. Mrs. Granville would be driven mad by having all five of her own kids plus Laura in the house. In fact, now that she thought about just how loud and manic that would be, Laura decided it would probably drive her mad too, and she was only eleven.

She heard the buzzing sound three times before she figured out what it was. Her bed made and toys tidily put away, she stared at her school bag. The buzzing was coming from there and the only thing it could be was her mobile phone. Undoing the straps of the old-fashioned brown satchel, she felt the short vibration through the leather and her brow furrowed. There were two things confusing her: Number one was the obvious one—everybody knew that no phones got a signal in the village, and she knew for sure that hers didn't work unless she was at school in Taunton, so the phone shouldn't be buzzing at all. The second thing was that school had been over for two weeks or more, so even if she'd left it on, the battery would have been dead ages ago.

Pulling it out, she stared at the lit-up screen.

`New Text Message.`

The screen looked slightly odd and it took a moment or two before she figured out why. There were no lines or bars on either side of the message, framing it. Which meant that the phone had absolutely no battery and no signal. She sniffed, not unduly concerned. It could also mean that her father's cast-off Nokia was finally dying. Phones did odd things as they reached the end of their lives. Everyone knew that. Screens came on and off and went funny colors. Maybe hers was just doing that. She pressed the open button.

`Do you want to come out to play?`

Smiling, a thought came to her. It must be Jimmy or Jenny. Their home phone must not be working either, so they must have tried their mobiles instead. Having tried to call after breakfast and getting no dial tone, Laura had been just about to grab her coat and head down to their house now that she'd done all her boring chores. Glancing at the top of the text, she saw there was no number or name to identify it. That was odd too. Her fingers moved deftly over the keys.

`Is that u jen?`

The phone buzzed again with a new message almost immediately after she'd pressed Send.

`I'm lonely.`

Staring at the message, Laura felt confused, but not afraid. It didn't sound like anything Jen would say, not even if she was mucking around. Maybe it was Jimmy? After all, who really knew what went on in boys' heads? And now that they were eleven the differences between the girls and boys were getting bigger. It wouldn't be long before Jimmy would stop hanging around with them and be up at Tucker's farm helping his dad with the lambing and bringing crops in.

`Jimmy?`

Sitting back on her ankles, she waited for the phone to buzz again. She didn't know why Jimmy would send something like that, either. When the vibrations ran through her fingers she almost dropped the phone.

New Message. Open.

`If you go down to the woods today, you're sure of a big surprise.`

This was not Jimmy. Jimmy would never write anything so odd, and even if he did, he wouldn't write it like that, with all the words in full. He'd write it in text. The words were familiar, and she found herself singing them in her head. The teddy bears picnic—definitely not something Jimmy would write about. The words looked creepy staring up at her, dark against the green screen.

`Who r u?`

Laura had heard of text-bullying at school, but never had any of it herself. Was this what it was like? She shrugged. She didn't feel particularly intimidated, just confused and a bit curious.

`Melanie. Come and play with me. I've got lots of friends for you to meet.`

Laura only looked at the message for a second before shutting it down, bored. Mind games didn't interest her. Whoever this Melanie was—and she must be one of the townies on holiday down at the caravan park or something—she was too weird for Laura. One minute she was lonely, the next she's got lots of friends. She punched in her own reply.

Dont fink so.

Pulling herself to her feet, she grabbed her parka from the wardrobe and put it on, stuffing her small purse into one pocket. The phone buzzed once more, and sighing, she opened the message. This game was getting dull.

But I want to play with you Laura. I've got things to show you.

For the first time, she felt a small shiver of fear trickle almost unnoticed down her spine. How had this girl got her name? Angry with herself for letting the stranger get to her, she left the message unanswered and shoved the phone in her pocket. Jimmy was right—townies were just plain weird next to country people.

CHAPTER TEN

Although the air temperature outside probably wasn't that cold, the force contained in the rising rage of the wind and the sheer volume of falling water choked any warmth from the summer's day, and Alex was chilled to the bone as she stumbled back into the familiar surroundings of Mary's kitchen. Maybe it was just the shock and the cancer; who the hell knew? Not her, that was for sure. At least she hadn't seen any imaginary children on her way home, so maybe she should just be thankful for small mercies. Letting Simon shut the door behind them, she headed to the stove to warm her hands on its surface.

"Is the phone back on yet?" Noticing that Mary wasn't in the room, Alex wondered if her aunt was even up. Well, she was going to have to get up soon, that was for sure. After Mary's experience in the garden the previous day and what the vicar had said before he died, Alex found the idea of her aunt being asleep and vulnerable in this house to be a little bit frightening.

Warn them. That's what poor Reverend Barker had said. Was Mary one of the people that needed to be warned?

"No." Paul stared at her and then Simon, his eyes wide and shaky. "What the hell happened to you two?"

Glancing down at her jeans, Alex could see the dark stains on her knees that had nothing to do with the soaking she had received outside, and looking at Simon in the bright light, she noticed the shadows of pink that lingered on his blond hairline. Had that come from her? From her own head when she'd clung to him? She wondered how many more ghosts of blood were visible on her and realized how they must look to Paul. Like veterans of some awful war zone. The kind of place Simon was used to.

"The phone line was down at the shop too, and then we thought we saw something at the church." Inside, she almost giggled. *Sure, we thought we saw something. Imaginary children pointing our way to dying men.* What would the police make of that? It would be her they'd be arresting.

"We went inside and someone had vandalized the altar, or maybe he even did it himself, who knows, but then we went outside and found Reverend Barker dying." She knew the words were coming out in a blunt flood, but she couldn't help it. "He either jumped from the bell tower or was pushed. And he said some strange stuff before he died. About that girl, Melanie Parr." She stared at Simon and then at Paul. "How the hell are we going to contact the police if the phones are off?"

Paul stared back at her for a moment, no outward sign of shock at their news apart from the telltale clenching of his jaw, something only she would recognize, and then he grabbed the hand towel and passed it to her.

"Jesus. Jesus Christ." He paused for a second and then drew himself up tall. "Yes, you're right, we'll have to find a way to get hold of the police, but you also need to get warm and dry." He stared at the stains on her trousers. "And you've been sick. I think a cup of tea for you."

As she squeezed the water out of her long ponytail, watching him putting the kettle on, she remembered just how much strength he had. Yeah, Paul could be a lot of things, but weak wasn't one of them. It was easy to take things out on the people you loved. An old cliché, but true. She'd been hard on everyone, and the shit in her life was nobody's fault. Except maybe Ian's, and that pain was too big to face.

Paul pushed his hands into his trouser pockets, making the roundness of his belly more prominent as it escaped over his waistband.

"Are we sure all the lines in the village are down?"

Alex shrugged in response. "If ours is and the shop's is, then I'm pretty sure they all are."

Simon took off his glasses and rubbed his face, leaning back against the kitchen counters. Alex thought he looked tired, and felt a pang of sympathy for him. It hadn't been much of a party weekend for him so far. His voice was still calm when he spoke, though. "I don't suppose there's a policeman in the village, is there?"

Paul's laugh was loud, short, and humorless. "You guessed right, my friend. We don't even have our own postman out here. I think the nearest police station is Taunton, and that's over twenty miles away." He gazed out of the small panes. "And I doubt we'd make it there in the car. Most of the roads will be flooded by now and more than likely we'd get stuck somewhere, even if we took the Land Rover.

A tingle like electricity ran through Alex's veins as a thought ate through her brain and straightness came back into her spine. As she moved nearer to the two men, her voice was excited. "No, there may not be a policeman, but I know what there is—there's a retired traffic cop. Daniel Rose."

Paul and Simon exchanged a look, and it was her cousin that spoke. "No offense Al, but I don't think—"

"No, you're not getting it." She cut him off, shaking her head impatiently. "Daniel Rose has a kind of CB Radio. He's a radio ham. Talks to people all over the country on it. Don't you see? If the phones are out, we may still be able to speak to the police!"

She looked from one man to another. "We need to get down there. For one thing, we can't leave the body out there in the elements for too long. If there has been foul play, the evidence will be ruined, and we need to know how to shut the place off so no one else has to go and find him."

Simon nodded, and this time his attention was fully back on Alex. Despite her earlier anger, she found that she liked it. She couldn't help herself. What a time to start finding men attractive. But then, her timing and choices had never exactly been perfect, had they? And she'd control it. She had to. It wouldn't be fair on anyone if she didn't.

"Come on then." He smiled at her gently and she wished with an ache that came out of nowhere that she could see that grin, whole and happy. "Let's go, lady, before we get too dry."

Nodding, she turned to Paul, who put back the mug that he was about to make her tea in. "Get Mary and we'll meet you down at The Rock. We'll probably need you to help let people know what's going on, and I don't think we should leave her up here alone."

"Okay, but then you're definitely going to get warm and fed. You're too thin these days, Al."

She smiled at her cousin, although his words twisted her stomach slightly. So the weight loss was starting to show. Well, she'd be getting a lot thinner in the next couple of months.

"Take the Land Rover; the keys are on the hook in the hall. It might be a good idea to have a car in the village anyway, and it's too harsh out there for Mary to walk. Not with . . . well, with the way she's been."

"I'll get her down there as quick as I can and see you in The Rock. If you're not there, then I'll leave Mary in the pub and walk up to Daniel's. Okay?"

Alex reached out impulsively and hugged her cousin. "Take care, Paul. Get down to the village as fast as you can." The memory of the vicar's destroyed body was too fresh at the front of her mind. *Come for us.* Who did he think Melanie Parr had come for and why? She zipped up her wet jacket. First the police, and then she'd start asking questions.

Paul pushed Alex gently to the door until she was standing next to Simon. "Now go, you two. We need the police here as soon as possible." He kissed her on the forehead, and for a second she felt as if she was a child again, and he the only big brother figure in the world worth having. Suddenly she didn't want to go back out there. She just wanted to stay here with her family, Paul and Mary, stay here and pretend that all was well in the world. The lips vanished from her skin leaving only a cool patch, and taking the moment with them. Without another word, she followed Simon back into the restless storm and whatever waited for them there.

CHAPTER ELEVEN

It took them about fifteen minutes to get to the Roses' old cottage, and during that time the air had darkened almost to black. Luckily they were just inside when the thunder ripped through the sky, cracking like a bullet fired in warning just above their heads. Alex jumped, even though they were within the warm confines of Daniel Rose's attic room. His wife was downstairs making a pot of coffee for them, and as much as Alex relished the idea of the hot liquid inside her, she wasn't sure that her damaged nerves needed the added caffeine. But she did need the normalcy of it. She needed the normalcy of *something*. At least she hadn't seen any strange children on this journey, although as the wind and rain had battered them, she'd had the spooky feeling that even the weather was against them. Simon also seemed preoccupied, but then, she reasoned, his day hadn't exactly been normal either. And looking at the man fiddling with the buttons on the huge array of dials, it seemed that Daniel Rose was starting to feel the strain.

The retired traffic policeman's face was serious and intense as he switched on his equipment, only the slight shaking of his hands belying either his age or his shock at the news of the vicar's death. Simon and she had told him everything—the words written in wax on the altar, how the vicar had been alive when they'd found him, and the words he'd managed to spit out before he'd died. Even without the added detail of messages in the night and children pointing the way, it was a chilling enough tale. And those details were ones she hoped to put behind her.

Daniel had said very little since bringing them up the old twisted stairs to his radio room, and looking at the lines in his face, which created a network of canyons and valleys in the loose skin, she wondered at the comfort she felt just by being in the presence of age and experience. It was a false security, of course; she knew that. She couldn't imagine that age would make much difference to fear. In fact, wasn't it children that were never scared of heights or death or anything real? Carry that idea further, and the elderly must be the most afraid of them all. It would make sense. Their dreams were dust, no time left to chase them; the future just held shadows and the possibility of pain. She winced at the stabbing ache inside. Maybe she and Daniel Rose had more in common than he knew.

Lightning chased its tail of sound through the playground of the sky, and the bulb above them flickered slightly. Simon stared at it thoughtfully. "That would be all we'd need. No electricity."

Daniel shook his head. "That's one worry you can let

go of, son. I've got a generator. So does the pub. Most people do out here. Those of us who have lived here a long time, anyways. The electric's more reliable now than it used to be, so it hasn't been used for a time, but I get it serviced regular. Habit, mainly."

"So, can you get the police direct on this thing?"

"No." Daniel looked up at Simon and shook his head. "No, the radio won't let us get into their bands. I can listen to them, but not transmit. I'll have to get hold of another ham and they'll have to fetch someone on the phone."

"Someone you know over the airwaves?"

Relaxing now that he was talking about something he understood, Daniel's voice slowed down and softened. "I think that'd take too long for what we need. We could waste time calling for people who aren't listening. I'll make a CQ call and see what we get back."

"CQ?" Simon was perching on the edge of the crowded desk.

"It means 'seek you,' just the ways it sounds. It's a general call. Anyone can answer. My aerial is omnidirectional see, sends out all the way round. Some bugger'll pick us up." He started to turn the dial, which whistled back at him. "Just let me get to the two meter band and then we'll be on our way."

Alex sat silently in the spare chair, watching the two men. Daniel had better be right. They needed to get the police out there, and if it took too long the storm would cut the village off.

"CQ, CQ, this is Golf Three Quebec Sierra Tango. Any station comeback?" Daniel released the microphone button and sat back. "Now," he muttered, under his breath, "let's be having you." He pushed the button down again. "CQ, CQ, this is Golf Three Quebec Sierra Tango. Any station go ahead."

The moment of silence seemed like forever. Alex touched Daniel's arm.

"Is that it?"

The old man smiled slightly. "No, it just means we've got to go looking for them. Don't worry. We'll get someone." He twisted the dial again, his head tilted to the right as if maybe his hearing in that ear was better, and the machine wailed at them as he searched the frequencies. Slowly, the noise faded. "Bingo." Out of the static came a conversation, tinny, but gloriously alive. Alex covered her mouth as she listened, her eyes glancing up at Simon's and seeing her excitement reflected there in those depths of blue. How good it would be to get help and pass this buck over to the authorities.

When a natural pause arrived between the two men, Daniel opened up the mike, cutting in.

"Sorry to interrupt, this is Golf Three Quebec Sierra Tango. I'm calling from Watterrow, Somerset. We've got a bit of an emergency here and need the police, but the phones aren't working. Are you close by?"

One of the two men came back straightaway. "I'm about ten miles the other side of Taunton. I know where you are. Is it something to do with this awful weather?"

Hesitating slightly, Daniel responded. "Likely a bit more serious than that. We need to get the police out here, especially before there's too much flooding. Can you call them for us? Tell them I'm a retired policeman myself. I don't want them to think we're causing a fuss over nothing."

"Roger. Keep this frequency open. Stand by."

Creaking the wooden door open, Daniel's wife, Ada,

carried through a tray with large mugs of coffee and a plate of sandwiches and held it out toward Alex, then Simon. "There you go."

Looking at the food, Alex felt her stomach turn. The pain that was literally eating at her, combined with finding the vicar dead, had destroyed her appetite. Still, she was grateful to take the steaming-hot liquid, enjoying the burning ceramic in her hands. She noticed that Simon didn't seem interested in eating either. Maybe he wasn't as tough as he appeared after all. Ada sat the tray down on top of the gas heater, and sipped her own coffee. The ham and pickle sandwiches remained untouched, and Alex figured that they all took comfort in their own ways. Maybe Ada's means of soothing herself was to prepare food, even knowing that no one was going to eat it. Daniel and Ada were both regular churchgoers, and the loss of Reverend Barker would have hit the couple quite hard. Alex wondered if, like her, the idea of the reverend committing suicide out of the blue seemed highly unlikely to Ada Rose. She imagined that it probably would, and perhaps it was contemplating the alternative that was adding to all their edginess. Why would anyone want to kill the vicar?

"How are you getting on up here?" Ada stared with concern at the back of her husband's head. "The storm's getting right fearful out there. I think some people may have lost a tile or two by tomorrow at this going."

Before Daniel could answer, the machine spat out the disembodied voice it carried. "Calling Golf Three Quebec Sierra Tango. Are you still there?"

"Still here. Go ahead."

"It doesn't seem to be your night. I've spoken to the

police. They can't get out to you at the moment. A highsider's overturned on the B2338 in the wind. That's the only road into your village isn't it? They can't—"

The voice was cut off by a high-pitched mechanical screech and Daniel's jaw clenched.

"Jesus, what's that? Feedback?" Alex could feel the roots of her teeth tingling with the sound as she flinched.

"I'm not sure." Daniel turned down the volume and checked the settings. "I've never had anything happen like that before." He clicked the button down again. "This is Golf Three Quebec Sierra Tango. Are you still there?" Only a crackle came back at them. "I don't understand it."

Simon sipped his coffee. "Could the storm have knocked the aerial out of line or something?"

Daniel let out a sigh. "It could have. Or the lightning could be affecting it in some way." He smiled grimly at them. "But I'm sure that we'll get them back. I may just have to fiddle around up here for a while."

Alex and Simon sat in silence for ten minutes, hoping in vain for another voice to join them through the hulk of metal that Daniel poked and prodded, before Paul turned up, dripping and windswept. Alex stepped out into the hall to speak to him.

"Is Mary okay?"

Paul shrugged, and exhaled. "Well, I'm not sure if 'okay' is the right word. But she's better than she was before. Maybe being in the pub will be good for her." He paused to take a mug of coffee from Ada, who'd been more than glad to have one more soaking stray to cater to. "How about you two? Did you manage to get hold of the police?"

Alex shook her head. "Daniel managed to get hold of someone on the radio, but there's a lorry overturned on the road, so there's no way the police will be able to get to us today."

"Jesus." He banged the back of his head gently and absently against the wall while absorbing the information, as if knocking for entrance to a secret passageway. "So, what are we supposed to do?"

Alex was saved from her inability to answer by Simon, who joined them, Daniel dwarfed in the shadow of his large frame.

"I guess we'll just have to move the body into the church and lock it up. I can't think of a better solution. Once we've done that, maybe we should ask the residents if they've seen anything or anyone unusual around. Maybe try and get down to the caravan site as well."

Alex knew he was thinking of the strange children they saw earlier, and she was too. It was easier to think of strangers doing something like that rather than anyone from the village, and maybe it was just a childish prank that went horribly, horribly wrong. "Maybe we should try to get people together in The Rock later. At least that way we can break the news to the whole village at once and stop any rumors or gossip."

Paul nodded. "And a drink or two at the end of this wouldn't go amiss, either."

At the end of this. Alex wondered exactly when "the end of this" would be. She couldn't forget the desperation in the vicar's eyes as his blood carried his last words to her. *Warn them. Come for us. Our sin.* Maybe it was nothing; maybe he was just rambling after lying broken and dying out in the rain for God only knew how long, but deep inside, in the part of her that truly accepted that cancer was killing her, she didn't believe that. Something else was going on in Watterrow, something she didn't understand, but something she was sure had to do with Melanie Parr.

Ada joined them in the corridor. "He's checking the fuses, but I'm sure he'll have it working again soon. He spends that many hours tinkering around in there that he can more than likely take that radio apart and put it back together again in his sleep." She managed a small smile at Paul. "How's your mother? Has her headache gone?"

Paul nodded, his eyes slipping slightly sideways. "Yes, but she's still not quite herself. She's having a sherry at The Rock."

"Well, I might just go and join her. I think a sherry would do me nicely right now. And Crouch will be happy for the profit."

Simon looked down at Alex. "Crouch?"

"Crouch the Grouch, we call him. He's the landlord."

Leading them down the misshapen stairs, Ada paused at the bottom to pull a coat from the closet, before passing the others theirs. The damp material was cold, and Alex was shivering by the time she'd got it on and done up, and she sensed that Simon must be feeling the same beside her. The idea of going back to the church and dealing with the body sent a wave of fatigue through her.

Simon zipped his coat right up to his chin, making his voice seem muffled. "When we ask people about what's happened to the vicar, we should mention that girl that went missing, Melanie Parr, to them. Maybe it's nothing, but it seems strange that your aunt mentioned her name and then Reverend Barker. Maybe someone will be able to shed some light on it."

Ada's face twitched and jumped as she stared at them. "Melanie Parr?"

Alex nodded.

"But she went missing thirty years ago. She can't have anything to do with this. She can't."

"Well, maybe, but maybe not. A few questions won't hurt." Alex pulled the door open, letting the storm's furious curiosity surge past them and peer noisily into every corner of the snug cottage.

Daniel had followed them down to see them off, and turning in the doorway, Ada clutched at the arm of her husband. "You didn't tell me. You didn't say anything about Melanie Parr . . . ."

Daniel ushered her out, and the rest of Ada's words were swallowed up by the wind.

Pausing for a moment to fall behind the older woman, Alex once again felt that there was something going on in her village that she wasn't a part of, but now she knew she was being dragged into it against her will. Her and Simon. Whatever it was about Melanie Parr that bothered these people, she was determined to find out.

CHAPTER TWELVE

The rain was hammering into the kitchen window as Kay stuffed dirty washing into the machine, and somewhere not too far away thunder rumbled toward them. For a moment she stared out over the garden. To her left she could make out the edge of the woods and felt just a twinge of maternal worry. They'd better not have gone into the woods, not with the storm whipping up as it was. She trusted Laura, she really did, and individually she trusted the Granville kids, but from her own childhood she could remember what it was like in a group of friends. It was easy to be persuaded and to get carried away by the collective mind.

She filled the soap section and pushed the On button, feeling the vibration through her hands as the machine tumbled into life. Emma would be fuming if they came home with muddy clothes. She had enough washing to deal with between the littlest ones and Dave's work clothes. On reflection, though, Kay was pretty sure the kids would stay away from the river and woods.

The kitchen table was still covered with breakfast debris, and putting the kettle back on for another cup of tea, she covered the jam and the butter and put the plates in the dishwasher. Thank the lord for modern appliances. She'd vacuumed yesterday so there was no need to do that, and once she'd sorted the washing and figured out what to cook Laura for dinner, the day was pretty much her own. And the wonderful thing about a rainy day, once you were over the age of about fifteen, was that it really did encourage you to do absolutely nothing. She'd got the new Martina Coles book from her book club and she hadn't started it yet, and that was looking like her plan for the day. To curl up on the sofa, maybe eat the bar of chocolate at the back of the fridge, and lose herself in the exciting big-city world of one of Martina's characters. There were definitely worse ways to spend the day.

Humming, she damped a cloth and wiped it over the wooden table. Maybe she'd even start the book before the washing was done. Sure, if she tried she could find a few more jobs around the house to do to fill the time—the bathroom, for one, always seemed to need cleaning, but she figured it would still be there tomorrow, and today she felt like having a lazy, indulgent day to herself.

The kettle finished its bubbling and she poured it over the bag, letting it soak for a moment or two before pinching it out between her forefinger and thumb, ignoring the heat, and dropping it quickly into the bin. Promising herself that she wouldn't touch it for at least an hour, she grabbed the large bar of Dairy Milk from the fridge and padded into the lounge, sinking into the well-worn couch. This was going to be bliss.

She had only finished the first chapter when her attention was distracted by the sound of something coming from above. What was that? It wasn't the banging she'd heard earlier; this was something else, like a voice. Putting the book down, she listened to the noises of her house. From the kitchen came the quiet whirring of the washing machine, but apart from that there was nothing. For once, even the creaks in the old wood and brick had subsided.

And then she heard it again. Was it laughter? Putting the book down, she stood up and frowned. Maybe Laura had brought the Granville kids around to play, but it wasn't like her not to say hello on her way in. And Laura was polite. She'd have asked her if it was okay, even though she knew that Kay was never likely to say no.

Leaving the lounge, she went into the hall and called up from the bottom of the stairs. "Laura? Is that you?"

It was gloomier in the heart of the house, with no large windows to allow in even the gray light from outside, and as the silence came back at her, Kay fought the temptation to flick the light switch. That would just be stupid and silly. It would be like admitting she was feeling nervous in her own house. And she wasn't. She definitely wasn't. Still staring upward, she saw a shadow darting across the landing. It was so fast she almost thought she'd imagined it. Maybe it was a cat that had got in somehow to escape from the rain.

Annoyed at her own inaction, she climbed the stairs, ignoring the familiar creaks, and took a few steps across the landing. "Laura?"

From somewhere behind the spare room door she heard a giggle. "Laura, this isn't funny." For the first time she felt a tingle of fear creep up from her toes. What was this? Although she was calling her daughter's name, she knew in her blood that it wasn't Laura up here giggling and playing games. Laura was a good girl.

The lilting voice danced out from the doorway. *"As I was going up the stair, I met a girl who wasn't there."* Behind the voice came a little girl, no more than ten or eleven, and staring at her. Kay's heart froze. It wasn't Laura. It definitely wasn't Laura; this was a very different little girl, and one that Kay knew. She had once known her too well. It couldn't be. It just couldn't be. *But it is. It's Melanie Parr.* Melanie Parr was dead and gone. Gone a long time ago, lost in the storm. Not hearing her own moan, Kay took a step backward, her eyes trapped staring at the perfect blond hair, and the kilt-style pleated skirt, and then the high white socks, one red shoe on, and one foot bare.

The Melanie that couldn't be smiled at her, white teeth sparkling in the gloom, and took one pace forward. *"I saw that girl again today."* She tilted her head and pouted, mocking Kay's fear. *"I wish . . . I wish she'd go away."* She paused to giggle that hollow laugh, and it seemed to fill Kay's head. *"Do you wish I'd go away, Kay? Don't you want to play with me anymore?"*

Kay shuffled further backward. This wasn't real. It couldn't be real. It was the storm bringing back memories, that's what it was, or maybe she was getting the flu and a fever, or maybe she had fallen asleep down on the sofa and this was all a very, very bad dream. The tears that were filling her eyes felt real, though. And staring at the girl in front of her, she didn't feel like a woman nearly forty, she felt like she was a child again, small and always scared.

Melanie slowly waggled a raised finger. *"Tut-tut, Kay Keeler."* The smile and tilt to her head remained, and Kay groaned again. Keeler. She hadn't been Kay Keeler for such a very long time. *"You told. You told on me and look what you did."*

They seemed to stare at each other for an age, Kay's eyes swimming with tears, and then from behind Melanie, from the doorways to the spare room and the bathroom, four more children appeared, one girl and three boys, their faces serious, their clothes, unlike Melanie's, muddy and damp. One of the boys was carrying what looked like Phil's fishing box, the size of it too big for the child, who could only have been about six years old. This dream was getting too real, and she wanted it over. "You don't exist," she mumbled to herself and to the gang of children in front of her. "You don't exist."

Melanie's smile stretched into a grin, and behind her the other dark-haired girl slyly giggled.

"Oh, but we do, Kay. We live in the storm with the Catcher Man. I've had such adventures with him, you wouldn't believe. And I've gotten oh so strong." She took a long stride forward and Kay yelped, reaching behind her for the banister to guide her to the stairs.

"And now I've come back to play. And your mummy's not around to run to anymore. I'm going to play with you all, Kay. I've already started, and now it's your turn."

Kay felt her feet tangling up under her, misjudging the distance between herself and the top step, and she called out as she tumbled, hands reaching frantically for the banisters as she rolled painfully past them. Her shoulder cracked against the wall and pain roared through her, stars shooting across her eyes. If this was a dream, then surely she should wake up now. Surely she should.

Above her, Melanie looked like a kaleidoscope of color as she stood at the top of the stairs. *"Shall we play fishing?"*

Hitting the hard wooden floor head first, Kay's world went black.

CHAPTER THIRTEEN

Alex had stayed in the church while Paul and Simon went to the graveyard to collect Reverend Barker, and although she was glad not to have to see his broken body up close again, she was happy when the two men appeared in the doorway. The church was giving her the creeps standing inside on her own, and looking at the vandalized altar, she couldn't help but feel as if the old building were accusing her of something. It was stupid, but she still felt relieved not to be alone anymore.

"I guess this is as good a place to put him as any." Paul looked pale as he lowered his end of the awkward bundle onto the ground in front of the first pew and Alex was pleased that the altar rug covered most of the body. She didn't need to look into his eyes again. Listening to the thud when Simon let go of the weight, Alex wondered if rigor mortis had set in yet. Or maybe he'd been through that and was coming out the other side? The morbid thoughts were unpleasant, but she couldn't stop herself. Maybe summer flies had already laid their eggs on him. It was funny how much she'd discovered about death these days. As if knowledge of its processes would somehow cause a miracle and she'd escape it. *Yeah right. That pain running through your bones isn't getting any better, is it?* She stared again at the bundle on the floor. *A few months tops, and I'll be seeing you, Reverend.*

"It didn't look like anyone else had been round there." Simon wiped the water from his glasses. "The body was untouched as far as I could tell."

"Good," Alex said. "However odd those children were we saw this morning, it wouldn't be nice for them to find something like this. Hardly what you want on your holiday."

"Is this written in wax?" Paul was staring down at the altar, color returning to his face. "What does it mean?"

Alex shrugged. "I'm not sure. It seems familiar, like I've heard it before, but I don't know where." She looked up at her cousin. "Do you think it could be related to that Melanie Parr girl?"

Paul's brow furrowed instantly. "Why would it have anything to do with her?" His tone was sharp and there was a slight hesitancy over the first word that hinted at his stutter.

"Well, her name was what Reverend Barker was trying to say when he died. Her name and then something about warning people. Surely there must be a link to these words."

"Or it could have just been the last rantings of a stark raving mad suicide. Have you considered that?" He spat the words at her and Alex recoiled slightly. What the hell was the matter with him? Why did he get so defensive every time that missing girl's name was mentioned?

"Yes." She kept her own voice cool. "Of course I have."

"Look, I'm sure you two can manage to lock this place up by yourselves. I'll walk down to the doctor's and let him know what we've done. He may need to come and see the body or something." He was calmer, but Paul still couldn't meet Alex's gaze. "I'll meet you back at The Rock." Nodding to Simon, he scurried back up the aisle and out into the rain.

Simon raised an eyebrow at Alex and she shrugged in return. It seemed that his friend had noticed Paul's strange behavior too.

"So, where do you think we'll find the keys?" Simon was obviously polite enough not to want to talk about Paul, and Alex liked that. "I checked his pockets outside, but they were empty."

Alex nodded past the choir seats. "He's got a small office out at the back past the vestry." It didn't seem like that long ago that she and Ian had sat in there and chatted with the vicar over their plans for the wedding. Bitterness tugged at her heart. Who was she kidding? It was four years and a lifetime ago. So much for "till death us do part." It turned out that her beloved didn't want to hang around for that bit. Sniffing, she pulled herself up tall. Screw him. Those days were gone. Long gone.

She led the way, warning Simon to duck through the low doorway as they found the vicar's office. After the cool emptiness of the church, the cluttered room seemed cozy and warm.

"There they are." Alex pointed to the large bunch of keys sitting on the desk. Picking them up, Simon paused. "Hey, come and look at this."

"What?"

"Look at the stuff on his desk."

Coming alongside him, Alex stared. A pad of paper was open with various notes written on it. At the top was the coming Sunday's date, and the bland scribblings on the sheet were obviously the beginnings of his sermon. The pen was placed on the sheet, cap still off, not neatly stacked with all the other pens in the tray, as if he'd been disturbed by something. Her eyes flicked across. Next to the pad was an open packet of bourbon cookies, and next to that was a mug, half full of cold tea.

Alex looked back up at Simon. "Well, I'm no policeman, but this hardly looks like the desk of a man about to commit suicide."

Simon nodded. "I agree. Even the way the keys were on the desk. It looks like he came in here to do some work, and then something disturbed him. I don't think he killed himself at all."

Staring once again at all the evidence in front of her, Alex couldn't help but agree. With what she knew about the reverend, she hadn't really believed that he'd commit suicide anyway, but now, after seeing his office, she was doubly sure. But it did leave an uneasy feeling in her gut. "If he didn't kill himself, then what the hell happened to him?"

Sighing, Simon perched on the edge of the desk. "Well, that's the million dollar question, isn't it?" He paused. "This whole thing seems really odd to me."

"How do you mean?" Alex pulled out the desk chair

and sat down, letting her grateful limbs rest. Tiredness had become a way of life, but the stress of the past day on top of it was taking its toll.

"Well, for a start, this Melanie Parr business. Don't you think it's odd that you didn't know anything about it?"

She shrugged. "She went missing before I was born."

"That doesn't matter. I would have thought that this was a pretty sleepy village, and something like that would have been talked about for years, wouldn't it? It just seems weird to me that no one even mentioned it to you."

"The country can be like that, Simon. Strange things happen out here. People are different than in the city. Out here we just get on with it, if you know what I mean."

He nodded. "Yeah, I guess so. But then your aunt being convinced that Melanie Parr spoke to her yesterday and then the vicar saying her name before he died and the way Paul reacts every time her name is mentioned . . . ." His voice trailed off. "I don't know what I'm trying to say."

Alex stared at him, her voice soft as she thought aloud. "I do. It's like they're all scared of her. Scared of her memory, at any rate. But why would they all be scared of a child that went missing all that time ago? It doesn't make sense."

Simon smiled slightly. "No, it doesn't, but nothing's making sense." He paused. "And I can't talk about things being strange."

"What do you mean?"

He looked awkward, as if he'd started saying something and now regretted it. "You'll think I'm crazy."

Alex laughed, but there was no humor in it. "Trust me, I won't think you're crazy. I saw a little boy at the church gate that disappeared into thin air, remember?" God, if he only knew the rest. He'd think she was barking. "Go on. What's bothering you?"

"It's about the children, actually. Something that I know can't be right, but I just can't shift it from my head." He sighed. "You know those two kids we saw out in the rain this morning and I said that one of them seemed familiar?"

Alex nodded. "Go on."

"Well, it's been bugging me all morning, and it was only thinking about Melanie Parr that it suddenly came to me. Where I'd seen his face before."

"You're just beating about the bush now. Get on with it!" Alex smiled, trying to put him at ease.

"I did some research for a series of articles on a missing child once. You know, other kids that had gone missing in similar circumstances. The final piece wasn't very good and never made it into the paper, but I did do some work on it. Well, the thing I guess I'm trying to say is that I'm sure that boy that we saw on the way to the shop this morning was one of the children I researched. His photo was on all the papers with those glasses on, and that sweater. It was a school sweater he had on over jeans, did you notice?" He didn't wait for a response. "I wish I'd seen it close enough this morning to see the school logo. But how odd to wear a school sweater on holiday."

Alex stared at the vicar's things on the desk, casually abandoned before death, then thought of the message scrawled on the altar.

"I don't think you're crazy. I don't think you're crazy

at all." She looked up at Simon. "That's not to say that I think you're right about the kid, because that's just not possible, but I do agree that there's some weird shit going on. When you heard me say something at the altar and I pretended I hadn't?" He nodded. "Well, what I said was, I couldn't move my legs. Look how they move now. The problem is, I don't know why I said it. It just seemed right."

They stared at each other for a second, and then Alex smiled. "Maybe it's the storm. Maybe it's made us all a little bit crazy." For a second she thought she might tell him about the little boy from the church gate, *her* little boy and how she'd seen him in her room the night before, but then stopped herself. Now that really would be crazy.

"You know the library here has a lot of old newspapers on microfiche. Nationals as well as locals. If that kid's face is really bugging you, then you can always stop by and have a look. No one will mind. And it may help pass the time if the weather leaves you stuck here with us for a couple of days."

Simon shrugged, looking slightly embarrassed, and once again Alex was relieved that she hadn't told him about her strange experiences of the night before. If he thought what he'd seen was odd, he'd think she was a freak for what happened to her.

"It was probably nothing, but we'll see. Maybe I will." He grinned. "It's probably just my old eyes and all this talk of missing children making my brain play tricks on me."

Standing up, Alex nodded sagely. "Yes, you look like you're getting on a bit. It's probably just a touch of dementia setting in."

"Great. A touch of dementia. Beautiful. Just what I need."

Alex laughed aloud. "Well, I think what I need is a glass of wine. It's got to be lunchtime already, and after the morning we've had, I think I've earned it. Let's go down to The Rock and find that grumpy cousin of mine."

"Good plan, lady. Good plan."

CHAPTER FOURTEEN

One of the things Laura loved about the Granville house was that it was always messy. Not dirty, but cluttered, and in the kids' rooms their toys were always out and sometimes their beds weren't made. Not even Jenny's or Jimmy's, and they were the same age as she was. She guessed it came from being part of a big family. There were just too many children to keep track of, and as long as they were all clean, dressed, and fed, then that seemed to be good enough for Mrs. Granville. It wasn't like being an only child. Yes, that gave you plenty of attention, but it also meant there was plenty of rule-obeying. Laura would never be allowed out of the house without having made her bed first. Still, that wasn't such a terrible chore, and her parents were pretty cool most of the time.

Another thing she loved about going to the Granville house was that it always smelled like cakes or cookies were being baked; a hot, sweet mouthwatering scent that hugged you when you stepped through the door.

And normally, it was because there was a batch of something delicious cooking in the oven.

Sitting on Jimmy's bed, the England football squad duvet crumpled up to make a cushion, that morning she could smell chocolate in the air.

"Is your mum baking again?"

Jimmy shrugged. "Yeah, but not for us. She's got some Women's Institute thing tomorrow, so she's baking for that."

Jenny rummaged in the bottom of the closet, yanking out toys in various states of disrepair. "We could play with Barbie and Ken." She blew a strand of fine, golden to ginger hair out her face, her ponytail untidy down her back.

"Yuk." Jimmy grimaced. "There is no way we're playing dolls." His own matching color hair was short and spiky and looked freshly gelled. The two may have been twins, but Laura could see their own differing personalities emerging as each month passed.

"You didn't used to mind."

He glared at his sister. "I used to be a kid and didn't know any better. Boys don't play dolls. And anyway, you always want to play stupid romance games with them."

Laura sighed. This was true. Jimmy didn't mind playing with the dolls when they were playing serial killers and stuff, but Jenny was growing up into a romantic and always wanted Barbie and Ken to get married. Laura liked both games, but she was glad Jimmy had said no. She wasn't in the mood for the dolls either.

Outside the sky was still dull gray. "I wish we could play outside. I don't want to stay in." However much they could never agree on what games to play inside, outside it seemed that the possibilities were endless and they always found something that they all wanted to do. Her coat was behind her on the bed, where little Peter was playing with an Etch-a-scketch, concentrating furiously on his clumsy scribblings, and she thought about the phone in her pocket.

"When the wind dies down Mum will let us out. And probably even if it doesn't. She'll go mad with us cooped up in here all day." Jimmy grinned cheekily. "We'll make sure she lets us out one way or another. If we play cowboys and Indians loudly enough round the house she'll pay us to leave."

Laura smiled, but she was still thinking about her phone. "This is going to sound a bit stupid, but have either of you had any texts this morning?"

Jimmy and Jenny both shook their heads. "Nope. My phone isn't even on. I never turn it on when I'm not at school. Don't see the point."

Jenny tilted her head. "Why?"

"Well, I got a few this morning. I didn't even know my phone was on."

"Who were they from? Anyone interesting?" Jenny wiggled one eyebrow at Laura, implying maybe one of the boys they had crushes on at school.

"No." Laura felt herself blush a bit. She didn't want to talk about the boys at school in front of Jimmy. "Not like that, anyway. They were really odd. From some girl called Melanie. Said she wanted me to play with her 'cause she was lonely." The twins stared at her, and she wished she hadn't said anything. "I ignored them, but I just wondered if you'd had anything like that."

"Maybe some kid from the campsite pissing around." Jimmy emphasized the swear word happily.

Laura had noticed him using more and more bad language now that they had moved up to the senior school. It always made Jenny roll her eyes and Laura thought that secretly made Jimmy enjoy it all the more.

"Yeah, that's what I figured."

"Let's have a look though. Did you bring your phone? Maybe one of us will recognize the number."

Laura yanked the handset from her coat. "I think the phone's dying though. I couldn't see a sender's number this morning." The screen was black, and she pushed the On button. Nothing happened. "The battery must have died." Peering at the small dead screen, Laura decided not to tell her friends that there hadn't been any battery or signal showing earlier either. She was already wishing she just hadn't mentioned the whole thing. She felt like she was making something out of nothing. "It doesn't matter anyway."

"I seen children playing. New children." Peter didn't raise his head but kept drawing.

"Sure you did, Petey." Jimmy grinned at his baby brother. " 'Course you did."

Peter shrugged slightly, as if he didn't care whether his big brother believed him or not.

Shoving the dolls back into the bottom of the closet, Jenny glanced at her Mickey Mouse watch. "It's nearly ten. Shall we go and see if Mum's cookies are done?"

"I thought you said they were for other people."

Hauling herself to her feet, Jenny looked impatiently at Laura. "This is Mum we're talking about. She'll have made thousands. Plenty for us!"

"We might even persuade her to let us go out now," Jimmy grumbled.

Getting off the bed, Laura looked at Peter. "You coming, or shall I bring you a cookie up?' At three, Peter's hair was still very blond, no sign of the red that marked his older siblings, and Laura had a real soft spot for him. She remembered when he was born, and she loved the way he just quietly got on with things, entertaining himself.

"Stayin,' " he mumbled, still bent over his battered toy.

"Okay." She kissed the top of his head and bounded down the stairs after her friends.

It was only as she disappeared through the doorway that he raised his head and looked out the window, his small blue eyes searching for something amongst the hedgerows of the garden and the trees of the woods beyond. "I want to go and play with the other children, Laura." His eyes glanced back to the door, disappointed she'd gone before he spoke. He then looked back out at the trees, then down at his toy, then back to the trees again. In his head he could see his bright yellow coat on the floor of his bedroom. All the others were downstairs. He could put his coat on and go out for just a minute. He wouldn't go very far. It was naughty to wander off, he knew that, and he wasn't a naughty boy, he was a good boy.

He would just go down to the end of the garden. Maybe just the other side of the fence and see if the children were there. And then he'd go back inside. That's what he'd do. He'd go back inside and have a cookie with Laura and Jenny and Jimmy. Staring out the window, he nodded as if someone had asked him a question, and then carefully put the toy down on the bed and padded toward his room.

The yellow coat was exactly where he remembered it, and his face concentrated, he slipped each arm into the appropriate hole, for a moment thinking that the back was going to be at the front; then he'd never figure it out and have to call for Jenny or Mummy. He smiled happily when the gaping opening was where it should be. Leaving it undone, not yet old enough to master the zip, he crept out into the hallway. His small, pudgy hand gripped the rail of each banister as he carefully came down each stair, trying to be quiet. Normally he would slide down on his bottom, but he was scared that might make too much noise. And he could see better through the banisters.

From the kitchen he could hear the others laughing and giggling as they persuaded his mother to hand over the hot baked oatmeal and raisin cookies, and for a second he was tempted to forget all about the other children and join them instead. They were talking about putting a movie on while waiting for the thunder to pass and he heard Laura mention his name and say something about taking some cookies and milk up to him.

Turning his back on the noise, as Mummy was saying that if he was hungry he'd have to come down and get one himself, he wasn't a baby anymore, Peter wished that Laura would come out and play with the new children too. He was sure that they wanted her to. Especially Melanie. Melanie said she wanted to be friends with everyone and there were some other new children that were three, just like him, to play with.

One eye fearfully focused on the kitchen, he pulled open the downstairs bathroom door and reached in to pull his Wellington boots out from their place with the others under the sink. His breath was coming in fast pants with the concentration of being so careful, and tucking himself under the stairs, just in case someone came out into the hallway, he tugged the boots on. He got them on the right feet through accident rather than planning and, ready to go, he peered round the edge of the stairs to make sure the way was clear.

Normally he'd go out to the garden through the back door in the kitchen; in fact, normally that was the only door they ever used, but that way was blocked, so he was going to have to use the front one. Stepping forward, he stretched himself as far on his tiptoes as he could go, small clumsy fingers grasping at the latch. For a second he didn't think he was going to make it and he'd have to reverse everything he'd done and run back upstairs, but then he felt the cold metal. Letting his feet do the work, he dropped back onto his soles, keeping his finger on the metal, and as he lowered, so did the catch, the door immediately swinging open with the wind from outside.

Smiling, he stepped out into the rain and shut the door as quietly as he could behind him. The water hit his face hard, but he was a country boy and the elements didn't really bother him, especially when the air was warm, and squinting against it, he trotted around the side of the house and down to the garden. He couldn't hear anyone coming behind him, but up ahead, just beyond the low back garden gate at the edge of the woods, he could see the children waiting for him. Four or five were peering out from behind the trees, but Melanie was right by the gate, no coat on and smiling at him, as if the weather couldn't touch her. Raising his arm, he waved excitedly. They wanted to play with him. Just him. And not because he had to tag along with Jenny or Jimmy or the others. They were going to be friends of his own.

The wind seemed to get stronger as he got closer to the gate, but Peter didn't mind. Melanie was waving him forward, having taken a step back toward the woods, and reaching the gate, Peter hesitated. He'd always promised Mummy that he would never ever wander outside the garden without her. His fingers toyed with the bolt impatiently. But he wouldn't go very far. And he wouldn't be alone.

Staring at the others waving him on, he smiled, pushed the metal open, and followed.

They were about halfway through *Scary Movie 2* when Laura felt the phone vibrating in her sweatshirt pouch, which was strange because she was pretty sure that she'd left it in her coat pocket on the bed. She was also sure that when it had gone off this morning it was the tone that had been on. Maybe she'd accidentally pressed a button when she was messing with it. She didn't feel convinced. What she was convinced about was that the phone had been dead when she'd tried to turn it on to show Jimmy and Jenny the earlier messages. So how come it was buzzing now?

She was curled up in one of the Granville's oversized comfy armchairs and the twins were stretched out on the carpet in front of her on beanbag cushions. Not wanting to draw attention to herself, not until she had something she could actually show them at any rate, she quietly drew the phone out. The screen shone brightly.

New Text Message
She pushed the open button.
If you tell he will die
She read it twice before the cold chill settled in her

young stomach. Once again the screen was empty of a battery reading or signal bars and there was no sender id. No name, no number. Getting up from her seat, she walked as casually as she could out into the hall and took refuge in the downstairs bathroom. Lowering the lid, she sat on the toilet seat, feeling its cool surface through her jeans, making her skin pimple. Her hand moved over the buttons and sent just one word:

Who?

This time the message sign didn't even come up, just the words, taunting her from the green screen.

Look and see.

The screen darkened for a moment, then flickered to life, the colors on the film bright, made more eerie by the silence. A blonde girl that looked younger than her was smiling at the camera and waving, her curls blowing out behind her head in the wind. It seemed like she was standing in the woods somewhere, but it seemed darker than it should have been and Laura couldn't figure out if that and the strange greenish tinge to the gloom was because of the phone or just the madness of these messages that shouldn't be coming through anyway.

The little girl—*is that Melanie?*—pointed to her left, and the camera panned to the left, and Laura had to put her hand to her mouth to stop herself from crying out. Peter's yellow coat was immediately recognizable, as was his blond hair and his sweet face, all crumpled and crying. Two older children, one boy who seemed to be wearing a school sweater and jeans, his glasses glinting even in the sickly gloom, and a girl in an old-fashioned pinafore dress, were holding each of his arms and smiling while someone else, Laura couldn't see who, threw small rocks at him. Peter squirmed as they hit his small body and Laura could see that he was crying out, confused and terrified by the pain, but the two children kept a firm hold on him.

The camera moved back to Melanie, who was still smiling, then the screen returned to an open text message. Whoever the girl was, she obviously wanted Laura to say something. And Laura knew what it was.

What do you want?

She could feel the two cookies she'd eaten gurgling and fighting to rise as bile from her stomach. This was stupid and crazy. Why would those kids have taken Peter? Why did he go with them? New words flashed up.

I want you to play with me.

Laura stared.

And you'll let Petey go?

Not if you tell. Bad things happen when you tell.

The world felt blurry at the edges and she couldn't really believe she was having this conversation.

Where are you?

The woods. Come now.

Where in the woods?

We'll find you. We want to play.

The phone went dead. Lights out, power off, and for a full minute Laura just stared at it. Part of her almost didn't believe the last few minutes had happened, but the trembling in her hands and the image burned into her eyes of little Petey crying as rocks were thrown at him told her otherwise. This was crazy and weird but it was happening.

Fighting the urge to run in a panic to Emma Granville, she stood on shaky legs, lifted the lid and flushed. There was only one thing she could do, and that was go out in the woods and find Pete. Whoever these kids were, they wouldn't know the local area as well as she did, and once she'd found the little boy she'd get away from them and come and tell her mum. She didn't know how they'd got her phone to work, but it was probably some bluetooth connection or something new that hadn't worked its way down into the country yet.

Taking a deep breath, she went back to the lounge. Jimmy squirmed on his old cushion. "You okay?"

"No, I don't feel too well. I think I'll go home."

Jenny sat up. "Yeah, you look a bit pale. Did it just come on?"

"Yeah. I'll just go and grab my coat. I'll call you later."

"Okay. Hope you feel better."

Laura tried her best at a weak smile, then turned her back on them, taking the stairs two at a time to fetch her coat. Jimmy's bed was empty, dashing her vague hope that Peter would be sitting hunched over the Etch-a-Sketch where they'd left him and this was all some kind of weird trick. She could just about make out the small dent in the covers where he had been sitting. This was real. He was gone. She stared out the window for a moment, the trees a blur in the rain, before heading back down the stairs and out into the storm.

CHAPTER FIFTEEN

Paul trudged carefully across the steep cobbled road, having left Simon and Alex warming up in The Rock with large glasses of red wine and a quiet but lucid Mary. They'd told him what they'd found in the vicar's office and he'd agreed that it didn't sound too much like a suicide to him, either. They'd stared at him as if hoping he could shed some light on it, but he didn't have any more of a clue what was going on than they did. All he knew was that Melanie Parr was long gone; maybe someone was playing tricks on them and one of those tricks had gone badly wrong with Reverend Barker. He didn't see the point in sharing what he remembered of the girl unless he had to. And as far as he was concerned, at the moment he didn't have to. Some memories were best left buried in the past where they belonged.

He paused, his eyes for a moment distracted by some movement in the gray air ahead of him. For a second he thought he saw a small group of children playing ring-a-ring-of-roses, but then, as he blinked, they'd gone. He stared into the rain, but there was nothing there but the uneven walls of the stone cottages. One still had a large black bin out in front from whenever the garbage men came. Maybe that's what he'd seen. Great. Now it wasn't just Mary seeing things, it was him too. Maybe it was something in the water. He blinked again, rain getting in his eyes. Or something in this bloody storm, which seemed to be getting worse rather than better. Still, an hour outside at most and then he'd be back in the warm, where he pretty much intended to stay until the rain stopped. Above his head the sky growled, but no lightning flashed. At least that was something.

Simon had offered to come back out and help him knock on doors to let people know to meet in the pub at four, but Paul persuaded him against it, saying that his friend needed to dry out and that there weren't exactly hundreds of houses to go to. It was a small white lie. Paul may have moved into the city, but he still understood country people. They were used to taking care of themselves. It was in their blood after generations of hard living, of working the fields and animals of the farms with no one but family on which to rely. They wouldn't like having some city man they didn't know telling them what to do. Some of them would probably even have a problem with *him*. He had moved away, after all.

Still, he thought as he looked up through the streaks of water to the lit-up windows of the gray stone building closest to him, he shouldn't have a problem here. He'd known Phil and Kay Chambers forever; from long before Kay Keeler ever considered kissing a boy, let alone becoming Phil Chambers's wife. They were two of the guests that should have been coming to his party the previous night and he'd been looking forward to seeing them again. The primary school days at Wivvy Local School were a long time past.

Not finding a bell through the gloom, he knocked loudly, just as he'd done as a boy. Phil's family had lived in this house for generations. His mum had been a schoolteacher and his dad worked with the dairy farms, just as his dad had before him. Phil may have broken the mold by becoming an accountant, but he still loved the country life and spent most of his summer weekends out fishing on the quiet river. It wasn't the life for Paul, but he could understand why his friend had chosen to stay. The country got into some people's blood and they'd never be able to shake it out.

With no answer coming, he lowered his head and peered through the letter box. "Kay? Are you in there?" His ear pressed to the small gap, he was sure he heard laughter coming back at him. Like a child's laughter. "Laura? It's Paul. Can you answer the door?" Warm rain trickled into his mouth.

Waiting for Laura to come downstairs, he felt slightly confused. Where was Kay? She surely wouldn't have gone out anywhere with the weather like this. Stepping back, he stared at the house. All the lights were on. Maybe Laura had friends over. The seconds ticked by, but the door didn't open. What was she doing?

Something in his peripheral vision snagged his attention, and he paused for a moment. *What was that?* The long low window at the front of the house was steamed up as if something were being boiled close to it on the other side. That couldn't be though, because

Paul knew that room was the lounge. What were Laura and her friends doing in there? Stepping closer, trying to peer through, he realized that letters had been drawn on the fogged-up glass. What the hell did that say? Irritated, he pushed the rain out of his eyes and stared.

Come inside Paul
Lets play fishing with Kay

What the hell were Laura and her friends doing in there? This wasn't funny. This wasn't funny at all. On top of everything else that had gone on over the past twenty-four hours, he really didn't need this shit from kids. He hadn't taken shit from kids since he was one, and even then it was only Melanie that had scared him. He pushed the thought of her from his head. She was gone. Dead and gone a long time ago, and good riddance to bad rubbish. If Laura Chambers and her friend were behind what happened to Mary and the reverend, then he was going to kill them himself. Even in his anger, the thought didn't sit right. *She's a good kid. You know that. Why would she be doing this?* Another thought chilled him. Maybe Laura wasn't there. Maybe it was someone else. But who? And why?

Turning back to the doorway, he raised his hand to knock again, but as he made contact with the wood, it swung away from him. The door was open. Surely it had been locked a moment ago. The bright hallway was a relief after the dullness of the storm, and letting his anger have more reign than the slight nervousness that nibbled at his insides, he stepped inside.

THE TAKEN

* * *

A sound. Someone downstairs. Is she dreaming? Every-thing seems swimmy inside, nothing tenuous, yet every-thing so horribly real in the blackness. Her head lifts slowly as she comes around, her mind fuzzy and groggy. What happened? Where is she? She tries to open her mouth, but can't, forcing her breathing faster from her nose, a small spray of mucus escaping. She feels it settle on her hot cheeks around the plastic stretched over her lips. Tape? Why is there tape on her mouth? Hazy memories of sitting down to read her book. Then she'd heard something. Gone upstairs. There were children up there. Melanie had been up there, even though she couldn't be because Melanie was long gone, and there is no Catcher Man, everyone knows that. Had she fallen? Her brain aches trying to think. Yes, yes, she'd tumbled down the stairs. Maybe she is still there. As she forces herself awake, panic sets in. Whatever this is, it isn't a dream. Or a nightmare.

"Kay? Laura? Anyone home?"

Hearing her name being called from the depths of the house, her eyes drift open and she tries desperately to hold her head up, not let it loll backward or forward as it is so keen to do. She must concentrate. Focus. Where is she? Fear tingles through her almost conscious being. For a moment she isn't sure of exactly where she is as her eyes move around the room. It's her bedroom, she's sure of it, she can see her dressing gown hanging from the back of the door, but somehow it all seems different. Not seen from this angle before.

A low moan growls in her chest, her heart beating faster as alertness returns. Her arms and fingers are numb, her wrists burning above her. The big double bed has been pushed to the wall at one side, leaving the space where she hangs from the beam now free from clutter. Rolling her eyes upward, she sees the rope tied tightly, trussing her arms, her hands, almost alien to her, swollen and blue. She tries to move them and can't. She feels detached, apart from herself, from these hands that won't do as they're told.

"Kay?"

The voice is slightly closer, she thinks in the kitchen, and for a moment her heart stops with fear, her eyes flashing to the door, to whoever is on the other side, before a drip of recognition cools her down. Paul. It's Paul. Somehow Paul is in the house. He can help her, he can untie her, he can. . .

Her excitement has made her wriggle slightly and pain taps gleefully at her insides, the numbness fading. There is cold, deep cold buried within, and she senses that something is horribly, horribly wrong and that Paul isn't going to be able to help her, whatever he does. Slowly, slowly she lowers her trembling eyes, not wanting to, oh god, not wanting to, but she has to see, she has to see if she is hurt.

Her breath is coming rapidly from behind the tape, the sound almost a snort, and tears form at the corner of her eyes as she looks, but there is too much to see, too much to take in. She sees where the line of her shorts was when she lay in the garden the day before yesterday, the tan developing as nicely as she'd hoped it would, and somewhere in her head she thinks wildly that next time she will be braver and just take all her clothes off, it's not as if anyone could see over the high wall and Phil would love it, not that they'd ever really had a problem keeping up the excitement in their mar-

riage. She sees where she's put a few pounds on her hips at that place where all men love it and all women want to look like boys, but she'll lose it by the end of the summer. . . . And then she sees, she can't help but see the tape, the strips of white surgical tape that cover her belly, some of the edges pink, pink with her blood, where it's oozing from her, and the sobs start to come heavier.

What have they done to her? What have they put inside her? This isn't real. This can't be real. Dead people don't come back. They don't come back and they can't hurt you.

Rolling her head back up, her eyes widen and for a second her sobs stop. Melanie is standing against the bedroom wall, her arms hanging down at her sides, where she hadn't been just a moment ago. The little girl smiles.

"But we're not dead, Kay. Not all of us. Some are just in between. And it's amazing what you can do in between if you really try." Her smile stretches and to Kay her red gums look like blood. Melanie looks toward the door. "I think Paul's coming," she whispers. "Shall we play fishing?" She looks back at Kay, raising one finger and waggling it very slowly. "You shouldn't have told, Kay. You should never have told." Still waggling that small finger, she disappears into the wall, as if she's stepped backward and through it.

Kay feels a moan build up in her chest and against the tape that is stuck so hard to her mouth as terror envelopes her. No no no, this isn't happening to her, not to her, not to Kay Keeler, who people say could have been anything she wanted, but all she wanted to do was marry Phil Chambers and have a family, and who was so lucky to get all she wanted from her quiet life, this couldn't be hap-

pening to her, not to her, dead people don't come back, there is no Catcher Man . . . For a moment, she shuts her eyes, unaware of the strange moist sounds escaping from her nose as she cries, and then looks down again.

Her vision focuses on the six or seven thin strands of something—is that fishing rope? LET'S PLAY FISHING, KAY—that have been twisted together, and they leave her stomach from the small gap in the tape to form a thicker rope, stretching out like a thin, dry umbilical cord directly in front of her. Her terrified eyes follow its taut line to the door handle only feet away.

"*Anyone home? Answer me.*"

Paul's voice is getting closer, in the hallway, and he pauses there for a second before she hears the creak as his weight hits that first stair. He's coming closer, coming closer toward her, toward the door, and with that thought everything stops. Suddenly everything is clear, so crystal clear she could be on the other side of the room looking at herself.

Everything is falling into place, and she screams, oh god she screams, and as the muted sound escapes in only a frustrated hum, her panic makes her move, and this time she doesn't care about the twitching of pain inside, she cares about nothing except that Paul is coming up the stairs. Her fixed eyes stare wide, as if she can will him to stop, to PLEASE GOD JUST STOP JUST STOP JUST STOP because the fishing wire is attached to the door handle, six strands, six strands of it, and what would be logical to be at the end of fishing wire, well, fishing hooks, of course, and oh god the door opens outward not in and the fish hooks were inside her and what would come out what would come out?

He is on the landing, she can hear his heavy cautious

tread and she is screaming inside for him to stop, to GO AWAY, to GET AWAY FROM HER and if she screams any louder she will explode, her head already twisting from side to side. Blood has started to dribble from the tape, she can feel it running down her naked legs as if her period had come, and he is only seconds away and she doesn't want to die, she doesn't want to die. This isn't how it's supposed to be, not for her, please god don't let her die, let her wake up now, please wake up now. Anything at all, just make this stop, stop right now and the handle is turning and all she can see is the rope and the handle, the rope and the handle and oh god this is really happening and there is the splash of liquid on the floor below as she lets go of her bladder and nononoNONONONOOOOOOOO . . . .

Paul reached for the old, round handle and twisted it, pushing hard. Nothing happened. It must be locked. Shit. Whoever was playing these weird jokes must be on the other side of that door, and despite his nervousness he just wanted to get to the bottom of it and let everything get back to normal. Still, it didn't stop him glancing nervously back down the stairs. He'd checked all the rooms downstairs pretty thoroughly and the landing below was empty, but he still shivered as if for a moment someone had been watching him. From the other side of the door he thought he could just make out that awful laugh he'd heard through the letterbox.

"Kay? Kay? Are you in there?" He banged on the wood. "Whoever's in there, I'm going to break this door down now, and then I'm going to want some answers!" The door didn't even rattle, and he stepped back confused. Even if it was tightly locked there would still be some give in it. He may not be very strong these days with his expense account lunches and too infrequent visits to the gym, but he was still a relatively powerful man and the wood didn't seem that thick. Could something have been pushed up against it? Maybe Kay and Laura had done it to protect themselves from someone else. Maybe whoever had scribbled that message in the window. But if so, why weren't they saying anything? *And how did anyone know I would be coming along? How could anyone have written that message with my name? Isn't that just a little bit weird? The kind of weird that made Mum run inside terrified yesterday?* His frustration was growing and he ran his hands over his drying face as he studied the door.

Glancing around the frame and hinges, he almost smiled. Of course. It opened the other way. How fucking stupid was he, he thought as he grabbed the knob again and yanked the door firmly open, ready to face whoever was on the other side.

It seemed for a split second as if there was some resistance, as if a small child had grasped at the handle and tried to stop him from coming in, and then it was gone. These strange old houses . . . The thought died before it really began, and for a second nothing seemed to make sense as he let go of the door handle, all his energy needed to understand what his optic nerves were desperately trying to process. He wasn't ready to face the person on the other side. Not ready at all. It was her eyes that he saw first, and it seemed that that was all he could see, would be able to see, despite the fact that his peripheral vision, almost tunnel-like, told him that Kay, Kay Chambers, his childhood friend, was hanging naked from a beam in her bedroom. But it was her awful eyes that held him, wide and terrified and so full of hate, hatred for him, above the tape that covered her mouth. His own mouth hung open as he stared, and as his brain tried to pull itself back from madness, he wondered if she was still screaming behind the shiny black gag.

A wet, slick sound tore his eyes downward and he started to moan, no tape to hold his anguish in. Something had come out of her, was still coming out of her, red and bloody like afterbirth, slowly slopping to the ground beneath her pale legs, trailing on the floorboards. A glint of steel flashed teasingly from its tangled nest within the shiny gray and pink mess that seemed to have crawled toward him and his mind struggled to comprehend its meaning, before looking back up at the twitching, defiled body strung up before him.

Kay's head was hanging down now, those death-watch eyes hidden from view, but the sight of one foot, her left foot dancing by itself beneath the redness, below the destruction of her stomach, made the bile burn in his chest. Rolling outward into the corridor, unable to trust his balance to keep him upright, and not wanting to collapse there where he stood, not amongst all that . . . he slid down the wall, his eyes squeezed shut. Hugging his knees to himself, he started to shake.

CHAPTER SIXTEEN

"Paul?"

Despite Simon and Mary's protests, Alex had come after Paul, hoping that maybe if they spent some time alone she might get him to open up about Melanie Parr and whatever it was about that long-gone child that bothered him so much. Keeping her head down against the torrent of rain, not really knowing why she was bothering since she was soaked through already, she pushed her tired limbs up the cobbled street. It wasn't like Paul to be so closed up, to have secrets that he didn't want to share. From the corner of her eye she saw that the door to Kay Chambers's house was slightly open. She paused for a second and stared at it. Maybe Kay had burned something baking and was letting fresh air in. Or maybe she'd let Paul in and he hadn't shut the door behind him properly. Looking up the street, there was no sign of her cousin—in fact, there was no sign of anyone; not even in the country would people go out in this weather unless they had to, and she figured he must be in with Kay.

She tapped on the wood. "Kay? You home? The door's open." Only silence answered her. "Kay? Laura?" Again nothing. Stepping into the well lit hallway, she left the door open behind her. "Hello?" The air felt damp, as if the rain had been slowly penetrating the opening for some time, and Alex moved farther into the house. The same uneasy feeling she had in the church was tapping at her heart and stomach.

"Kay? Paul?" Her voice dropped from a shout and she fought to keep it above a whisper, her nerves jangling slightly. It was the middle of the day—what was there to feel nervous about? Oh, I don't know, she answered herself, children that visit in the night and disappear, dead vicars, people obsessing with a dead girl. What's there to be nervous about in all that? Her inner sarcasm made her smile a little. Irony was something she was getting good at these days, even if it did tend to be tinged with bitterness.

The kitchen was empty except for the chill of the fresh air that had taken up its surly residence, lingering on the surfaces just long enough to deposit the damp carried on its back before moving relentlessly on. The wood of the door frame was cold beneath her touch as she ran back into the hall, a morbid shiver running down her spine. Cold as death. As if any warmth of life had left the house itself.

Standing at the base of the stairs, she stared upward for a second before starting to climb, not calling out this time. Kay was probably just having a nap. She knew the other woman wouldn't be upset at Alex wandering around her house given the circumstances, but Alex still felt like something of an interloper as she made her way up the creaky stairs.

Halfway up, she froze, a giggle wafting down to her. An awful giggle followed by whispered words that she couldn't make out. Her ears strained to hear. Who was that? *It's the giggle you heard last night. Inside and outside, then inside the closet. The one that scared the little boy so much. She doesn't know you can hear her. She doesn't know you're in between.* Pushing the thought that she didn't really understand to one side, she concentrated on what was real, what she could feel, the thick solid banister under her fingers. It felt cool against her hot skin.

As she rounded to the second flight, Paul's huddled figure came into view. For a horrible moment, Alex's breath caught in her throat at the sight of his body curled in on itself protectively against the wall above her, so still, so lifeless, and her legs pushed faster to reach him. Flashbacks of finding the vicar burst into life behind her eyes. *Not again. Surely that couldn't happen again.* What was going on here?

"Paul?" This time she could barely force a whisper, and her hand shook as she reached forward to touch his shoulder.

His arm was warm, and as his head rose slowly, Alex felt her breath run out of her lungs. "Oh God, Paul, you scared me. Are you okay? Are you okay?" Crouching beside him, she clutched at his face, wanting so desperately to feel the warmth of his skin, the softness of his cheeks. His eyes were hollow sockets, the color almost drained from their pupils, and he groaned, twisting his face away feebly, the weight of his skull heavy in Alex's arms. She pulled him back to face her, her anxiety making her almost aggressive.

"What happened, Paul? Where's Kay? Where's Laura?"

He met her gaze for a moment before his eyeballs rolled backward, back toward the door.

"She's in there. She's dead."

His emotionless words hit her hard, as if the air in them were punching her backward. "Kay's dead? But she can't be." Alex stared at Paul waiting for some kind of response, but he kept his eyes away from her, still focused with almost lifeless dread on the open bedroom doorway.

Pulling herself to her feet, feeling them shake slightly below her, Alex glanced into the bedroom. For a second she felt the world shift beneath her as she looked into the nightmare that had been her friend's death, and for a second she thought the grief might be overwhelming, destroying whatever was left of her spirit inside, but as she forced her eyes to take in the full view, a coolness washed through her as if the rain had somehow finally seeped inside her skin. *This can't touch me. This is done. This can't touch me.* In that instant her own clarity, her sudden composure, terrified her as if she was the still center of a storm.

"Where's Laura, Paul? Did you see Laura?" Her voice felt like it was coming from someone else, but it was strong and calm. She stared at her dead friend, whose future she had envied, like she'd envied everyone she knew over the past few months, the irony not lost on her. Kay, who'd been so full of life, was dead and gone;

but Alex, riddled with cancer, was still living. They all fought their own battles, but they were all dust in the end. It was all just a matter of time. Paul stayed silent, but he shrugged slightly, and Alex wondered what damage had been done to him in that split second. How many more battles would he have to fight inside because of this?

She looked down the corridor, and seeing the closed door to Laura's room, made her way toward it, the colors on the walls seeming brighter, like she was even seeing more clearly. *Maybe you're not reacting like other people would because you're not like them. How about that? Not anymore. Not like Kay, but not like them, either. Paul and the others can't hear the clock ticking as loudly as you can. You're in between.* She reached for the handle.

"*Nooooo!* No! Don't touch it! Don't touch it!"

Forgetting about the door, forgetting about everything as Paul's scream slashed at her, she spun around to see him stumbling to his feet, those agonized, urging eyes pleading for her to freeze where she stood.

"What? What is it, Paul?"

Shaking his head, his words came in sobs. "I opened the door." His eyes wandered to Kay's room before bringing their sorrow back to Alex. "Don't you see? I opened the door." He paused before repeating the words in a whisper to the chill air. "I opened the door."

Alex looked back at the floor in Phil and Kay Chambers's bedroom. The metal hooks flashed a grin at her before she took in the twisted threads of limp wire weaving their awful story. She looked up at Paul and saw the full horror of what he'd unwittingly done etched in his expression. Her stomach clenched. *Maybe I am capable of reacting after all.*

Paul's eyes met hers before they both turned to look at the girl's bedroom door, and it was her that spoke first.

"We're going to need a ladder."

CHAPTER SEVENTEEN

Having got Simon out of the pub, her shaky expression telling him that way too much was wrong here, they fetched Daniel Rose, who was still trying in vain to get any sort of outside contact from his radio. They sent him to gather the villagers to the pub. There was a sense of urgency now. What had happened to the vicar could have been a trick that went wrong, but what had happened to Kay was calculated and terrible. And if it could happen to Kay, then it could happen to any one of them.

Pulling Paul out of the house, Alex tugged the door locked shut behind them. No one else needed to go in and see what they'd seen. Crouch was fetching his long ladder from the coal shack at the back of the pub, and it was inevitable that as people came down to the pub, they would wonder what the hell was going on at the Chambers's place. Beside her, Paul froze. "It's gone."

"What's gone?"

"The writing on the window. When I came down

here there was writing in the window. Like finger writing in steam. It said, 'Come inside, Paul. Let's play fishing with Kay.' And now it's gone."

Alex stared at the smooth panes of glass. They were clear. "Why would someone write a message to you on the glass? How would anyone know you were coming?"

Paul let out a long sigh. "Because there is some very weird shit going on." He stared at Alex. "Don't you think?"

Standing there in silence, Alex couldn't deny it. But she knew that whatever it was, it had to have something to do with that Melanie Parr girl. It just had to. And when they had everyone together in the pub, she was determined to find out what it was.

She had tried to pull her thick, long hair into a makeshift plait, but strands blew loose in the wind, dancing around her head as she stared up at where Simon and Crouch were trying to balance the creaking ladder against the uneven cottage wall and the slick cobbles beneath their feet. Water stung her eyes, forcing them shut.

Was little Laura hanging up in there like her mother? Who would do that to a child? *Maybe another child.* She thought of the frightened little boy who had appeared in her room, and again at the church, and the two stranger children they'd seen on the way to the shop. And then there was the giggle she'd heard at Kay's house, just like the one that had woken her the night before. Who was that? *You know damned well who it was. You just don't want to admit it, because then you'll have to admit that Paul is right and there's some crazy shit going on here. But you know who it was. It was Melanie Parr. The Catcher Man brought her back. How about that for an answer? Just how much can you blame on the morphine?* Staring, she watched Simon take a first tentative step up the slick rungs of the ladder. What was happening to the village tonight? And how were they supposed to stop it?

James Partridge came alongside her, silently watching the activity. He was a quiet, dependable man who never spoke much, but when he did there was a soft warmth in his tone that let you know still waters could sometimes run deep.

"What's going on in there, Alex?"

She glanced up at him and watched the rain run through the crevasses of his weathered face, trying to avoid his eyes as he studied her.

He didn't wait for an answer. "Your Aunt Mary don't seem too well, either. My Jan is sitting with her, but she won't say a word."

Alex's eyes drifted back to the ladder and watched as Simon started to climb more confidently, the base held firmly by Crouch and Tom, old farmer Tucker's eldest.

She didn't look at James, but just followed Simon's feet, rung by rung, as she spoke. "Kay's dead." Her voice was almost as soft as his, and he leaned so close to hear her that she could feel the vague touch of his breath warming her face. "So is Reverend Barker. And we're trying to find out what's happened to Laura." This time she did look at him. His dark eyes were wide, but he stayed silent as she spoke. "What's going on? I don't have a fucking clue. But I wish I knew. I really, really wish I knew." Turning away, she stepped forward, needing a small space of her own, but he stepped up beside her.

He kept his eyes forward and his voice low. "Do you

think it's got anything to do with these strange children in the town?"

Alex stared at him. "What do you mean?"

He swallowed, hesitant. "Seems the town's been full of children since the rain came. Jan saw a few hiding in the trees when she went out to round up the chickens. Thought she was seeing things when she told me, but I've changed my mind now. Seen a few today, myself. Playing games on street corners, mainly dressed wrong for the weather." He looked down at Alex, unused to this much speech. "I couldn't help but feel they were watching us. Watching and laughing." He paused. "And you might think I'm crazy for saying this, and perhaps I am, but one or two of them seemed ever so familiar. Like I'd seen their faces somewhere before."

Alex stared at him for what seemed like a very long time. "I don't think you're crazy. I think it might have something to do with the children. I just don't know what. Or maybe we're both crazy. Who knows." They stood in silence after that, just watching and thinking.

Simon was almost level with the window and Alex's heart started to race as he took the last step and leaned forward, peering into the glass. He seemed to stare for an eternity before straightening up and starting his descent. Alex met him as he reached the ground and grabbed at his arm. "Well?"

He shook his head, his face full of disbelief. "She's not there. She's not in there." He looked back up at the window. "If she's not in there, then where the hell is she? Where is she?"

There were still standing there gathered round the ladder when Daniel Rose ran down the street toward them, the awkward movement of an old man who'd done little running in too many years.

"We've got a problem." Staring at the red of his face, Alex couldn't make out what was covering it more, rain or sweat. "Little Peter Granville's gone missing. Emma's almost hysterical, poor thing; doesn't know how long he's been gone. Dawn Wilbur's helping her get the other kids together, and then they're coming down here."

Alex's heart sank. Petey could only be about three or four. Why would he wander off on his own? "Laura's missing too."

Daniel stared at her. "Emma says that Laura was over playing with her kids this morning, and then after a couple of hours said she wasn't feeling well and left. Maybe wherever they are, they're together."

Alex peered frantically into the rain. God, she hoped that Laura and Pete were together. At least the little boy would have a chance in this weather with someone else. The sky had darkened so much with the weight of the storm that she could barely see the end of the street. "We've got to try and find them. We've got to."

James held her slim shoulders. "We can't go looking in this rain. Not while it's so dark. We got no chance of seeing anything, let alone finding anyone, and the weather'll make it too dangerous. Let's at least talk to the other Granville children first. They may have an idea where they could have gone." He looked up at Daniel, who nodded.

"He's right. We can't search in this, Alex, not without any idea of where to look. I'll get back and keep trying the radio. We've got to get hold of the police somehow."

Alex suddenly wanted to scream at them for their calm demeanor as they talked to her. Turning away from Simon, ignoring the offered crook of his arm, she risked slipping on the cobbles and strode back to the pub, needing a couple of seconds to vent her anger. They were right. She knew they were right. But that didn't make her feel any better. Hearing Simon's feet coming quickly behind her, she sped up, reached for the heavy wood, and swung the door open into the warmth and light of the pub.

CHAPTER EIGHTEEN

Jenny and Jimmy were clutching each other's hands so tightly that Alex could see the whites of their knuckles screaming through the skin as they sat down at a table in the restaurant area of the pub. Emma was in the bar, still crying, while Crouch tried to get her to drink a brandy, and someone had gone out to check that Dr. Jones was on his way. Emma Granville was definitely going to need something to help calm her down if Petey didn't get found soon. Especially if and when she heard about what had happened to the vicar and Kay.

Taking Jenny's spare hand, Alex rubbed it gently. "I'm sure Pete's fine, really. But we need to know if there's anywhere that he hides or if he's got any places he likes to go to play."

Jenny didn't speak, but Jimmy shook his head. "Pete never goes off by himself. He's not like that. Never." The boy's eyes were shaking, challenging Alex to accuse him of lying. He was angry, she could see that, and he didn't have anyone to vent his anger and emotion on.

If he wanted to snap at her, that was fine. She could take it. She decided on a change of tack.

"Laura's missing too. She was at your house this morning, wasn't she?"

Both children nodded.

"What time did she leave?"

Jimmy shrugged. "Not really sure. She was fine and we were watching a movie to pass the time till the rain stopped. Then she went to the bathroom. When she came back she said she wasn't feeling well and was going home." His voice broke a little. "I wasn't really paying attention."

Jenny suddenly let out a small gasp of air. "There was something odd, though. But it's probably nothing."

"What?" Alex leaned forward slightly. "What was odd?"

"Well, when we were sitting upstairs she asked if we'd had any text messages. She said she'd had some odd ones this morning. But when she tried to turn the phone on to show us, the battery must have died."

"I thought you said there wasn't any signal out here."

"There never is." Jimmy shot Simon a glare. "We never normally turn our phones on unless we're at school. No point."

Alex focused on Jenny. "Did she say who these texts were from?"

"I can't remember. A girl. She said she wanted Laura to play with her."

"Melanie," Jimmy cut in. "Laura said the girl's name was Melanie and she was lonely."

Pulling her hand back from the girl's, Alex stared at Simon. Melanie. Melanie Parr. Once again this missing girl seemed to be at the center of an awful event. What was happening? Surely the village wasn't being haunted? It couldn't be. That kind of shit just wasn't real. The same questions flared back at her from Simon's eyes.

"We need to get to the bottom of this."

Simon nodded. "I know we said it was pointless going out and looking for the children in this weather, but if no one can get a car out with the roads flooded and that bloody overturned lorry, then I think it's time someone tried to get out on foot. Is there a way through the woods or something that Paul and I could try? At least that way we can shout for them and try and get help."

"Yes, you should be able to find your way through. If Paul has kept his childhood bearings, that is." Standing up, Alex left the children with Dawn Wilbur and went with Simon back to the bar. "I'll stay here, and when we've finally got the villagers gathered I'll see if I can push them for information about Melanie Parr. And see if anyone knows anything about these creepy children."

"What's going on?" James Partridge stood between the two of them.

"Paul and Simon are going to try and get out of the village through the woods. The road is blocked, so no one can get out that way, plus the river will have flooded it by now. We really need to get the police here." The words sounded good, but Alex wondered just what the police would make of what was going on in the sleepy village of Watterrow. Two deaths and the rest of the people seeing things. She and Mary weren't the only ones to have had weird experiences in the past twenty-four hours. There were too many people looking troubled and staring into their drinks dotted around her in The Rock, their eyes slipping from each other, for that to be the case. There was something secretive about them. As if they thought that something was very wrong with their head or themselves. She knew that look. She'd worn it too many times since the clock started ticking loudly inside her.

The villagers that were just suffering from the shock of finding out about Kay and the vicar were chatting animatedly to each other. How awful, how terrible, who could possibly be doing this in their village? All normal hyper reactions. She remembered it from 9/11. It was the rest that made Alex think that whatever weirdness had gripped the town, ghostly or not, it was holding it tightly.

"Alex?" Paul's grip on her arm brought her back to the conversation at hand.

"Sorry, I was just . . . well . . . just thinking, I guess."

"We're going to go out in two pairs. Simon and I will take the route out by the old tin mines, which should lead us close enough to Wivvy, and James and Tom Tucker reckon they know another way that will bring them out by Bampton somewhere. One pair should find their way out, and going two ways will also give us more chance of coming across the kids."

"Sounds good." Even Emma Granville was looking calmer knowing that someone was going to be out in the woods looking for her baby, or at least getting some help. "I'll check on Ada and Daniel and then maybe get some food going here. You guys should at least take a flask of something to keep you warm if you get lost."

Simon grinned. "Is that the hint of a maternal streak?"

Despite the fact that they were meant as a joke, Alex felt the words like a slap in the face. Maternal streak?

Ha. What would be the point of that? It was her repro-
ductive system that was killing her, after all.

"No." Her voice was chilled. "Just practical thinking."

For a second she enjoyed seeing the wobble on Simon's smile as he tried to figure out just what he'd said
to piss her off, and then the pettiness of it overwhelmed her. Kay was dead. The vicar was dead. And
more than that, how the hell was Simon supposed to
know about her? She gave him a wan smile. "And men
are rubbish when they get a cold."

The four men were ready to leave with rope and
torches when Crouch tentatively suggested that one
pair take the shotgun he kept behind the bar, and the
other a large knife. Paul and Simon stared at each
other for a moment before Paul nodded toward Tom.
"You take it. I haven't shot one of those things since I
was a kid. I'd probably just blow my own foot off."

Nodding, Tom gripped the gun and held it over his
shoulder. "At least you'll know if we get in trouble. Even
in this weather, you'll hear it if I have to fire this thing."

Paul looked down at the large kitchen knife in his
hand. "Well, I guess if we get into trouble I'll just have
to scream my head off." He smiled. "Which won't be a
problem."

Listening to their banter, Alex felt her heart racing.
She wasn't sure that guns and knives would work with
whatever they were up against. "Just get out of the village and get some help." She paused, watching them
zip up their coats and get ready to head out into the
encroaching dark. "And take care."

CHAPTER NINETEEN

Simon set a brisk pace along the stretch of pavement, Paul indicating where they should turn to take the shortcut around the back of some of the houses and out into the woods. As soon as they stepped off the concrete and onto the soft earth, Simon felt the ground working against his feet and his heart sank. It was going to be hard work. According to Paul, they had at least three or four miles to go, most of it uphill. Still, he didn't shorten his stride. The quicker they got through the trees and to the next village the better.

The rain pattered heavily through the leaves above them, running together and falling in weighty drops, and Simon paused to zip his coat right up to his chin. Paul was a few paces behind and as he came alongside, Simon could hear his friend was already a little out of breath. Behind them he could see the lights glowing from The Rock and for a moment wished that he'd stayed in that warmth. Whatever was going on in this strange little town was really none of his business.

And then he thought of Alex. There was something about her that connected with him and he hoped that maybe when all this was over he could persuade her to go out on an old-fashioned date with him. So maybe this shit was his business a little bit, after all.

He looked at Paul, his cheeks puffing as he breathed. They'd only walked about fifteen minutes and still had a long way to go. If he didn't have Paul with him, Simon figured he'd make the journey in pretty good time, but he knew that his friend wasn't going to be able to match his own pace for long.

"You okay, mate?"

Paul nodded. "If you mean will I be able to keep up, then yes. I'll give it my best shot. I don't want to be in these woods any longer than I have to. Not in this weather."

They walked side by side in silence, picking their way through the patches of slippery leaves and slimy tree roots, all the time their feet sliding half a pace back with each step. For a while there was just the sound of their own breathing and the weather; the village behind them had totally disappeared. Simon sniffed and broke the peace. "You know this town, Paul. Who do you think is doing this stuff? You don't really think kids could have done that to Kay, do you?"

Paul laughed, but it was devoid of warmth. After what had happened to him today, Simon thought it would be long time before he heard Paul's rich, earthy, devil-may-care laugh again.

"What's so funny?"

Paul trudged ahead. "Trust me, you really don't want to know what I think."

"If I didn't want to know, I wouldn't have asked."

"I should have known the little cow would come back. I should have known it." Paul's voice was weary, and Simon grabbed his arm, forcing him to stop and look at him.

"What are you talking about?"

"You want to know who I think is doing all this? Melanie Fucking Parr." Simon shook his head. "That's crazy. Melanie Parr's dead."

"Maybe she is. And that scares the shit out of me, because she was scary enough when she was alive." Paul's voice was getting louder, somewhere between a laugh and a shout. "And now she's leaving messages in windows, scaring old women, leaving her name on the fucking vicar's dying breath, and if she's dead then I don't know how we can stop her, because Melanie never got bored of playing games. *Never.*" He took a deep breath, calming himself. "And I think she's going to play with us until we're all dead, just like her." He stared at Simon. "Now you can call me crazy if you like. But you didn't know Melanie Parr. You didn't know what she was capable of."

The stillness uncomfortable, Simon started to walk again, his long stride matching his heartbeat. "What did you mean? Last night you said you barely remembered her."

Paul sighed. "I lied." Grimacing, he matched Simon's steps. "Although I wish it were true. She was an evil little bitch. She made my life hell." He sniffed, the exercise having made his nose run. "Not just mine. Most of us kids. She scared us."

Despite himself, Simon couldn't help but feel disappointed in his friend. Secrets and lies. Everybody had them. "Okay, so tell me about it. Tell me what she was like, what she did. I think it's about fucking time someone started saying something about her."

For about five minutes, Paul stayed silent, and then, as if having made peace with himself and the memories he was dragging back to the forefront, he began to speak. Despite his city lifestyle having taken its toll on his body, he didn't get out of breath as he climbed the muddy inclines, reaching for a branch here or there to ease his way, speaking quietly and clearly. It was as if he were so far in the past he'd forgotten how out of shape the Paul of the present was. It was Simon who was sucking oxygen hard into his lungs, keeping alongside, listening to his friend bringing Melanie Parr back to life.

"When Melanie and her mother arrived in the village, it caused quite a stir. Us kids were only seven or eight, but even we could tell. You know, listening to our mothers talking in that really excited, serious way women do when they're gossiping." He smiled slightly, immersing himself in the memory.

"Mrs. Parr was very glamorous. There wasn't really anyone like that in the village or even in Wivvy, not that was part of our day-to-day lives. She dressed like someone out of the movies, or at least it seemed like that to us. I guess looking back, she was just a city girl with a few nice dresses and a couple pairs of high heels, but compared to the sensible shoes of the farmers' wives and women like my mother, who only really dressed for church on Sunday's, she may as well have been Marilyn Monroe. Alex's mum, my aunt Alicia, was beautiful, but in an ethereal way, not red-lipped and nail-varnished like Mrs. Parr."

"And of course, Mrs. Parr was a divorcee. The rest of

the country might have got their heads round that issue, but in this part of the world marriage was still for life. She seemed dangerous and exciting to our mothers, and they decided that the best way to get close to her was to ensure that we all got close to Melanie." He smiled slightly. "There were a lot of tea and garden parties that summer, and whether we wanted her to or not, Melanie Parr became part of our gang. I guess we didn't mind at first; I don't remember minding, I just remember thinking that she wasn't really like us. Even when she was laughing, it seemed she had a secret, but then I was never sure of kids when I first met them. I'd get all shy and then my stutter would get much worse." He ignored the water that strayed into his mouth. "God, I was a geek. But me aside, I don't remember any of us thinking anything very much about her in those first few weeks. Ironic really, considering how she fucked about with our lives so much in the couple of years that came after."

Simon's foot sank suddenly, and in danger of sliding downhill with the mud, he grabbed a thin sapling, bending it under his bodyweight, and yanked himself free. "Who was in your gang?"

"Most of the kids from the village. Me, Tom, Kay, her sister, James Rose, a few others. Alex, of course, was a few years from being born at that point. She was lucky enough to miss out on all this. The rest of us all went to the primary school in Wivvy, but before then there'd been a nursery in Watterrow, so we'd played together forever. It was easy. All our families knew each other. We were always in and out of each other's houses, playing in the farms and the woods. We had so much energy in those days. But our games were pretty simple until Melanie started playing. She liked to play games with your head. I don't think any of us liked them. Or liked ourselves for playing them."

"What kind of games?" Simon was relieved to feel the ground level out slightly. They were definitely making better time than he'd thought they would, Paul not slowing them down. And at least his story was taking both their minds off the growing ache in their legs and the thought that there might be two children lost in the woods somewhere.

Again Paul let out that dead laugh. "What kind of games? Twisted ones. The kind you would never tell anyone about. Like when we built the pirate station out on the river. Kay wasn't really happy about it. She didn't mind playing on the bank, but she was scared of water then. Think she always was. We never really talked about it after that. And you know how it is. The older you get the harder you try to cover your weaknesses. And we never really talked about the things that happened back then. When Melanie was gone it was easier to just try and forget them.

"Anyway, Melanie persuaded her to swim over to this raft thing we'd built that was tied to an old oak tree on the other side leading up to the woods. Kay was really scared and shaking, but Melanie was good at making you do stuff." Darkness bent his brow. "And then using it against you."

He paused a moment before going back to his story. "She said it would be good for Kay. Help her get over her fears. Said she'd swim with her. The rest of us waited on the bank."

"Who else was there?"

"Me, Tom Tucker and Joe. I'll tell you about Joe in a

minute. Anyway, they get to this raft, which was really no more than a few branches and logs inexpertly tied together, and we all start cheering and Kay almost relaxes, when all of a sudden, Melanie lets go of her, dives down and swims back to us, climbing out with this great big grin on her face.

"Kay was yelling for her to come back, clutching at the biggest log, which looked like it might come away from its binding, she was holding onto it so hard. Tom was about to get in the water to go out to her when Melanie spoke in that clear butter-wouldn't-melt voice that she had. 'Maybe we'll leave you there, Kay,' she said. 'How would you like that? Do you think you could get back here by yourself?'

"I could see Kay looking around her, and for a minute it looked like she was sure she could swim that far, even with her flailing doggy-style strokes, and then Melanie carried on, all smooth and confident, saying stuff like, 'Did you feel the tug of the current, Kay? I had to fight it helping you over there. It wouldn't take a second for it to suck you down, pull you under, not with the way you swim. You're weak, Kay. The river would drag you down. Down to the weeds that'd wrap round your legs and hold you tight. And then none of us would be able to help you, no matter how hard we might want to. All that water going into your lungs as you try to breathe. I wonder what it feels like.'" Paul shook his head, irritated at his own inadequate retelling.

"It's difficult to explain why she was so effective. It was something in her voice. It made you believe in her, just for a little while. 'Maybe we'll just sit here and watch,' she said, and we did. Me and Tom sat down and enjoyed Kay crying and begging for help. Joe grumbled for a bit and then squatted beside us. After half an hour, even though it was a warm day, Kay was shivering. That river was cold, the summers are never long enough to warm it up properly, and her feet were going numb.

"Joe started cursing under his breath, not fascinated by this, not like the rest of us, not at all, but Melanie just watched Kay, her blond hair tucked carefully behind her ear and her voice normal, as if she were talking about anything, and that made it scarier, and she said, 'You'll never make it back now, Kay, will you? You're too cold. Your muscles just won't work properly for you. It's just about time now. Just waiting. Will you let go of the wood now, or in an hour? How far will you get before you sink? How long can you hold your breath under water? Which of us will try to save you first? All these questions, and the outcome will be just the same. Water in your lungs.' "

He looked up at Simon, searching for some kind of understanding. "I mean, we were eight years old. Have you ever heard a child talk like that? She mesmerized us."

Simon didn't know what kind of comfort he could offer his friend except just listening, and Paul looked back down at his feet.

"It was weird. It was like I wasn't myself and Kay wasn't Kay. Watching her panic, her fear, and knowing that we had the power to prolong it or stop it, released some kind of primal thing in us. I can't explain it and part of me hated it, but god, I was eight years old and it was the closest to a hard-on that a kid of that age can get. And it was Melanie that was doing it."

Rain ran through Simon's hair and almost into his eyes, but he didn't really notice. He was absorbed in the hot sunny day of over thirty years ago. "What happened? I mean Kay didn't drown, so did she swim?"

Paul shook his head. "No, she couldn't have let go of that log if she tried. It was Joe. He spat on the ground at my feet and dived in. It took him ten minutes of gentle coaxing to get her to put her arms round his neck and let him swim her back to the bank. I don't know how long we'd have been there if he hadn't. And I don't really know what would have happened. It was like the minute he got in the water, the spell was broken. I was young, and it only took that few minutes before she got out of the water to convince myself that I had been only seconds away from doing the same, and it was just a silly joke, and no one would really have let her drown, but looking back I'm not so sure. Something dark happened that afternoon. Something dark that Melanie let out from inside us.

"When she was a little calmer and warmer, Joe took Kay home, and me and Tom and Melanie wandered back in silence. I think Tom was trying to figure out what had just gone on, the same as I was. Only Melanie didn't seem to care. She'd just enjoyed the game.

"I thought that would be the end of Melanie being in our gang. I mean Kay was hardly going to want her around after that, but I underestimated Melanie. I think that afternoon was almost like a little test she set us, and we all passed. Except for Joe. You see, the next day, it was me that Kay wasn't talking to. Melanie had told her that it was all my idea, it was my idea to scare her and Melanie had just been a pawn in my game, with her innocent face and angel-blond hair, and she felt so bad about it, but that she knew how Kay could get me back, and Kay was too mad to really think about what she was hearing, and Melanie said why didn't they go into my house and steal my mothers purse, take the money and leave the purse in my bedroom, and wouldn't that be fun as well as revenge? It was so easy for them; no one locks their doors around here now, let alone then, and they did it bold as brass while we were all in the garden relaxing. They just snuck into the house and did it.

"My father was still alive then, and I got the belt like I'd never had it before. I couldn't sit down for nearly a week. Couldn't stop crying, either. My dad just wasn't like that; he wasn't the violent type. I think it hurt him as much as it hurt me, but it didn't hurt either of us as much as it hurt my mother to think I'd done something like that to her. And how could I explain that I hadn't?

"And then Melanie came to see me, and told me that Kay had done it, she knew because Kay had told her, and she'd seen the lucky trinket silver horse my mum kept in the small key ring of her purse in Kay's bedroom, and why didn't we go and have a look?"

Paul let out a small sad laugh. "Can you see where this is going? So, of course, I did go with her and take a look, sneaking around someone else house without a care, as if I did it every day of the week, even though I'd never have dreamed of doing it before that, not without Melanie there, and lo and behold, there was my mother's charm, sitting on Kay's bedside table. And of course, Melanie had a way that I could get right back at Kay." He stopped walking and leaned against a tree, taking a deep breath.

Despite his eagerness to get to the other side of the woods, Simon was pleased to pause for a moment, needing to rest his legs too. He didn't speak, not wanting to interrupt Paul's flow. "She really played us well. I don't know how many of us kids she got like that, but it wasn't only me that couldn't look people in the eye during that time. She loved making us hurt each other, and then she loved our guilt. Christ knows what she would have become if she hadn't disappeared.

"The only kid I know she didn't get to was Joe Barnes. Joe was a city kid too, and his family hadn't been here long before Melanie and her mum arrived. They lived out past Venn cross, a few miles up the road, but Joe always came down to play with the Watterrow kids. Joe's dad had just bought the old petrol station up there. It had been a local family business, and some of the older generations were a bit put out by it. Didn't really like the idea of Londoners coming in and making a killing out of selling vital supplies.

"Of course, that wasn't what was happening. Joe's family barely made a living, let alone a fortune, but the bare facts never win over xenophobia, and a lot of people boycotted them. Still, the Barnes's persevered, knowing that people would come round in the end, and in the main they were right.

"Anyway," he continued, his breathing was becoming more labored now as they approached the top of the muddy slope, "one day after school, about four months into all this craziness, Joe came to see me. He said Kay had been talking to him, crying in fact, and saying how she felt bad about the purse and the stuff she'd done to some of the other kids with Melanie and that it was beginning to really frighten her, and did I know anything more? Had Melanie made me do anything to anyone?

"At first I didn't know what to say. What did he mean Melanie had been there when Kay stole my mother's purse? That couldn't be right. But then it all started to make sense. After all, Melanie had been there when I'd defaced Kay's sister's doll collection and left the marker pens tucked in Kay's favorite bag, where I knew her parents would look. In fact, it had been Melanie's idea. And then I thought of all the other things I'd done with her over the past few months, to people I knew and didn't know. They'd all been Melanie's ideas. Heat crept up through me from my toes, a shaky, scared kind of heat.

"Suddenly, I felt dirty. Dirty and ashamed, because I'd enjoyed a lot of what I'd done. Despite my vague fear of Melanie, she hadn't really made me do those things—she'd just made me *want to do them*. She'd made me feel it was okay to do them, and then I'd enjoyed it. Sneaking into people's houses and causing havoc. Leaving a trail of blame. There was something exciting about the whole thing.

"I remember Joe asked me two or three times if I knew anything about it, standing there on the playground, all serious, because he was going to tell his parents about it because something should be done about her because she wasn't right. *She just wasn't right.* Those were his words. She *just wasn't right.* He tapped the side of his head while he said it.

"I stood there and watched him for two or three minutes, my head cataloging all the awful things I'd done over the past few months, some just pranks, and some bad enough to make me hang my head with shame even all these years later, and fear rose in my stomach, a bad fear, the fear of all those things coming out, the fear of the look on my parents' faces. I couldn't get found out. I couldn't. And what could I say? I'd done things in his house and around the garage that I'd let other people take the blame for. Sprayed things. Nasty things on the wall. I think they'd probably made Mrs. Barnes cry. How could those things become known? Nothing could be worse than that. Not to me. Not then. So I did the stupidest thing I've ever done—I shook my head as if I didn't know what he was talking about, and then I walked away.

"I told Melanie what he was planning. I had to. I couldn't deal with it. She just nodded, and then she went to Kay's house. I don't know what she said to her, I never found out, but it was enough for Kay to go to Joe's and persuade him not to tell his parents. It was the day before his ninth birthday. We were all invited to a party at his house on the Saturday. It never happened."

Simon could see trees bending in the wind up ahead of them. God, it seemed the storm was getting stronger with each step. How much farther did they have to go? "So what did happen?" He raised his voice slightly, battling the weather.

"Joe had a cat. It was an old moggy thing. I think the Barnes had it from before he was born. It must have been about fifteen. And God, it was huge. All day it slept while the family were out. Slept and ate, and saved its energy for when Joe was home. Joe made out as if he didn't really care about the cat one way or another, but we all knew that was just a fat lie. He loved that cat. What kid doesn't love their pet? Anyway, the night that Kay persuaded him not to tell about the Melanie stuff, Joe's cat didn't come home. Poor kid probably stayed up half the night waiting for it to come in. Cats that old don't normally like spending the nights hunting, not when they can be curled up on a nice warm bed, and I don't think that lazy old moggy was any different.

"The next morning, Joe didn't turn up at school. I figured that it was just that his family had let him have the day off school for his birthday and didn't think anything of it, but when I got home, my mother and Aunt Alicia were in the kitchen, both as white as a sheet. My father was cursing, slamming down his whisky glass, still in his work clothes from the dairy farm, saying it was about time people got over their prejudices and if they could do something like this to a nice family like that then what the hell would happen if a Negro ever dared to want to live a nice quiet life in the country? What the hell would happen then?

"It took him a couple of minutes before he realized I was there. I asked what had happened and my mum said that something bad had happened at the Barnes's garage and Joe and his mum had left. His dad was going to stay on until the garage was sold. I remember that my heart started beating very, very fast and asking what, what had happened that was so bad that Joe would leave without saying good-bye. My mother and aunt tried to stop my father from telling me, but he said I needed to know, I needed to know what people were capable of, and then he told me what had happened to Joe's cat.

"When Joe had got up on his ninth birthday, the first thing he'd done was go outside to see if he could call the cat in, worried about the daft thing, his head probably full of fox attacks. According to my father, Joe had noticed something odd about the wooden sandwich board down in the drive that declared the garage closed every evening. And, when he got there, he found he was right. There was something odd about it. Something horribly odd about it.

"His mother's scream joined her son's when she ran outside to find out what on earth was making him yell like that, and it was only the arrival of his father that got them both away, having to literally drag the crying Joe inside. You see, the cat had been nailed by each paw to the wood, its head lolling backward, betraying its broken neck. But the worst part of that unnatural tilt of the head, and the bit that probably made Mrs. Barnes scream so terribly loudly, was that the cat's eyes were gone. Cut out of its head, only dark bloody sockets where they should have been. And underneath the dead cat someone had written in the cats own blood, two simple words—Go home. Finger writing. Just like the message left for me in Kay's window. Anyway, those two words were enough. The Barnes decided to follow those instructions. They left."

Paul leaned forward against the wind and Simon did the same. The ground was soaking, and they both sunk two or three inches into the mud, the cold creeping into their shoes. Pushing himself forward, Simon listened to Paul's almost monotone voice, as if he were spitting this story out from somewhere it had been locked away inside him and he just wanted to be rid of it.

"I stood there in that kitchen and didn't know what to say. I don't think I've felt anything like that since. Not until this, anyway. I remember thinking that I was going to pass out right there on the floor and that it was really going to hurt if I landed on my face. I remember trying to speak, desperately trying to push the words out, but they were trapped inside. I can't explain how frustrating that is. Only stutterers know just how mad that makes you when your throat and mouth seize up on you like that, and everyone looks at you with pity and impatience, waiting for you to make some kind of sound so they can at least have a go at finishing your words for you.

"Of course, it probably wouldn't have been so bad if I had known what I was trying to say, but I didn't. There were too many things going round in my head—Joe, Melanie, all of us, all of the crazy things we'd been doing, and how Joe had gone without even saying good-bye. That was like someone had punched me. I think that down in my subconscious I was hoping that Joe would be the one to get me out of this mess. And now he was gone."

Simon kept his eyes on the row of trees that bobbed up and down with each of his labored steps. "Did you ever hear from him?"

"No. I used to think about him a lot, though. Especially after Melanie vanished. I think he knew it was her that had done that awful thing to his cat. He was bright enough to figure it out, especially since he thought she was crazy anyway. I guess he just decided that enough was enough. Just like his family did. Anyway, standing there in that kitchen, with the family staring at me, probably wondering what the fuck I was trying to say, and why was it affecting me that badly, all I could see was Melanie's name almost painted in red behind my eyes. I turned and ran out of the house and didn't stop running until I'd got to the cottage Mrs. Parr was renting right out on the edge of the woods.

"I went round to the back and through the door and straight up to Melanie's bedroom. Sweat was pouring down my face, my skin throbbing with the exertion, and as I burst through the room, there she was, sitting cross-legged and still on her mattress, surrounded by her claustrophobic collection of golden-haired dolls that looked like china versions of herself. And she wasn't alone. Kay was there, and Tom and James Rose and a couple of smaller kids who were too young to hang out with us, I think they were old Alice Moore's nephews come to stay for a while. And they all were staring at Melanie, all changed from when we first met. Kay's eyes were lost in the dark circles that surrounded them, and Tom's bottom lip was raw from where he'd been chewing it nervously, a habit his mother had worked so hard to get him out of when we were five or six.

"I didn't say anything, nobody did, and then Melanie grinned, and reached beneath the largest doll and pulled out a plastic sandwich bag and held it up. The cat's eyes were in it, all shiny and slithery and round, with long cords—I suppose they must have been optic nerves or something, attached to the back, bloody and pink. Melanie just smiled and said, 'Anyone want to feel them?' Jesus, I've never got out of anywhere so fast in my entire life. I could hear the others right behind me, Kay already crying, but I didn't wait for them. I didn't even stop when I got outside, but ran the opposite way from the village and into the woods, eventually crouching behind a tree, throwing up, and then sobbing my heart out."

Simon stopped, cursing slightly as he almost lost his shoe in the mud, leaning on Paul's shoulder to retie it. "God, what an awful child."

"That was really just the beginning. Until that point

she'd been *using* us to play. After that she began playing *with* us. Tricks, dangerous tricks, tricks that left you hurt and bruised and bleeding. It was fucking horrible. I would wake up at night almost not able to breathe. Sometimes, she'd leave you alone for a month or so, and you'd just start to relax, and bang, she'd be back. Broken glass in your sandwich, or something like that. And we were all so scared of her, of what she was capable of, and what she knew we'd done, what evidence she had on us, that there was no way we were going to tell. Remember what it was like as a kid? Adults were part of a different world. They couldn't do anything for us, not really."

"Jesus. Jesus Christ." Simon stared at Paul, wondering at his friend's childhood.

"Yeah. It wasn't good. It wasn't good at all." Simon could see Paul's eyes, bright white in the darkness as he spoke. "And then one day she disappeared in a storm. Gone, just like magic. For a long time, I used to imagine her coming back to get me in the middle of the night, and then slowly the dreams faded and life went on. But I think what Mum said last night is true—the dead never really leave us. And now it seems that Melanie's come back to get us, after all."

Shaking his head, Simon turned his attention back to making his way over the wet ground. Ghosts didn't exist. The idea was crazy, really crazy. "How far now?"

"Once we get over this ridge we should pretty much be free of the woods. Not far. A few hundred yards or so."

After ten minutes or so, Simon's thighs were burning with the exertion of scrambling up the muddy slope and his hands were filthy from where he'd stumbled occasionally onto the ground, but at last, up ahead he could make out a break in the trees.

"We're nearly out." Paul nodded, and leaning forward, the wind seeming stronger even through the protection of the trees, they pushed themselves forward. Simon squinted against the rain. Surely the storm couldn't be getting worse? And how the hell was the wind coming at them so fast? They weren't out in the open. His feet slid slightly in the mud and he felt Paul grab his arm to steady him. He took three more steps forward before a gust of wind sent both of them tumbling backward, branches slapping at their skin as they fell through the trees.

"What the hell is going on?" Dragging himself back to his feet, Simon had to shout, and even then wasn't sure that Paul could hear him. The wind was howling, dragging up the heavy wet leaves from the forest floor and launching them at the two men. It had gone from a breeze to a gale in seconds, and Simon grabbed Paul, pulling him behind an ancient oak tree to stop them from being thrown back the way they'd come. The weather roared at them, forcing them to huddle together.

Paul peered around the edge of the bark, his eyes wide. "Look! Look!" He jabbed one finger forward, pointing toward the edge of the wood, where the ground cleared into a field. Where they should have been walking the last stretch to Wivvy. Simon glanced around the other side of the trunk, his fingers gripping the bark. Just what the fuck was that? Blue light flashed and crackled through the last row of trees, dancing madly from one branch and twig to the next and back again. Was it some kind of electrical storm?

How the hell was it happening just along the perimeter? Christ, he'd never seen anything like it. If it was some kind of lightning, wouldn't the branches be burning?

Looking to his left and right, trying to shield his eyes from the battering wind and rain, he could see the same electricity running through all the trees in that last row, the blue lights bright in the gloom. Whatever it was, he didn't fancy walking through it. Not with all this water around. Shit. If they were going to get out of the forest, they weren't going to do it this way. Not without getting fried. Feeling the strength of the storm, he wasn't even sure they would make it back to the pub. Beside him Paul's face was lit up with dreadful wonder, and Simon shook him to get his attention.

"What do we do now?" He was shouting, but couldn't hear his own words. Paul just stared at him.

"Is there a shelter near here we can get to?" He was screaming the words out, halfway through the sentence when the wind suddenly stopped, his words filling the silence. His face tingled with the sudden release from the attack on his skin. He stared at Paul, neither men needing the tree for support anymore, the rain just falling gently through the trees, the air still. Just what the hell was going on?

Cautiously stepping backward, Simon could see the blue crackle still running through the boundary trees. Despite the strange calm there was a palpable tension all around them. From somewhere behind him a giggle ran through the trees and both men spun round.

"Laura? Laura? Is that you?" Shadows seemed to dart through the trees and bushes around them, but there was no answer to Simon's shout. The giggle came again, but this time from a different direction. After a second it was matched by another, maybe a boy's, and then another, higher and lighter. Younger. Spinning round, Simon was sure he saw a flash of shoes and legs darting through the trees. And then a bare leg. Something and nothing. There but not there.

"What the fuck is going on?" Simon stared at Paul.

"Games." Paul barely whispered the word, his eyes darting from tree to tree. "She's playing games."

"What do you mean?"

"I don't think she's going to let us leave the village, do you?"

Simon looked back at the electrified trees, and then stared back at the silent wood around them. "This is a really fucked up situation. Really fucked up."

"Yes, it is. But I think we'd better try heading back to the pub. Maybe get to the Tucker place. That's closer." He stared at Simon, his eyes blank, and then into the waiting trees. "Let's just hope we get there."

CHAPTER TWENTY

In the clearing there is perfect stillness, and despite the gray of the sky above, no water falls here. He lets out a sigh that shakes the trees and then sits down heavily on the dead trunk, which had fallen some time after his last visit to this place. Not that he's sure how long that is. Time has little meaning for him. He just knows there have been other people, other ways, and long periods of dark slumber.

He rests his heavy head in his hands, the long leather coat creaking with the movement, and beneath his fingers feels the smooth ridges of his naked skull. For a moment he shuts his eyes, enjoying the darkness. If only there was more of it. There had been peace in the darkness, he was sure. Beside him, the ground falls sharply away, declining steeply without warning, and below there is only a small ledge before the torrent of the river. He can hear its angry flow, just as he could that last time he was here. When he had given her the choice she expected. When he had saved her.

Again he sighs, graying the grass beneath him. Within a day it will wither. And then no grass will grow in that patch again. He can feel the grown people in the woods, stumbling backward and forward trying to find their way out, but his storm would keep them in. He would keep them in until she was done with them.

Inside, in the vast empty spaces where universes could exist, he feels an ache. She disturbs him. She disturbs everything. Slowly over the years she had suckled at his power until now, when he was no longer sure who commanded whom. She had wanted revenge and he had allowed it, not understanding the complicated, exhausting network of human emotions, so far away from his own existence, but hoping the satisfaction would dull her angry fire and let there be some peace again.

He can feel the children tingling on his skin, far away but with him. He can feel their discomfort and their joy and their unhappiness and wonders how that came to be. It used to be that he could barely feel them at all after he saved them. He would just carry them with him, inside. But then her voice, the first voice he could remember for such a very long time, had burst through. And then she'd become stronger. And then she'd wanted to play with the other children and it didn't seem so much to allow, not for her, not at first.

But now she is bringing children into the in between and he can feel her pulling away from him. If he was capable of fear, he would be feeling it. The in between is his domain. It always has been. It always would be. The Catcher Man and the in between. As one.

Staring down at his heavy boots he listens to the river as it endlessly passes by. Perhaps it was a mistake to al-

low her to return. To interfere with things. Perhaps he should have kept the storm moving, seeking out the screams of the lost and the hurt and the nearly gone. He should have realized that to pause here would release too much power, power that a creature like Melanie would absorb and use. Maybe she had known it all along.

This was where they'd worshipped him all those years ago, begged him to bring children into the world with them, to make them catch. He remembered warmth then. Warm air and warm naked women on the forest floor. Then slowly they called for him less. And then as the years eroded everything but his name, they changed him. They put him in the storm and made him take children from the world. The change means nothing to him. But he knows he is tired. So very tired of existing. Of carrying the children and their pain.

He wonders if he will change again if they linger here much longer. He wonders how much Melanie has changed from lingering here. For a moment that could be a minute or a century he considers gathering them in and moving the storm on, leaving her business unfinished. But he is tired. And the stillness by the ravine is peaceful. Almost like the dark. And in that unsettled space inside him, he wonders if he still has the power to gather her in.

CHAPTER TWENTY-ONE

Despite her protestations Crouch had poured her a brandy, and sipping it, Alex looked around the small pub at the many familiar faces. The landlord had opened up the double doors into the restaurant, and from her stool at the far side of the bar she could see to the back of it, where a couple of the older kids were dozing, their heads lolling against each other. Children had that wonderful way of dealing with shock. Sleep it off. She let the golden liquid slide down her throat. That would be nice. To be able to sleep it all off.

As soon as she had finished her potted history of what had happened to the vicar and Kay, Ada Rose had scurried into the kitchen to make sandwiches, and Alex smiled through her tiredness. Yes, they all had different ways of reacting. Some were just sitting quietly, holding hands; others had convened at the bar talking loudly and some even laughed. Shock was a funny thing. Emma Granville had taken all the younger children upstairs and was settling them in to sleep with the help of Dr. Jones, and Alex had been glad to see him go, if only for a while. She didn't like the way he'd looked at her. He could hear her clock ticking too. Well, he could spend his time worrying about calming Emma down for the next hour or two at least. Her need was more urgent than Alex's.

There was a hum of conversation around her that she was too tired to focus on, and she knew people needed a few minutes to let the chill of reality sink in before they started with questions. She hadn't mentioned Melanie Parr yet. Would she find out what that little girl had to do with all this?

Glancing around, she noticed the pinched faces as some of the villagers gazed out of the windows. A lot of the locals were spread out there in their isolated farm homes. Their families who were safe in the pub were right to be worried. She was frightened for all of them, those inside and out.

The door from the kitchen swung open and Ada came through carrying two catering trays of sandwiches, which she deposited on the low table in front of the fire, and Alex called Crouch over again.

"Ring the bell, will you."

When there was silence, she looked at Crouch, but he nodded her on and he was right to do it. She was more likely to get information out of the people than he was.

"I know it's a shock to you that Kay and Reverend Barker are dead. God knows, it's a horrible thing that's happened to them, but our main focus until the police can get here has got to be trying to find Laura Chambers and little Peter Granville. Those of you, who like me have lived here all your lives, try and remember anywhere that might be a good place for someone to hide out. Any old barns or anything. They've obviously gone somewhere, and hopefully, since Laura was at the Granville's this morning, they're together. If the police get here soon, then we want to be able to give them as much help as possible when searching." Her voice sounded confident and she almost believed in it herself.

A murmur of agreement spread around the room, and Alex saw a couple of people taking sandwiches. It was a good sign. The shock was wearing off and was being helped by the promise of activity. The world always felt better with a plan of action.

A hand tentatively went up—it was Alice Moore, from the post office. She was sitting in the low chair next to Mary's by the open fire, and she looked more fragile than she had when Alex and Simon had tried to use her phone that morning. But then, they were all changed from those few hours ago. "What is it, Alice?"

The older woman nervously chewed her bottom lip. "I know this probably isn't important to you right now, but I can't stop thinking about it." She fiddled with the necklace that Alex was sure was a crucifix. "But what have you done with the . . . the bodies?"

A hush fell. Alex's voice was firm. There was no easy way to put it. "We've left them where they are. We moved the vicar into the church and covered him, but Kay is still where we found her."

"But that's awful!" Alice glanced around her and her throat was working as she spoke, as if chewing on her distress. "Shouldn't we take them somewhere? Especially Kay . . . we should do something for Kay. We can't leave her. Not like that."

Voices were rising around her and Alex called for quiet, but the indignant conversation didn't stop until Crouch reached across the bar and rang the bell again, this time loud and angry.

"We've got to leave them where they are. The police will want to examine the crime scenes exactly as we found them. We've probably destroyed some evidence as it is." Alice's eyes were wide and welling up, and Alex's tone softened slightly. "Remember what the reverend would have told you. They're gone. It's just their earthly remains that are left. No more harm can come to them now. Now we have to worry about the living."

There was a moment of silence and Alex felt some of the tension slip out of the room. Maybe country people were more pragmatic about death, or maybe nobody really wanted to go into the Chambers's house and cut Kay down. That was probably closer to the truth.

"But who would want to do that to anyone? And why here?" Alice Moore called out, and was immediately seconded by others.

Not having the energy to shout over them, Alex waited until the voices had lowered to a hum. God, she was tired, and the pain inside her was starting to burn upward from her pelvis. She needed painkillers, but she was damned if she was going to ask Dr. Jones. She'd get this out of the way and then see if Crouch had any behind the bar.

Taking a deep breath, she let the words out. "This isn't just bad luck. And I don't think that Kay and Reverend Barker were just random victims. Horrible as it sounds, whoever's doing this is doing this to us on purpose. They were chosen for a reason. Now, maybe Kay didn't know what that reason was, but I think the vicar did. He said some things before he died. Some things that we have to make sense of." She paused. "And some of this stuff may not make sense. Not in the traditional sense."

"He was still alive when you found him?"

Crouch's voice carved into her from behind. "God, how awful."

"There was also a message left in the window at Kay's house."

"She's come back. I always knew she would. She's come back." Rocking backward and forward, perched awkwardly on the old two-seater in front of the fire, Mary muttered aloud and only stopped when Alice wrapped her arm around her, her grip perhaps a little too firm. Still, although she fell silent, Mary's lips continued to move, mumbling silent words.

"What's she talking about?" Dave Carter, a retired pilot who'd only recently moved into the village, seemed to speak for all, as once again the sea of skin, worn and smooth, looked at Alex expectantly.

"I don't know. But I think this might all have something to do with a little girl that went missing years ago. It sounds crazy, but nothing else seems to make much sense. Mary thought she saw her in the garden yesterday. And the vicar said her name when he was dying. Melanie Parr. And he said we had to warn the others. That she'd come for us. Mary said that the Catcher Man had brought her back." She paused. "Neither of those names meant anything to me until Paul told me Melanie had gone missing in a storm years ago."

As she spoke her eyes wandered around the room looking for signs of recognition or reactions of any kind. Some looked puzzled, especially those younger than her; some just looked tired and frightened and wanting answers; but on the faces of those older than herself, some not that much older, a guarded look had crept in. Some of those faces surprised her. Ada and Daniel Rose had exchanged glances before their eyes slid to the floor. Alice Moore's hands fluttered to her throat and Mary's rocking increased. Yes, something was being hidden.

"What did the message say? The one you found at Kay's place?" Even Crouch's ruddy complexion seemed harder, more defensive.

"Paul found it. It was written in steam on the window, but god knows how it got there. He said that it said, *Come inside Paul. Let's play fishing with Kay.* It was gone when I arrived." Crouch looked disbelieving, but Alex pressed on. "I know it sounds weird, but Paul wouldn't make something like that up. And there are other things that are wrong. There are children in the town. Children that shouldn't be here. We've all seen them. Haven't we?" She glared around, knowing she was in danger of making a fool of herself, but tired of pretending that everything was okay. "I know James Partridge has, because his told me." She stared at his wife, who ducked her head. "And I think if we all started being honest, we'd discover that strange children aren't the weirdest things that have been going on."

Again, a series of furtive glances scurried backward and forward across the bar. Yes, she'd made her point.

Mary turned around, clutching the back of the sofa, hands like desperate claws in the fabric. "It's all real. She's real. The Catcher Man brought her back. He knows. *She* knows."

Ada stormed over to her, and Alice twisted in her seat as Daniel's wife shook the hysterical woman by the shoulders. "Stop it, Mary! She's gone! She was gone a long time ago. Stop it now! It's done. It's all done."

Alex stood up from her stool. What was winding these women up? What was making Ada so angry?

"What does she mean, 'The Catcher Man knows'? Knows what?"

"She doesn't mean anything. She doesn't know what she's saying. The Catcher Man doesn't exist. He never has. He was made up by someone generations ago. He was just a stupid, stupid story told to scare children. That's all." Ada looked around her as she spoke, seeking support from those around her. She found it in the nods of those whose expressions Alex didn't trust. She'd lived alongside these people all her life, and now she wasn't sure she knew them at all.

Looking at Ada's defiant expression, she let out a humorless laugh. "Well, something's real now, and it's scaring the shit out of me, I don't know about the rest of you." Alex's words echoed around the room, challenging the women from a different generation, and she stared at her aunt, whose gaze slipped away to the fire, guilty and burdened.

Chapter Twenty-two

There was a long silence after Alex spoke, and from deep within her, Mary felt an ache for her niece. Alex was looking at them all like they were strangers, and she could understand the young woman's hurt. But they weren't strangers. They just carried secrets, that was all, and didn't everybody? Theirs were just darker and maybe better hidden than most. Hidden to protect those they loved.

The warmth from the fire barely penetrated her skin and Mary wondered if she'd feel this cold, this detached from the world for the rest of her life. Sighing heavily, she decided she didn't really much care either way. Melanie would be waiting for her out in the storm, of that she was sure, and if it was up to that little girl, that little *monster*, then they'd be meeting again soon enough. And then it would be Ada's turn. She looked around her at the bar, where it seemed that everything was standing still and waiting for her to decide what to do. If she was gone, and Ada, then who would be left that would be strong enough to tell? To finally let their awful secret out and put an end to this terrible tale?

Ada had released her grip on the back of Mary's chair, but was still standing behind her, awkward and out of place. Mary wondered if Ada was having the same dark thoughts she was. And Alice. Poor Alice.

Her limbs aching and heavy, Mary turned and stared at the two old women, shaking her head. "You just don't understand, do you? She's come back. And she's taking her revenge on us." Her shoulders slumped slightly, as if the small outburst had drained all her energy. "And maybe we deserve it. The secrets may as well come out now as when the police come. Maybe if we tell, then this might all stop." Her breath hitched slightly. "At the very least, it might all stop for us." She glanced at Alice. "Don't you think, dear?"

Alice was comforting herself by stroking Sailor, Crouch's cat, who, woken by the noise from his slumber by the fire, was winding himself through and around her legs. But Mary thought she saw a slight nod and wondered for a moment if Alice was the best of them all, keeping that inside, letting it worry away at her and yet never saying a word, despite that she could have done so with no shame to herself. She really hadn't been part of it.

"What do you mean?" Dave Carter moved away from the bar, lowering himself into the one empty chair near Mary. Alex came forward too, and it seemed to Mary as if she were about to start some old-fashioned story telling, which perhaps she was, taking them all with her as she drifted backward, back to another time linked so definitely with this here and now, and yet so distant, so already done, so *cannot be undone*.

She smiled at Dave Carter for a moment, her face beautifully serene, before her vision floated somewhere in the space above the harsh outline of the energetic flames, where the promise of light was welcoming and soothing. There might not be that much time before Melanie came to visit her or the police arrived, but there was all the time in the world for her; enough time to say what needed to be said. She wondered how the story would taste when she regurgitated it. Her voice was smooth as she started the release, and she led them back into the past, melodically, like a children's storyteller, and then she was there, or should she say *then*, the sweet smell of damp air around her, skin itching with oppressive heat. Her muscles didn't ache anymore, the years lifting from her flesh and soul, her hair long free as her heart speeded up.

Resting her chin on her arms, Mary leaned on the back of the sofa and gazed out the cottage window, her legs tucked under her. It was just too hot, and the thin layer of sweat that seemed to constantly cover her itched at her scalp. Occasionally her eyes drifted over to where Alicia was playing the piano, and she idly wondered why her younger sister's hair didn't ever stick to her head or look greasy with this oppressive weather.

She normally found Alicia's music soothing, but something about this unpleasant heat was leaving her irritated. She stared at the gathering gray clouds above the house, now spreading across the village. It would be a couple of hours before David came home from the farm, so there was no point in thinking about cooking yet. Not that on a day like this any of them would be particularly hungry, and that was fine by her. The idea of standing for any length of time over that stove was enough to make her jaw twitch with annoyance.

No, she thought, running her hand through her sticky hair, salad and cold ham would do them all today, even Paul. Her eyes wandered across the familiar scenery outside, looking but not really seeing it as she thought about her son, and she didn't hear the sigh that escaped her, low and haunting.

What was the matter with him at the moment? He'd lost weight, and although even she would have to admit that he'd had a bit of puppy fat to lose, there was something radical, painful even, about the way the pounds had dropped off. He had shifty eyes too, these days. Only ten, and yet already she was getting the feeling that he had secrets from his mother. Not allowed in the bathroom, not allowed to see him getting dressed. So much of their relationship had been disallowed. Maybe that was just his age, but something wasn't right. It seemed like something was eating him from the inside out. And not just him, either. All his friends were different these days. They'd changed over the past year or so, since that Joe kid left. They'd all got so serious, so intense.

Grayness absorbed the sky, pressing down on the roof of the old cottage, as Mary's mind skipped over the issue of Paul's stutter. She didn't want to think about how bad that had got. She'd tentatively asked the doctor about it, her own face twitching as if by raising the question she had betrayed her child's sense of privacy, and that if he'd found out then he'd never forgive her. The doctor had smiled sympathetically at her and put it down to his age, all those hormones starting to fire up, and she'd accepted that, trying to push aside the argument that there was more to it, that ten was too young for 'all those hormones.'

Her gaze drifted back to Alicia, not wanting to look anymore at the aggressive weather that was gathering outside, and something about her ethereally beautiful sister added to her irritation, and she allowed it to run for a moment. Sometimes it seemed so unfair that Alicia, the late-in-life and unplanned youngest daughter of their dead parents, was beautiful and talented and unburdened with the realities of domestic life. Men constantly fell in love with Alicia's sweetness and that rare talent she had, but she almost floated over them, sometimes lingering for a moment, but never enough to form a relationship. God, she wouldn't be surprised if after all these years of marriage, even her own husband didn't occasionally think of Alicia when they were panting together in the dark. They were happy as happy goes, but Mary knew she'd never been the type that caught a man's eye in the same way as her sister did, and love him as she surely did, David was only a man.

Yes, sometimes she thought Alicia had it too easy. Alicia, who lived in her own little world, just her and her beloved music. She played in the concert hall in Taunton sometimes, and the breathtaking quality of her work there kept the steady stream of well-to-do children from the town coming out to the village for their private lessons. There were more than enough for her to pick and choose, and that kept the fees high. No one could deny that she was worth it. She was almost as talented a teacher as she was a musician.

The sweat at the back of her knees was making her too uncomfortable and standing up, Mary gave her sister a smile she didn't feel. Something was definitely wrong in the air today and it niggled at her insides, the cottage now claustrophobic, the music too loud in her head. The back of her legs ached from crouching in the vegetable garden that morning and she needed to stretch them.

"I think I'll go."

Alicia just nodded, smiling her sweet smile from beneath that soft ash-blond head. Raising her hand to give a small wave, Mary caught sight of her fingernails and the earth that still lingered underneath, despite the scrubbing she'd given them. For a moment it seemed they summed up all that was different between her and her beautiful sister—earth and air, real and unreal. With that thought, her irritation disappeared. Yes, she was real. She wouldn't trade her life and all its imperfections for Alicia's. Alicia made music. She, Mary, had made Paul, her beautiful baby boy, and nothing, no symphony or concerto, could ever rival that.

Alicia was lost once again in the keys, at one with the music, and picking up her cardigan and tying it around her waist, Mary snuck through to the hall and let herself quietly out the front door. The humidity hit her as soon as she stepped into the quiet village road, and as she walked downhill toward the pub and post office, the midges from the river formed an increasingly busy halo around her head. Walking faster, the sweat building on her scalp, her skin itching with the imagined attention of the flies, she didn't see the figure that was running toward her, panting, eyes wide. The woman had called her name several times before Mary stopped cursing under her breath and looked up. It was Charlotte Keeler.

"Mary! Mary! I've been looking for you everywhere." Her face was wild, shaking with emotion, and Mary held her arm.

"What is it? What's the matter?"

"You have to come to the house. Something's hap-

pened to Kay." Her voice was choking. "She has burns. Burns!"

"What?" The air seemed like glue around her now, impeding her understanding.

"And there's more." Charlotte's eyes almost shimmered. "For you, too." She froze, staring at Mary for a moment, before turning her head. "Come on. Everyone's waiting at mine. You need to hear . . . you need to . . ."

Before Mary could ask a question, Charlotte's ample figure was disappearing ahead of her, running back down the steep cobbled road to her own house. As Mary moved to catch up, her head was filled with her boy, her Paul, his stutter, his weight loss and the dead look in his eyes whenever she dared to ask him what was wrong.

The Keeler's old stone house should have been pleasantly cool even on the hottest England summer's day, but as in Alicia's cottage, it seemed that this strange brewing storm had pervaded the thick centuries-old barriers of protection, filling the rooms with its unnatural damp heat. It didn't stop the chill shiver that prickled across Mary's back as she looked down at the small burns and bruises on Kay's arms. Her mind still spun with the story that Kay had told the vicar, that he had told Charlotte, and who had now told her and the other mothers that had arrived during the past few minutes.

How could it be true? How could any of it be true? How could she believe that Paul would be so afraid and not tell her? She glanced behind her as she heard Ada Rose gasp, and then turned her attention back to Kay. The burns on the child's limbs were crudely formed and they glared angrily at her, crushing her disbelief with their glowing presence.

It had started with the cat, Kay had told the vicar, Joe Barnes's cat. That's when it had all really turned nasty with Melanie. Mary's brow furrowed. Could a child really have done that to an animal? And why, for God's sake?

Her stomach sickening, Mary turned away and sat on the arm of the sofa.

Ada joined her, speaking in a low whisper. "Thank God she's had the good sense to tell. Thank God—"

Mary cut her off. "She didn't tell out of common sense. She had to. Have you seen that burn on her right arm? It's infected. She probably kept it secret for as long as she could, but look at her. I wouldn't be surprised if she was running a bit of a fever."

For a moment the two women said nothing, huddled together in what was becoming a crowded living room. Charlotte had stopped crying and was applying some ointment to her daughter's arm, Enid Tucker helping her. The vicar sat back, awkwardly sipping tea, uncomfortable amongst the increasingly tense women. He was still a relatively young man, not much older than Mary herself, not yet of an age to be sexless, benign.

Ada chewed her bottom lip. "She said Melanie Parr did it, made them do it or whatever." Her eyes were hollow. "Do you think . . . do you think that James or Paul . . . ?" The question hung unfinished.

Mary stared away from her friend. "Do you mean will our children have bruises and burns under their clothes?" The whisper was all she could manage. "Yes. Yes, I do." All of Paul's strange furtive behavior, the increased stutter, the dark rings under his wide eyes, it was all making sense. It all fitted together with the madness that Kay had spilled out to the vicar, the madness that he had brought to share with her mother, the mad-

ness that had been these children's world for all those
months. She looked again at the child sniffing in the
chair in the far corner. She still looked so afraid, and
that made Mary's anger rise.

Didn't Kay think they could sort it out? That these
grownups could sort it out? And if Kay was afraid, then
how did James and her Paul feel? Kay was over a year
older than them. They were all older than Melanie Parr,
for Christ's sake.

Mary leaned forward. "Where's Melanie now, Kay
dear?" Her voice was low, but strong, and she waited
for Kay to wipe her eyes, hiding her impatience for the
answer.

"She's up at the ravine. On her own up there." She
couldn't meet Mary's eyes, anybody's eyes, but stared at
the carpet, her voice expressionless.

"The others have gone back down to the river to play.
Melanie likes to be on her own sometimes. Says she
has things to do that we wouldn't understand. Says her
mother don't mind her being on her own. Thinks it's
safe next to the city. She says she's not a scaredy-cat like
we are. She don't believe in any Catcher Man." Kay nervously glanced at her mother.

Raising one hand, she covered her mouth, her fingers
twisting the upper lip almost subconsciously. Mary's
heart sent a pang of emotional pain to her cramped
stomach and it reverberated back as she looked at the
nails on those young hands, bitten down until the edges
were raw, strips of skin torn from each side. Just like
Paul's. How was it that they all let it pass? How was it
that they didn't say something? To each other at least, if
not to their precious children directly.

Looking at Ada, Mary saw her own guilt in the

woman's face. And Charlotte's as she nodded in their direction, signaling them into the adjacent dining room. Reverend Barker took the seat next to Kay and started talking softly to her. Leaving them behind, Mary noticed the flash of anger the girl gave him and she understood why. He had broken her confidence by telling her mother what she had shared with him, and she hated him for it. And behind that hate was fear. Gritting her teeth, she followed her friends into the room next door.

When Mary closed the heavy wood behind her, there was a moment's pause and then the women let their anger hiss itself out in a whirlwind of whispers.

"I can't believe this! I can't believe it."

"It's not normal. How do you punish someone for that? How? God, I'd like to wring her little neck."

"Where did Kay say she was? In the woods?"

"Up by the ravine. On her own."

A flash of eyes passed around the occupants of the room.

"Do you think we should go up there? To the clearing?"

"I told Paul not to go up there—the banks are too steep and it's too far from the village."

"Stop it Mary, it doesn't matter. We went up there as children for God's sake, why did you think our kids would be any different?"

"So what should we do?"

Perhaps in another time or another place someone would have suggested they should go and talk to Melanie's mother, but it didn't enter their heads. Mrs. Parr wasn't one of them—she had city blood in her veins and now that blood was spoiling their country like a disease, making their peaceful haven unsafe.

"I know what I'd like to do. I'd like to go up there and

put the fear of God into her. I want to make her cry. I want to make her feel as bad as my baby."

"Then why don't we? Why don't we go up there?"
Silence.

"What? What do you mean?"

"Let's do it. Let's go up there and teach her a lesson she won't forget. We never expect them home before tea-time. Maybe she won't head back to the village for a while. We could get up there if we go now."

"But what will we do? We can't hurt her. We can't . . ."

"Calm down. I don't mean hurt her. But scare her."

"Her mother'll go mad when she tells her. Wouldn't you? We won't get away with it."

"I don't think Melanie will tell. What's she going to say?"
A pause.

"And even if she does tell, we'll deny it."

"I just keep seeing those burns and bruises."

"She has scars too. Didn't you see?"

"And it won't only be Kay."

"We owe it to them to go. We owe it to our children to sort it out."

The air was filled with breathing, harsh and hot. No words were spoken as the agreement was made, and it was Charlotte that reached the door first. Mary stood behind her as she called into the doorway of the lounge, her voice tight.

"We're going out. Can you stay here with Kay?"

The vicar was out of sight, but his muffled reply was still audible. "Where are you going?"

Charlotte's fingers gripped tighter on the wood of the door. "To the ravine."

There was no reply from the vicar, and Mary wasn't surprised. What was it he'd said about Melanie when he'd finished telling Kay's story? 'The child is an abomination.' No, he wouldn't argue with what they were doing. He may have taken to the cloth, but he was a country boy at heart. He understood about taking care of your own.

Striding grimly back up the hill, it seemed to Mary that the grayness had sunk from the sky, sticking to her, the feeling unpleasant and unnatural like static prickling her head. It was only half an hour since she'd left Alicia's cottage, but it seemed so much longer, and as she passed it again, the troop of women heading for the steep woods that started not far from the back of the small row of buildings, the soft strains of music escaped and wafted around her, breaking the spell in the air, allowing the first drops of heavy rain to fall.

Despite the increasing weight of the falling water, the ground was still solid enough for the women to climb the steep slope without sliding backward at each step. Mary felt her breath roaring inside her, her lungs burning like they were cracking with flame as they stretched with the unexpected exertion she was placing on them, but her legs were strong and she kept up the pace easily. You didn't grow up around farms without being a little bit hardy. Even delicate Alicia had strength in those slim limbs of hers. Maybe it was something in the air.

Above them thunder growled to life, and despite the anger and hate that filled her, Mary hoped that wherever Paul was, he'd head home now. In the woods the sky seemed almost black, the early afternoon becoming twilight around them. This was shaping up to be a bad storm, malevolent and vicious.

The four of them had spread out as they climbed, and it was Charlotte, looking absurdly out of place in her housedress and flat sandals, the clothes sticking to her form underneath in the onslaught of the rain, who stopped first. She smiled, pushing the lank wet curls out of her face.

"Hello Melanie, we've come to see you." Her voice dripped with honey and acid, enough to send a shiver down Mary's spine as she looked up to the top of the bank, only a few feet away.

The small blonde child must have decided that being in the woods in the middle of a thunderstorm wasn't the best idea and had started her journey home. Not so keen to be in danger herself, then. Sitting where the ground became level, she had been putting on her shoes and socks. One shoe on, she stood up and looked down at the women. Mary watched the change of expression on that perfectly beautiful face—at first a sweet smile, then twisting into puzzled concern. Maybe she could smell their anger; maybe even at ten she knew there was something wrong about four grown women coming out in a storm without even a coat, out to the children's territories, to places they had probably forgotten about twenty years ago. Still though, she didn't move. Not yet. Her confusion was still waiting to turn to fear.

Mary felt animal blood rushing through her veins, exciting her, making her heart throb in her chest. Looking at the flush faces of her friends, their shining eyes and parted lips, she knew they could feel it too. They were a pack. A pack of wild animals protecting their young. At first she felt like a lioness, growling and proud. She followed Charlotte's lead and picked up a fallen branch, watching Melanie take her first hesitant step back into the clearing, dropping her forgotten shoe, which tumbled past them down the slope, the women starting to circle the small pretty girl, who was rapidly losing her smug expression.

Mary wondered if they were more like hyenas, bitter and cruel, snapping and snarling at their weaker prey.

She pushed the thought down as she smiled at the child backing away from her. Well, so what if they were? They weren't going to do any real harm. Just scare her a little. Well, maybe scare her a lot. And she deserved it.

She raised the stick and swatted at the girl's legs, forcing her to jump backward to avoid being stung by the branch.

"What's the matter Melanie? Don't you want to play? We thought you liked a bit of danger." She lifted the thin branch again, and across the clearing, Ada Rose cawed, high and victorious.

"Jesus Christ. What happened?"

Dave Carter's voice broke into Mary's train of thought, bringing her roughly back to the present. As an ache ran up her arm, she realized how tightly she'd been gripping the arm of the chair. Telling it all, however, wasn't as bad as she'd thought it might be. Relaxing her fingers, she felt her age settling back into her bones, no animal blood rushing through her veins any longer.

She wished the fire would warm her more, down in the core where she needed it. Still, no matter. Not much longer now. Looking down, the gnarled sinews on the back of her hands and arms reminded her of the woods. The damp smell still lingered in her nostrils after all these years, especially tonight, brought back to vivid life.

She sighed. "What happened? It's so difficult to tell. We became *like men.* You know, how they behave in a gang, at a football match, in a crowd, where terrible things happen. We became a collective mind almost. No individual thought. Not in those few minutes, at least. Not when it got out of hand." She paused, brow furrowed, trying to think. "Not that there was really time for things to get out of hand. It all happened so fast. I think these things tend to." Smiling, she looked at the frozen faces around her. "Cliché, but true."

Her mouth felt dry and she needed something to help mellow her soul and give her the strength and courage she wasn't sure she had.

"Get me a gin and tonic, will you please, Crouch? Make it a double." Rising quickly, the man didn't argue with her and she waited silently till he brought the tall cool glass back, pouring only a small amount of the tonic in and taking a long slow sip, wanting the spirit to burn her throat. To purify her voice.

Carter leaned forward in his chair, repeating his question.

"So? What happened?" His voice was eager, and Mary wondered for a second if she could hear the edge of the hyena in it. Not that there was any real surprise there. Nothing about people had surprised her for a long time. Except perhaps their gritty need for survival. Well, she was getting over that one.

"We panicked her, that's what happened. I don't know who caught her legs with their stick first; whoever it was I'm sure didn't mean to, but once it was done, once she'd yelped with that first sting of pain, well . . . it was like a veil came down. Did *I* hit her? Probably. Almost certainly, but I just don't know. I'm not lying when I say I don't remember. I remember most of that day clear as a bell, couldn't forget it if I tried, each image is etched into my head, burned there, filling my dreams, but not those few minutes. They're gone."

From the corner of her eye, she could see that Alice was looking up, drawn into the story too, the part that she hadn't known, the hour or so before she became involved, only once before heard, many, many years ago. She looked better than she had in a long while. Maybe the telling was doing her good too, poor soul.

"We weren't hitting her hard. Just those kind of stinging shots, the sort children do to each other, almost like tea towel slaps, but we *were* scaring her. Because grownups didn't do that kind of thing. They weren't supposed to. And I think she could see our knowledge, that we knew about her, and that scared her. Maybe out there by the ravine, she thought we were as capable of evil as she was.

"We had closed right in on her, laughing and whooping, soaking wet and loving it in a strange way. We must have looked like some kind of crazy witches out there in that clearing. We must have looked like that to Melanie anyway, because she stepped further and further back, desperate to keep out of our reach, terrified of what we were going to do to her. She kept shuffling backwards until she was right by the drop away into the river."

Mary paused, her eyes almost shut, remembering the expression of surprise on that forever-ten face as the wet ground behind Melanie crumbled and she tumbled backward, her arms flailing forward trying to hold onto the air. Mary's wrinkled face flinched as she remembered how none of them had reached to grab her, their own shock freezing them, the rain that attacked them and their anger all forgotten, their vision filled with those pinwheeling arms and small, stretched fingers.

She let the words out that were eating her inside.

"And then she fell. She was gone, screaming backwards over the ravine."

CHAPTER TWENTY-THREE

"Oh Mary, oh sweet Mary mother of God . . ." The words were like punches coming out of Enid Tucker and Mary, the Mary that was never going to heaven, not anymore, the Mary that was here full of flesh and blood and fear, wished her friend would just shut up, just please shut up.

Leaning carefully over the edge of the drop-off, Charlotte beside her, Mary could see Melanie's twisted body on a small ledge a few feet above the torrent of the rising river. The girl's eyes were wide and terrified, her lower body bent out of shape.

"Melanie? Melanie? Can you hear me?" There was no animal in Charlotte's voice anymore; she was all human, all pathetically human and full of realization. The small voice drifted up to them, jagged and wet.

"I can't move my legs! I can't move my legs!"

Turning round, Mary saw Ada Rose desperately searching the ground around them for something long enough to reach the ledge, which was a good ten feet below them, and wanted to scream at her that it was useless. Ada knew as well as she did that there were no twigs or branches at their feet that were going to be able to go that far.

The air above her flashed bright before thunder raged again, the downpour that surrounded them stinging at their skin, sucking the warmth out of them. She shivered.

"It's no good, we'll have to go back for help. We need a rope." She had to raise her voice to make it carry over the sounds of nature that screeched in her ears and pulled at her hair.

"Melanie? Melanie?" Charlotte screamed down to where the girl lay, the water of the river steadily rising. Coughing and spluttering came back at them, the little girl crying.

"I can't move my legs! I can't feel them!"

"We're going to get a rope. You've got to hold on! We'll be as fast as we can. Just please hold on!"

Listening to the panic in her friend's voice, Mary squeezed her eyes shut for a moment, wanting to keep them that way, to block this nightmare out forever. To make it so it never happened. Her heart thumped too hard, and behind her lids she pushed away the tears that came with the truth that she couldn't ignore. It would take too long to go back to the village. It would take too long. The freezing river was rising too fast. It would overwhelm her. Drown her. To go back to the village would take too long for Melanie.

She felt a hand on her arm and reluctantly opened her eyes. Enid was tugging at her. "Come on, Mary. Let's go. We need to hurry."

For a moment the pointlessness of what they were doing was on the tip of her tongue, but then she bit it back. She just wanted to get away, to get away from there.

None of them volunteered to stay, to wait with Melanie, and her small cries of "Don't leave me alone! Don't leave me!" were the last Mary heard from her, carried carefully on the wind, the words mercilessly clear.

If only as she ran down the bank, her feet twisting and turning as she stumbled from going too fast in the rain, the life bursting inside her, if only she'd known then how long she'd be hearing their echo.

Charlotte had fetched dry towels for each of them while checking that Kay was sleeping upstairs, but Mary's sat on the chair beside her untouched. It didn't seem right to take that comfort, to have that warmth. The silence in the confines of the small lounge was putting her teeth on edge. How much longer? How much longer?

The women had all been exhausted when they'd staggered back to the village, so it was Reverend Barker who'd left ashen-faced with the rope, running through the storm back to the ravine. One more guest at the party.

Alice Moore had been emptying the small post box at the far end of the village, the one the farmers used when they didn't want to come down to the post office. The small sack of letters she clutched almost fell from her hands when she saw them, shocked at their bedraggled, haunted appearances.

Letting the others go past, Mary had asked her to gather up their children and get them to help sort the post or something. Anything to keep them occupied. Just for an hour or so. Alice had wanted to know why, and her whole body shaking, the words surreal, Mary told her, needing to tell someone. Nodding and quivering, agreeing to do as she was asked, Alice aged thirty *years in that five minutes of intense listening, and watching it happen broke something inside Mary. Alice Moore would never have children of her own. She wouldn't even think of it, not after that day.*

Breathing almost against her will, Mary let her head rest in her hands, not wanting to look at the faces of her friends, and they not wanting to look at her or each other they listened to the tick of the clock in the hallway and waited.

Eventually the door creaked open and the vicar was back, soaking and muddy, the rope dangling impotently from his hands. Forty-five minutes had passed since they left the clearing. Shaking his head, he sank into the old hard-backed chair in the corner. His voice was dull, empty. "She's gone. She was gone when I got there. I called and called, but there was nothing. I dropped the rope over the side until it hit the water and shouted and shouted. But there was nothing."

The silence that followed threatened to eat Mary up. Her head buzzed as the truth sank in. Melanie was dead. She'd known it. She'd thought she'd known it, but this, this final confirmation was almost too much to bear. What had they done? Oh Christ, what had they done?

"I think I may be sick." Ada rocked slowly back and forth.

"What are we going to do? What on earth are we going to do?" Enid Tucker chewed the skin at the edge of her fingers, something that took Mary back to when they had been children themselves, the tears prickling behind her eyes.

Charlotte stood up and crossed to the window, staring at the rain that pummeled the old square panes of glass, accusing them with what it knew.

"Go home and have a bath. Give your children some tea. We'll meet again when our husbands are home."

"Where?"

"I don't know." She shrugged and it seemed to Mary that the effort took all of her energy. Before she could stop herself, the words were out.

"I'll speak to Alicia. I'm sure we can go to her cottage. We don't want to be where the children can hear us."

The silence confirmed the plan, and Mary pulled herself to her reluctant feet, wondering how she was going to be normal, wondering how she was going to make Paul's tea, and smile and listen while looking for burns and bruises and hearing the echo of that little girl's panicked screams ringing constantly in her head, monster or not. Suddenly the reality of the future pierced her insides. As the women filed out into the rain, they knew the world had changed. Nothing would ever be the same again.

Mary took the last swallow of gin, enjoying the slight hum it had created inside her. Maybe she'd take another upstairs. Yes, maybe she would. But first she had to finish her tale. And finish it she would.

"We argued long into the night, once we shared what we'd done. The men couldn't believe it. Sometimes I think they never really did. It was easier not to, and men aren't good at dealing with such things. They didn't want to see the cruelty that we were capable of. Surprising really, because women are so much harder underneath our soft skin." She smiled wistfully.

"We were hard that night. Our guilt had turned to self-preservation in the hours we allowed ourselves, those hours in which the cold truth sank in. She'd hurt our children. She'd forced us into it, and after all, it was an accident, so why should we have to suffer more? She was an evil child. If she could do that to Joe Barnes's cat at her age, then what would she grow up into?"

She raised a wry eyebrow. "Anyway, of all of us law-abiding adults, it was only Alicia who insisted that we should go to the police. We should explain ourselves. We would live to regret it if we didn't. She stuck to her guns for hours, wouldn't budge, not until I cried and cried, begged her to just keep quiet, asked her where was the harm in that? I beat her down with sisterly love."

Throat tightening, Mary forced herself to continue. "She changed after that. She still played the piano, gave lessons, but the fire in her music was gone. She didn't play for pleasure anymore. I don't think she found pleasure in it, or wouldn't allow herself to enjoy it. She . . . how shall I put it, she sought solace with people she barely knew, with *men* she barely knew. At least one of those helped her produce the lovely Alex." Looking up, she sought out her niece, but Alex wouldn't meet her gaze. No matter. It was to be expected. "No one frowned on Alicia for that, for her single-motherhood. We carried her sins, you see. We caused them." She sighed.

"Alex revived her for a while, but not for long. Her guilt turned to disease and that took her from us."

Her cheeks were wet with silent tears. "We killed her just as surely as we killed Melanie. An accident, but our fault all the same."

She sat in silence for somewhere between a minute and an eternity, staring into the flames and slowly settling back into the present. She could hear Alice's breath hitching as she sobbed beside her, and Mary squeezed her knee. "It's all right, Alice. None of it was your fault."

"But the dead can't come back, Mary." Under the hardness of Ada's voice there was a slight tremble. "No matter what we did. Melanie Parr's gone. Dead and gone, and I'm glad!"

Mary wasn't the only one to hear the slight edge of hysteria in her old friend's voice. Alex finally raised her head, and it hurt Mary to see the sadness and shock on her face. The truth hurt, there was no denying it. And more often than not it was the innocent who felt the pain most. "Why don't you go home, Ada? Help Daniel get that radio of his working."

Alex turned to Crouch, and Mary noticed the man couldn't look her in the eye, as if he was somehow ashamed *for* her.

"I need a shower. Can I use one of the rooms?" He nodded before opening the cupboard and pulling out a key. She lowered her voice slightly. "And a couple of Paracetamol if you've got some. Make that four if you can. Save me asking for more later."

Taking the packet from him, Alex turned back to face the silent throng. "I don't care how crazy it makes me sound. This village did something terrible to that little girl and now she's come back. And we can either ignore that and carry on dying or try and think of a way to stop her. It's up to you." Mary felt her heart ache as her niece headed upstairs without even a backward glance.

After Ada had left and Alex had gone upstairs, the tension eased out of the room a little. For the younger villagers that had known nothing of Melanie Parr or whose relatives had not been part of the events of thirty years ago, Mary's retelling had been awful but unreal. As if Melanie herself had never really existed except in this awful tale and the outcome of it couldn't touch them. Perhaps that was the way it always was with these things. Nobody every truly believed the world existed before they were born. A world without yourself was never easy to picture, especially for the young. Slowly the quiet hum of conversation filled the bar, although no one seemed too keen to come close to Mary, everyone avoiding guilt by association.

Beside her, Alice was still crying and Mary sighed. It had been a cathartic experience for both of them, and despite her pain, Alice would survive. The story, their history, was shared, and she would realize that her guilt in it all was not so very great. People would forgive her, and then maybe she'd eventually be able to forgive herself.

Scanning the room, Mary sought out the dishevelled figure of Dr. Jones, and was pleased to see him sitting alone. She stared at him until eventually his eyes met hers, and she signaled him over. There were things she needed to know and there was no more time to wait. Dave Carter had moved away, and the doctor took his seat, awkward and embarrassed. Mary found she didn't care much either way about his disapproval. He wasn't country born and bred. He didn't know how tough country life made you. She stared at him for a moment, taking in the weakness of his chin and jowls, and knew that after all he'd just heard, he'd tell her what she wanted to know.

"Tell me about Alex." There. The words were out.

The doctor looked into her calm eyes, and this time didn't offer platitudes. Maybe after what he'd just heard, he'd decided she could take it straight. And he was right. That's what she wanted.

"She's dying. Ovarian cancer. She's known for a while. She's got a few months. No more than six."

"Thank you."

Nodding, Mary rose, hoping that only the stiffness in her back gave away the sudden grief, stronger than any physical pain that ripped through her. Still, it would be gone soon. For all of them, life was only fleeting. A breath, a whisper, and then nothing.

Going behind the familiar bar, she poured herself a large brandy, slipping the small serrated knife that Crouch used for slicing lemons into her cardigan sleeve unnoticed. Yes. Everything was as it should be.

"I'm going to have a hot bath." The doctor dragged his eyes up to hers from his seat, and nodded.

She smiled gently at him, forgiving him, forgiving all of them. "Don't disturb me unless it's really necessary."

Feeling the comfort of the knife against her wrist, she headed upstairs.

CHAPTER TWENTY-FOUR

By the time Simon staggered onto the gravel of the Tucker's home, Paul a few steps behind, his legs were like jelly and they were both covered in mud and exhausted. The gloom of the day was becoming dusk and very soon it would be pitch-black. Staring at the light coming from the house ahead, he felt relief flood through him, and only then realized how tense he'd been. A house. Normalcy. That was what he needed. Surely once they were inside any thought of ghosts and memories of giggles and strange electricity would fade. That would be good, because when grown men started believing in ghosts it was time to doubt their own sanity.

"Let's hope Enid Tucker's got the kettle on. I'm gasping for a cup of tea." Paul sounded as tired as he looked and Simon could empathize. Ever since they'd arrived in Watterrow weird shit had taken over, and although the rain had slowed it had still been a hard slog trying to find the farm.

"I'm hoping for a brandy, myself. Maybe in a coffee." Simon grinned at his friend, and Paul nodded.

"Yep, that does sound good." Paul's voice was distant and he looked up and around him as if something weren't quite right.

They were approaching the house from the side and the sound of their shoes crunching against the stones seemed too loud in the silence, almost hurting Simon's ears with the invasion of noise. They reached the front porch door and finding it ajar, Paul stepped backward, looking around the farmyard, puzzled.

"That's what's missing. The dogs."

"What dogs?"

"The Tucker's dogs. Tinker and Jess. They'd normally be out here saying hello."

Simon shrugged, looking out into the emptiness around them. "Well, it's been raining. Maybe they're inside."

Paul shook his head. "They're farm dogs. There's no way old man Tucker would bring them in. They're working dogs, not pets. They live outside and use that lean-to against the main house as their shelter."

"Well, I guess that's where they are then."

Paul didn't look convinced. "Maybe. But those two dogs are friendly. The rain wouldn't have stopped them from coming out to meet and greet."

Turning, he scanned the horizon. "That doesn't look good, either."

Simon could hear the tension creeping back into Paul's voice and he looked up at the fields behind the house, the side away from the woods. The sheep were still out there on the hills, the lambs seeking shelter at their mothers' sides.

"What is it?"

"Surely in all the thunder and lightning of the past twenty-four hours Tucker would have brought them in. Even if young Tom was down in the village and not there to help, old Tucker would have brought them in himself. He is too proud not to. He wouldn't want anyone to be able to say that he couldn't look after his animals. Farmers never leave their animals out in weather like this. Never." Paul looked up at Simon, and then at the back door of the house. "I've got to tell you, I'm getting a bad feeling about this, mate."

Nervousness creeping into his soul, the ghost in the woods suddenly seeming much closer, Simon pushed the back door slightly. Paul stepped through first.

"Hello? Tom? Enid?"

Despite his trepidation, Simon had expected at least one of the elderly couple to answer Paul's shout, but there was no reply. Stepping across the threshold as quietly as they could, neither man spoke as they quietly made their way into the hallway. Simon could hear his heart beating. Maybe they just hadn't heard Paul, that was all. That was all, surely. Or maybe Tom and James had been there and the four of them were heading back down to the pub. If the other two had come across the same problems he and Paul had trying to get out of the woods, then that was a distinct possibility. He felt a twinge of relief. That had to be it. That would also explain why the dogs weren't there. They'd gone with their master.

A television blared some old black and white cowboy film at him from the room to the left, and Simon followed Paul as he headed toward it. If the Tucker's were all heading down to the pub, then why hadn't they turned the TV off first? It didn't seem right. He couldn't imagine his own mother leaving her house with the box still on. It wasn't something that generation would do.

Just inside the lounge doorway, Paul suddenly stopped.

"What? What is it?" Simon couldn't help but whisper as he came alongside Paul. Staring in front of him, he could just see what must have been old Tom Tucker's head over the top of the armchair, wisps of gray covering his mainly bald and shiny scalp. The old man seemed to be sitting very still. Too still. His heart froze. This wasn't right.

"Tom?" Paul's nerves jangled in his voice. "Tom? Are you okay?"

Both men came around to the side of the old green velour chair, Tom Tucker's face hidden from them as it hung down.

"Could he be sleeping?"

Paul stared at him as if he were mad, and down in the pit of his stomach Simon knew that wasn't true, but it wasn't until Paul tentatively shook the man that the reality screeched at them.

Old man Tucker's head rolled sideways in a mockery of looking at them, and swearing under his breath, Paul fell backward from his crouching position.

"Jesus." Simon couldn't think of anything else to say, but it was patently obvious that the Lord had had nothing to do with whatever had gone on.

Tucker's eyes bulged from their sockets with frozen fear and his tongue reached out, purple and distended, swollen to twice its normal size.

Swallowing the urge to run, squeezing the door shut

on panic, Simon caught his breath before touching the man's hand. It was still ever-so-slightly warm.

"I don't think he's been dead too long."

Paul nodded, and Simon wasn't too sure whether he could see a slight relief in his friend's face. Relief that they hadn't got here a little earlier and had to face whoever, *whatever,* had done this.

Leaning forward, Simon studied Tom more closely. Around his bruised neck hung a tie, a striped one, maybe even a school tie, and someone had strangled him with it. He thought of the children in the village. And the children in the woods. Just what the fuck was really going on here?

Getting slowly to his feet, Paul shook himself slightly. "If Tom is here and dead, then where is Enid?" The two men stared at each other. For a second, Simon almost said something about her perhaps having left the farmhouse and going to the village, but he knew it would be crass. They both knew that if her husband was in the house and dead, then it was likely that she would be too.

"I guess we'd better go and look for her."

Leaving the sitting room behind, Simon smelled the damp around them, his senses fully alert and awake. The back door must have been open quite a while for the weather to have crept into the heart of the house. *Or maybe Melanie brought the storm with her. Maybe she brought the storm and a friend with a school tie.* He pushed the thought aside. He didn't have a clue what was happening, but he was damned if he was going to scare himself with thoughts like that. He didn't need it.

Steeling himself, knowing that Enid would have to be here or upstairs, he followed Paul and stepped onto the old tiles of the large kitchen. The side door was wide open and a pool of water had gathered in the doorway. His eyes scanned the room, absorbing what they saw.

A pan of potatoes sat drained on the side by the store, their fluffy edges declaring them cooked. Had Enid opened the door to let out the steam from cooking? Or maybe she'd opened it to run. And maybe she'd gotten away and was lost out in the woods somewhere, going around in circles just like they'd been a short while before. Simon could see it playing out in his head. Tucker's face going blue as he choked, one arm waving at Enid, urging to her to flee, to save herself.

Moving to the other side of the large oak table, his images of Enid Tucker's escape vanished. Enid hadn't run anywhere. Her large, homely frame, still dressed in her housecoat, lay face up on the hard floor. Around her head was a halo of blood that must have flooded from the deep and untidy gash in her throat. Her glassy eyes didn't have the expression of fear that her husband's death mask wore; she merely gazed at the ceiling in mild surprise. Feeling numbness creeping up his limbs, as if the cold were spreading from the tiles beneath, Simon stumbled backward, hands reaching behind him until he felt the cool edge of the sink in his grasp. Leaning against it, relieved that Enid's body was no longer in direct view, he shut his eyes in an attempt to dispel the dark spots that played at the edges of his sight. So much for being shock hardened. *Not quite so brave as you think, are you? Not when the world has changed the rules and children come back from the dead and the forest stops you from leaving town.*

He sucked in a long, shaky breath and opened his eyes again.

"Let's hope your mate Tom made it out of the forest. He shouldn't have to see this."

Still staring down at Enid's body, Paul shook his head. "If we weren't allowed to leave, then Tom and James won't be, either."

Allowed to leave. Simon wished Paul would stop talking like that.

"But you're right," Paul continued. "Maybe we should go outside and wait for them. Tom shouldn't come in and find his parents like this." Turning his back on Enid, Paul rummaged through the old cupboards under the sink and after a few moments pulled out a large square flashlight. It wasn't the sort favored in the city, but much larger, it's square face six or seven inches across. It got a whole lot darker in the country. He flicked the button and the light blazed. "Thank fuck for that."

Shutting the cupboard, Paul took half a step outside and froze. Even in the darkness that was rapidly falling Simon could see the color drain from his friends face. "Oh god."

"What?"

"Look. Look what's written here."

Simon came alongside him and stared at the open back door. Despite the rain and the way the blood had run, blending some of the words together, he could still read the scrawl. If he looked closely enough he could still see the imprint of the small finger that had written it.

Tom Tom the farmers son
Can you finish what
your mam begun?

215

"What the hell is that supposed to mean?"

Paul shook his head. "I don't know."

"Doesn't the rhyme go 'Tom, Tom the *piper's* son?'"

"Yes. She's changed it. She liked rhymes and songs." Paul was staring at the words, his voice breathy. "She liked to add her own bits in. Change them. All kids do."

Simon didn't like the chill that gripped his insides. He didn't need to ask who the *she* was to whom Paul was referring. "I wish you would stop talking about her as if she were still alive. That little girl's dead. You know that as well as I do."

Paul smiled at Simon as if he pitied him. "Yes, I do. I know she's dead. But it seems that death doesn't have the limitations it used to. Not in Watterrow at any rate. Not today."

Simon shook his head. "I worry about you, Paul. Believing in ghosts. What you told me about how she was as a child is pretty rough, but to think she's come back from the dead is a little far-out, wouldn't you say?"

"So what's your answer, Simon? Have you got something practical to offer? People are dying, and these are no ordinary killings. There were the lights in the woods." His eyes flared slightly, the whites shining. "And don't try and tell me there was anything ordinary about those. Or the messages she keeps leaving." He sighed. "And all the bloody children."

Paul turned away, flicking the switch on the flashlight, sending a white beam out into the courtyard. Simon stepped up alongside him. The light put them both in shadow, their faces outlines against the dark, and Simon was pleased. He didn't want to see Paul's face and he didn't really want Paul to see his own troubled expression. The wind was calm, but the rain was still coming down heavily and Simon felt cold to the core. He hoped that Alex and the others had stayed inside the warmth of the pub. They should be relatively safe there from whatever was doing all this. *Relatively.* The word didn't give him much reassurance against the madness that surrounded them and suddenly he wanted to get back to The Rock.

He thought about James Partridge and Tom Tucker wandering out in the woods in the dark. If, crazy as it sounded, that strange electricity was running through the entire edge of the trees, then they wouldn't have been able to get to another village, either. So they were on their way to the Tucker's or headed back to the pub. He hoped it was the latter for the younger Tom Tucker's sake.

"How long do you think should we wait for them?"

"I guess we'll give it twenty minutes or so. They both know the woods as well as anyone, so I can't see them getting lost. If they haven't turned up after that, then I think we should go back. It's nearly dark now, and even with the torch I'll find navigating our return a bit tricky."

Simon said nothing. The idea of stumbling around in the dark and wet all night wasn't appealing. Especially if they came across those giggly children again. Funny how he'd stopped thinking they'd come from the local caravan park. It seemed everyone had ditched that idea, but no one was going to talk about it. If they talked about it, then they'd all have to admit to thinking like Paul.

Paul turned the flashlight off to conserve the battery and neither man spoke, leaning against the damp outside walls of the house, the yellow glow of the kitchen light leaking no farther than the window, as if the wattage didn't have the power to spread the beam through the old pane of glass, leaving them once again in the gloom. The two strange children that he'd seen that morning on the way to the post office kept appearing in Simon's head, especially the face of the little boy.

Shutting his eyes, he leaned his head back, the rain running both over and under his glasses. He needed to concentrate on that young face. Behind his lids he rewound the morning's events. The two children had been playing on the corner of the street in the rain. Patty-cake. That was it. The girl was older and dressed more strangely, and the boy was younger. About eleven? Yes. That would be about right. He was wearing glasses, cheap but not the kind of huge NHS monstrosities Simon had been forced to wear as a child. The boy's glasses had wire rims and thinner lenses. In his mind's eye he could see the kid's mouth moving, reciting the words of the rhyme, his accent jarring with his playmate's. Yorkshire, that was it. Simon felt his heartbeat increase slightly. It seemed as if the name were lingering somewhere in the back of his mouth, there but not yet ready to come forward. What else had the boy done? Alex had said something to them about going home or not wearing the right clothes, he couldn't remember exactly, and then—the memory seemed to play out in slow motion—the boy had pulled a New York baseball cap out of his back pocket and tugged it onto his head.

Jesus. Jesus Christ. For a second he wasn't sure whether he felt hot or cold, the realization hitting him like a cricket ball in the face. *The baseball cap.* That was it. The boy hadn't smiled this morning—that was what must have stopped him recognizing him straightaway. In the photo that covered all the national papers during the first few days after he disappeared back in 1990, little Alan Harrison had been smiling. He'd had his glasses on and his Yankees baseball cap firmly on his head. His distraught mother said that he'd been wearing it the day he vanished. It was his favorite possession, brought back from a holiday abroad with his dad. *Alan Harrison.*

"Oh fuck." Opening his eyes, he pushed himself away from the wall.

Paul spun round. "What is it? Have you seen something?"

"No. No . . . I've just figured out who one of those kids was that I saw this morning." He could feel his hands shaking. "It was Alan Harrison."

"Who's Alan Harrison?"

Simon half-laughed. "It's crazy. *I'm crazy.* Alan Harrison went missing in nineteen ninety. His picture was everywhere. I know that was him I saw this morning." He paused and stared at Paul. "But how can that be? How the hell can that be?"

"How did he disappear?" Paul's voice was more energetic, but he didn't sound surprised. But then, Simon figured, Paul seemed more accepting of this whole fucked up situation.

"It was a weird one. Fucking horrible, actually. He had been over to a friend's house to play and went missing during his bike ride home. The police found his bike all bent up on the side of the road like it had been hit by a car."

Paul flicked the switch on the flashlight, lighting

them up, his eyes more alive than they had been since the awful events at Kay's house. "I remember it. Didn't someone come forward a few days later saying that he had run him down?"

Simon nodded. "Yeah. But the man was insistent that he didn't move Alan. In fact, he said he didn't even stop the car after he'd hit the boy. His passenger supported his statement and the police couldn't find any evidence of the boy in the bloke's car or house. It was like someone came along and just took him." He shook his head. "Who the hell would steal an injured child? That was the sickest bit. Who would abduct a kid in that state? The man had been going at over forty miles and hour. The boy would have been severely injured. The state of his bike gave that away."

Paul smiled, but the expression shook at the edges. "Don't you get it yet? Melanie said to my mum that the Catcher Man brought her back."

"What the hell are you driving at?" Simon had taken acid once at college and had felt reality as he knew it terrifyingly slide away from him. Now, standing there in the rain, he felt his stomach lurch in the same way.

"The Catcher Man steals lost children and then they're never found. That's what my mum said. That's what we were brought up to believe."

"But that's crazy! That was just a story made up to scare you into not wandering off."

"Is it?" Paul stepped up close, his face only a couple of inches from Simon's, as if physically making him focus on the truth. "You've just said that the boy you saw this morning disappeared sixteen years ago. And I know, and so do you deep down, that Melanie Parr's at the bottom of these fucking horrible deaths." He paused, and Simon could see the rain running through the tired lines in his friend's face. "What if the Catcher Man does exist? What if all these kids in the town are children that have gone missing over the years? What if he takes them and keeps them with him?"

Simon tried to pull away, but Paul wouldn't let him. He kept seeing Alan Harrison playing patty-cake with that girl in her formal clothes. Was that the outfit she went missing in?

"Christ, Paul. How am I supposed to believe any of this?"

"Look. If you'd asked me yesterday morning if I'd believed in ghosts, I'd have laughed in your face. I'm a feet firmly on the ground person. But now?" He shrugged. "All bets are off. All I can believe are the things I see and hear. And you'd better start doing that too or else you really will go crazy." He turned around, flashing the light out in front of them, and his voice softened. "You know, this part of the world is strange. History runs over a thousand years deep here and some of that history is pretty cruel. Blood was shed in human and animal sacrifices. Women were burnt as witches. But under all of it was a strong belief in the pagan gods. I guess it's like that in places where people are so close to nature. Maybe all of that allows things to happen here. Maybe the sheer belief of those centuries of people brought the Catcher Man to life. Who the hell knows?"

He turned back around and Simon didn't think he'd ever seen a saner looking man. Paul stared at him. "And if your eyes are telling you that you saw Alan Harrison on the street this morning, then for fuck's sake, believe them."

Simon stared at his friend, a cold sick feeling settling in his gut. "Come on, then. Let's go back to The Rock and let this insane drama work itself out. We can't do anything about Melanie Parr here."

They trudged silently back through the forest, the flashlight beam barely touching the country night, doing their best to ignore the giggle and sounds of movement that appeared so close and yet out of reach. At one point they froze as the echo of a man's scream reached them, and Simon grabbed at Paul's arm. "Was that Tom or James?"

Paul shrugged, pulling his friend onward. "I don't know. Whoever it is, we can't help them." Thankfully, the scream was cut short and for a while there was just the sound of their own labored breath as they fought the treacherous wet ground beneath their tired legs. Just as they clambered up the last peak before the lights from the pub called out to them, a wail slid through the thick old tree trunks. *"But I don't want to play . . . I don't want to play . . . Melanie . . ."*

Listening to the terror in that lost voice, Simon stared at Paul. The only thing to believe was their eyes and their ears, wasn't that what Paul had said? Neither man spoke and Simon turned to look down at the pub. He'd never been so pleased to see a place in all his life, and shutting his ears to Tom Tucker's torment, he broke into a trot, half-running, half-stumbling out of the woods and back into the village.

CHAPTER TWENTY-FIVE

Although The Rock was traditionally a pub rather than a hotel, it did a good trade in guests in the summer months and the rooms were cozy and clean. Stepping reluctantly out of the shower feeling as if she would never wash Mary's story away, Alex reached for the thick, wide towel and walked into the bedroom to dry off. Pressing the textured material to her face, she shut her eyes and relished its clean smell. It was the kind of smell that took you back to the carefree days of your childhood, the fresh warmth making you smile and feel safe. Although after what she'd just heard, maybe it was only her in this village that had been allowed innocence as she grew. Well, that may have been the case, but she was making up for it now.

Allowing herself only a moment of the towel's comfort, the feeling too bittersweet to last, she moved it to her hair and rubbed vigorously, studying herself in the mirror. So far, not too bad, she concluded. She had always been slim, although now her limbs were veering towards thin and maybe her ribs were just a little too prominent above her jutting hips, but she still had shape.

Looking analytically at her hips and breasts, she dropped the towel on the bed, letting her wet dark hair hang loose and wild around her face, its length tickling her back. How long would that last? How long until she became 'painfully thin'? Wasn't that what people called it? She smiled at the irony. She'd taken four of the eight painkillers Crouch had given her, but they hadn't kicked in yet. Yes. She was beginning to understand pain. No more innocence for her. Paul had been robbed of his childhood, and she of her adult life. No one got away unscathed.

Peering more closely into the mirror, she wondered whether her face had thinned or whether that was just her imagination, darkly rotting her flesh away from the inside. She felt she was definitely looking older, and dark circles hung from her eyes, enhanced by the day's events. Looking into her subtly dying reflection for a moment, the fear gripped her again, but she pulled its fingers away, one by one. Things were worse for Kay. Worse for the reverend. She met her own green gaze and spoke to it.

"I'm still alive. Right here and right now, I'm still alive. And that's all that matters."

The knock at the door made her jump.

"Wait a minute!" Not remembering whether she had locked the door when she'd come in, she darted into the bathroom and grabbed the dressing gown hanging there, pulling herself into it. By the time she reached the handle, she'd tied it.

Simon stood in the doorway holding a plate of sandwiches in one hand and trying to carry two glasses of wine in the other. He waved the plate at her. "Could you?"

Smiling, she took the plate. "Thanks, but I'm not really hungry. Did you manage to get help?"

He looked tired, the bags under his eyes almost matching her own, and he shook his head. "No. No, we didn't even get out of the forest." He paused, and she sensed there was more to his story than he was letting on, and she realized that she didn't care at the moment as long as her own flesh and blood were okay. There'd been too much death and dying. The details could wait until later. "Is Paul okay?"

He nodded. "Yeah. Yeah, he's fine." His eyes slipped away. "Crouch just told us what Mary had to say about Melanie Parr. Paul wanted to speak to her about it, but apparently she's asleep. Are you okay?"

"Yes, I guess so. I've slept for an hour or so." She paused. "Look, can we just leave all this at the door for a while and pretend the world is normal. I really need that. More than you could know."

"Sure. I think my brain needs a time-out from ghosts and secrets too." He grinned at her, for a moment shy and embarrassed under her gaze, and she felt her defenses crumbling. *I'm alive. Here and now I'm alive, and that's all that matters.*

"Do you want to come in? I may not be hungry, but I could do with that wine."

Following her in, he gave her the glass and stood awkwardly at the end of the bed as she sat down. Sipping the red liquid, she watched him. Yes, she liked him. She liked his goodness. She could see it in him. She raised an inner eyebrow at herself. She also liked his eyes and his smile. In fact, she pretty much liked everything about him.

Tonight they were all on a level playing field; she could feel it in the stormy air. The natural world had shifted and all their clocks were ticking loudly. Kay hadn't been expecting hers to stop, but stop it did. Had she heard it loudly railing at her as she hung there in her bedroom listening to Paul's feet on the stairs? Probably. Surely everyone heard it in the end.

Well, she'd had enough of listening to that sound in the dark, alone. Tonight, she was just the same as everyone else, and what was wrong with wanting to be normal, just for a few hours?

As if feeling her scrutiny, he put down his glass on the small sideboard and took a step toward the door. "Maybe I should go back downstairs. You're obviously just out of the shower. Probably need some time to yourself."

"I want you to stay." She stood up, her face serious. "Stay with me." She took a step forward so they were so close they were almost touching and looked up at his face. "I don't want to be alone tonight. And I don't want to be with them downstairs." But even that wasn't the truth of it. Not really. And this wasn't the time for coy game playing. "I want to be with you."

Behind his glasses, the blue eyes studied her face with that almost unreadable openness, and she heard his breath suck in, his nostrils slightly flaring with the action. It seemed to her, as the pressure of his silence made her skin shiver beneath the robe, that for a moment both of their clocks had paused. Nerves and excitement gnawed at her belly. It had been a long time; *such* a long time when compared to what was left, and her sudden need for company, for intimacy with someone, with this man, surprised her.

"So . . ." She couldn't look at him as she struggled to keep her voice under control. "Are you staying?"

He raised a hand and one finger traced the line of her cheekbone, his eyes following the movement. "You're so very lovely. Even after all this, you look beautiful."

She watched his mouth move, drawn to its perfect shape, lips neither too full nor too thin, and his proximity twisted the ache inside her belly. Reaching up, her fingers slid around to the back of his neck and curled into his almost dry blond hair. She smiled, her excitement releasing the intensity of the moment.

"You're not so bad yourself. But are you staying?"

A grin stretched across his face as he pulled her closer. "Oh, yes. I most certainly am."

They kissed, gently at first, and the feel of his soft lips on her mouth as his tongue talked expertly to hers made warmth flood to every extremity of her body. Moaning slightly as she pulled at the buttons on his still damp shirt, she tried to kiss him harder, but he pulled back, teasing, his breath brushing over her, his lips like shadows glimpsed from the corner of her eye, there and not there, just touching her enough to send bolts of lightning racing through her system. Oh god, it felt good. So good. Almost too good.

His mouth never leaving her skin he pulled off his shirt, and she felt him shiver as she ran her fingers up through the coarse, darker hair of his chest before he pushed her gently backwards onto the bed.

For a moment they lay there quietly, Simon leaning on one arm as he kissed her beneath him, pausing and smiling softy as he took off his glasses, before his mouth moved down to her neck and into the hollow of her collarbone. Shutting her eyes, she arched her back up to him as his hand slid down and unwrapped her from her dressing gown. The emptiness of the air around her tickled goose pimples onto the flatness of her stomach, but it was Simon alone that caused her nipples to harden under the warmth of his kisses. She gasped as he nibbled at her, his hand reaching for her other breast, squeezing and twisting, applying just the right amount of pressure to send waves of pleasure down between her thighs. If he wasn't careful, she was going to come before he'd even touched her. How the hell was he staying in control? She couldn't even hear his breathing speeding up. His calmness excited her further and she spread her legs, inviting his hand into the core of her.

Momentarily ignoring her openness, his mouth moved back toward her face, leaving a cool moist trail in its wake. His tongue pressed into her mouth, and as he did so, she felt his fingers sliding into her, pushing her lips apart, a slight hesitation the only sign of his surprise at finding how wet she was, how ready for him. Lifting her hips, she pushed herself onto his large hand, crying out at the feel of his fingers working inside her as his thumb gently rubbed on the bud of her clitoris. Their kissing was more urgent now and she squirmed onto her side, her own hands moving, one frantically working to undo his trousers, the other reaching up to feel his face.

He pulled slightly away from her to tug off his jeans, yanking himself free and abandoning them on the floor, but his eyes stayed on Alex's, their blue now hazy, his urgent breathing matching hers. His arms wrapped around her as he tumbled her over, rolling on top, and she could feel him nudging at her inner thigh. Reaching down, enjoying the feel of his thickness in her hand, she guided him, eager to feel him inside. Slowly he pushed himself forward, his body shuddering with pleasure, his lips meeting hers as they gently moved together, fitting so perfectly she could almost feel every ridge of him as he moved in and out, her hips greeting his every thrust, not just for the physical pleasure, but for the joy it brought her soul, lighting up the dark spaces, annihilating them, if only briefly.

His movements became stronger and she held his face in both hands, their panted hot breaths blending invisibly together like their bodies were, her words dancing in the air from inside him.

"My turn." They were both nearing climax and she smiled as she pushed him onto his back, straddling him, impaling herself on him. This was one she wanted to control. There was so little she could control anymore. Taking his hands and placing them on her breasts, needing him touching her, she shut her eyes and rocked her hips back and forward, her own fingers reaching between her thighs, the waiting having lasted too long, her building orgasm attacking her from too many angles, and as she moved faster and faster on top of him, his groans matched her own as he pulled harder at her nipples, until all she could feel was his throbbing penis inside her and her own muscles contracting around him as she came in an explosion, her hands grasping for his and clutching them, their fingers intertwined, he still moving under her, keeping the delicious waves of her orgasm invading her every cell, until he reached his own release in the wake of her satisfaction, pulling her forward and holding her to him. They lay there wrapped in each other, her hair tumbling over him as she buried her face into his chest, until both their breathing returned to normal. When she kissed him, it felt bittersweet.

The digital clock beside the bed was flashing 2:00 A.M. and sipping the red wine, her head leaning back into the crook of Simon's shoulder, Alex felt safer and more relaxed than she had in months. The rain still pattered heavily on the small glass window, but the energy and anger had gone from it, washing the thunderous lightning away.

Simon's arm was around her and his fingers absently ran over the skin of her upper arm. "What happened with your husband?"

The question was light, but Alex felt her defenses bite at her. "Why? What did Paul say?"

"Nothing. Just that you'd broken up a few months ago out of the blue." He'd obviously heard the note of aggression in her voice, because he twisted to see her as he spoke. "Sorry. I didn't mean to pry. It just came out. Guess I can't believe that someone would let you out of their life without a struggle."

Letting the warm red liquid explore her mouth, Alex hesitated before swallowing. Part of the truth wouldn't hurt, she reasoned. And anyway, it would stop him from wanting any kind of future with her. Suddenly, the remnants of wine tasted bitter. Her tone was harder than she meant it to be, a little of the pain escaping.

"He left because we found out that we couldn't have children. No. That's not exactly right. He left because we found out that *I* couldn't have children."

Simon said nothing for a moment, and she was glad

he didn't try to tell her how sorry he was or give her any platitudes about how it didn't really matter. She would probably have laughed and he wouldn't have understood. She was well aware that her inability to bring forth life really didn't matter anymore.

"He left because of that? Just upped and left? Not much of a husband."

He left because he was a coward. She pushed the thought aside, tired of it long ago. She was better off without Ian. It'd taken her a couple of months to figure it out, but she'd woken up one day and found the love had vanished from inside her. Maybe it had never really been there. Only the wish for it.

"No, he wasn't. Anyway, it was easy for him to leave. He'd just got a job in Taunton with a big firm there. He asked for a transfer to their Birmingham branch and they obliged. I guess he figured that was far enough away." Ian had fled to the land of Spaghetti Junction. He didn't even like driving. God, she'd wasted her life on him. She let out a deep breath.

"As separations go, it was all very neat and tidy. The cottage was my mother's, so it belongs to me. In fact, he didn't want to take anything apart from his car. Just packed his suitcases and left." Her slight laugh was hollow. "Guilt does make people less obsessed with material possessions." There was a sense of irony about Ian's not wanting to take anything, which hadn't been lost on her then and wasn't now. It seemed that he'd been rubbing salt into the wound. It wasn't as if she'd be needing it. She shut her eyes for a moment. Darkness was in danger of creeping back into the night, and she didn't want that. She didn't want all those other things to spoil these few hours with this man.

"Can we leave it now? It's the past. It's done."

Simon kissed the top of her head. "Sorry. Not my business. And not important." He stroked her hair, twisting the soft strands in his fingers as if trying to tie himself to her. "I've been thinking. Do you fancy getting together and maybe having a picnic in the sunshine?" They listened for a second to the melodic accompaniment of the rain. "If and when the sun shines again, that is."

Alex rolled over so that she was leaning on his chest facing him. Her stomach was knotting and unfurling like an eel. God, this was hard. "Is that your way of asking me out on a date when this is all over?" She reached up and kissed him gently, her voice soft. "Because if it is, let's just take it as it comes, shall we? This isn't the time for making plans. Okay?"

Nodding, he returned her kiss. "Sure. No problem." He flashed her a cheeky grin. Too cheeky. He was a bad liar and she could hear the disappointment under his words as they ran from that perfect mouth. She could feel it breaking inside herself too. But she could cover it; she had to.

Forcing a giggle, she pulled the covers over her head, teasing his stomach with her tongue.

His voice was muffled. "Umm. What are you doing?"

Enjoying the warmth of his skin next to hers, she slid herself further down the mattress, her mouth working constantly as it slowly but surely sought out its target. In a few eager moments, she found it.

The amused words seemed to come from far above her. "Oh. So that's what you're doing."

This time the giggle erupting from her full mouth was genuine. She was alive. Here and now she was alive. And that was all that mattered.

CHAPTER TWENTY-SIX

The teaspoon nearly slipped out of Ada's hand as she dried it, her eyes darting backward into the corridor. God, she was jumpy. She looked at her hand with mild disgust. Her grip was worthless enough as it was these days, and when she'd heard the downstairs bathroom door slam shut, whatever control she had over the creaking joints and muscles in those fragile twigs was lost. Placing it carefully on the outdated and chipped work surface, her heart paused for a second before she got the pounding under control again. She was too jumpy. It wasn't as if she were even alone in the house. God, she was acting like a child, and her childhood days were long past.

Shutting her eyes for a moment, she waited until relative calm settled in her core. Daniel had no doubt used the downstairs bathroom earlier and opened the small window, now allowing a gust to drag the door shut. She looked down at the ancient, withered hands that she sometimes couldn't believe were hers and almost laughed at herself. Almost. She wasn't quite ready for that yet. Her nerves were still too jangly and her mind was burning with the possibilities of what was happening to her community.

But there would be a logical explanation, wouldn't there? There always was at the end. It had to be a deranged fool on the loose doing this to them. That's at least what she'd been trying to tell herself until Mary had unleashed their past to all who would listen from her fireside seat in The Rock. And now? Well, it was like a spell had been broken. All those years of silence. Gone. Mary's speech had forced her to face up to what was going on around them. To make her really see.

She stared down at the film settling on the strong tea she'd just made for Daniel and wanted to cry. As they'd walked back from the pub, side-by-side and soundless through the night, she'd felt that tension creep back between them. A tension from thirty years before that they'd both fought so hard to put behind them. Daniel had gone straight up to his radio room as if she hadn't even existed, and maybe she didn't to him. Not anymore. She glanced over at the window and the darkness outside, feeling it reflected in the sudden emptiness of her soul as if now that the women's secret was out, there was nothing left to hold her together.

The irony was that tonight she needed her husband more than she ever had before. She'd needed to talk to him about some of the things that had been said. Daniel might not be convinced that there were supernatural forces afoot in their hometown, but Ada was terrified that he was wrong. But then Daniel had always been so grounded that a part of her wondered whether he'd even believed what had happened all those years ago until he'd heard Mary regurgitate it earlier.

Sipping her drink, she couldn't quite bring herself to go upstairs and face his coldness. Not yet. It was what Alex had said about the children that bothered her. The strange children in the village. She shivered slightly. Despite her own defensive denial at the time, she knew that poor Alex was right. She herself had definitely seen them, both earlier in the day and also on her way down to The Rock. Children that were *out of place*. That was the best way she could describe them. Out of place and watching her, too quietly and confidently for normal children. Peering out from behind buildings or just standing still and staring, there had been something wrong enough about them for her to want to talk to Daniel about it. But then the madness of the rest of the day had taken hold and there just hadn't been time.

She'd thought she was too old for this kind of fear, but over the course of the day it seemed that panic had only been an unexpected shadow away, caught in a glimpse from the corner of a tired eye. Since the discovery of the vicar and throughout the tumble of events since, the arthritis in her joints had flared up as if trying to distract her and the pain had been so much that she'd been afraid to stop moving in case she hadn't been able to start again. Would she get any sleep at all that night or would there be too many flickers of the past coming back to haunt her as she tried to doze and drift? Brief glances of blond hair and angelic features. Melanie Parr. Laughing, always laughing.

She sighed as she moved into the hallway. Maybe she shouldn't have snapped at Alex like that, but she couldn't help it. Alex was too young to know, to *understand* the sacrifices that had been made all those years ago. And it hadn't been meant. That was all that had kept her going over the years and she imagined it was the same for the others. *There was nothing angelic about Melanie Parr, and it wasn't meant.* Not much of a way to get through life, but country people were hardy. They knew how to cope. *She* knew how to cope. And she would damn well learn to cope with it again.

Her eyes drifted back to the empty blackness of the night through the window and, lost in her disturbed thoughts, it took a moment before she heard the steady drip of water. Where was that coming from? Turning, she looked to the taps of the kitchen sink, but they were shut tight. She listened again. Wherever it was coming from, it was inside the house. Mildly irritated, this combined with the bathroom door slamming convincing her that Daniel had left windows open somewhere, the torrent from outside no doubt soaking the carpet, she stepped into the hall. And then the world stopped. It seemed that Mary wasn't so crazy, after all.

Melanie Parr stood in the hallway, her clothes and hair soaked from the storm outside, water dripping from the hem of her skirt and forming a large pool beneath her on the polished wooden floorboards. *If I don't get that up soon it'll ruin the polish.* Ada's eyes stared at the water, and the feet at its center. *One shoe on, one shoe off.* Somewhere inside her breath rattled too fast in her lungs, the beating of her heart uneven. A dull ache shot down her left arm. She thought that maybe she should scream, but the tightness in her chest wouldn't let the air out.

She stared at Melanie, who smiled at her, water dribbling over her bottom lip as if a whole river were in her mouth, spilling out in a steady waterfall and running down her clothes. Melanie's grin stretched as she spoke, her words gurgling so that Ada wasn't sure if she'd said, *"It's time to play"* or *"It's time to pay,"* but as the long-gone child took a step toward her, her cold, blue hands reaching out, Ada decided, from somewhere within her terror, that it really didn't matter. Both were probably true; it was just a matter of perspective.

Alex woke up the way she had in the first few terror-filled days all those months before: with a sudden, sharp intake of breath, her torso reaching upward, heart beating so fast that for a moment she couldn't let the air out of her lungs for the tightness of her ribs. Eventually, her eyes focused on the room around her instead of the horror that had allowed itself free rein in her mind as the subconscious ruled. Her hair felt sweaty and greasy against her head and she pushed it away from her face. Her skin was clammy under her fingers too. *That was bad. That was worse than it had been in a long time.*

As if a remnant of her dreams needed to remind her that the nightmare still existed in the daylight hours, a sharp knife twisted in her lower gut, forcing her to curl up in the sheets, her knees tucked beneath her chin, eyes squeezed shut. It was several minutes before she could open them again, the pain easing to a tolerable level. Maybe not something she'd have considered bearable a year ago, but she was learning fast that your limits could change. *Part of the adaptability of the species; the good old human race.* She still had a couple of months before things got really bad. The tears she bit back had nothing to do with the pain and everything to do with the sudden blackness she saw in the future. A few months and then . . . nothing.

Frustrated, she sat up again, ignoring the ache of everything that was her, body and soul. *It was the dreams. That was it. That's what had made the fear rear its ugly head. Think of Simon. Think of last night. Still alive. Here and now.* Glancing down, she could see his sleeping form in the gloom of the dawn, his body turned away, lost in his own dreams or nightmares or just the blackness of unconsciousness. His back looked broad and strong and she wondered just how much those shoulders could carry. How would he cope if she told him the truth? You never could tell with people. Maybe he wouldn't find her attractive anymore. After all, who wanted to fuck the living dead?

Biting the inside of her mouth, she looked toward the sound of the rain pattering steadily against the window, knowing she was being unfair. But it was hard to be otherwise. Life was unfair. Too unfair. Slowly peeling the covers back, not wanting to wake Simon, she eased herself out of bed and carefully pulled the remaining few painkillers out of her jeans pocket. At some point she was going to have to go back to the farmhouse and pick up her morphine. Nothing else was even going to touch the sides of her pain. Still, the over-the-counter pills were all she had for now. She padded silently to the en suite bathroom, and leaving the light off, shut the door, just making do with the pale light coming through the small bathroom window. Running the cold tap, she scooped a handful of water to swallow the pills with and then ran some through her hair before standing upright, enjoying the trickle of the water as it made its way down her naked body and staring out into the heavy gloom. Laura was out there somewhere with little Peter. How were they feeling now? Were they even still alive?

Standing there in silence, she could almost hear the ticking of all of Watterrow's clocks, each man, woman, and child's individual timepiece working away, *unwinding*, a cacophony of heartbeats that slowly came together as one, as if the village were one entity instead of a hundred or so tiny, inconsequential lives, breathing toward their eventual ends.

"Alex."

The urgent whisper of her name came out of nowhere and she spun round, her eyes frantically taking in every corner of the bathroom. It was empty. Her own heart and its tiny, inconsequential beat now drowned out the collective as she stood frozen and wide-eyed. There was no one there. *Oh shit. Here we go again.* Her mouth dried.

"Alex."

The word came from behind her, and she turned again, this time expecting to see someone or something other than herself staring back from the bathroom mirror, but it was only her own trembling eyes and half-opened mouth that greeted her. Who the fuck was calling her if there was no one there? *Maybe it's Simon. Maybe he's woken up. Maybe your fucked up body is playing tricks on you and it only seems like the voice is coming from in here.* Stepping forward she tugged open the bathroom door and looked into the bedroom. Simon was still lying on his side, unmoved from when she'd left. She hovered in the doorway, most of her unsurprised to see him still sleeping, immune to everything. *Because it wasn't Simon's voice, was it? And you knew that. It was the voice of a child.* Still, she took a step forward, wanting to wake him, wanting to flick a switch and bring some bright yellow normalcy back. Suddenly her urge to touch him and feel his warmth was overwhelming.

"Don't wake him, Alex!"

The urgency in the hissed voice stopped her dead, and despite the ache of loneliness inside, she slowly turned again toward the bathroom. Through the doorway the room's emptiness taunted her, but stepping back into it, she felt her heart calming. Maybe this was madness. Maybe this was a dream or nightmare. But whatever it was, she could deal with it. She was dying. She had terminal cancer and whatever was going on in here couldn't compete with that. She pushed the door closed behind her, shutting Simon on the side of sanity. "Where are you? What do you want?" Her own whisper seemed to fill the void in a way that the other hadn't, as if it wasn't anchored to the here and now.

"We haven't got much time. Look up, Alex. Look up."

Her eyes lifted and her breath caught. The little boy that had come to her bedside was lying on the ceiling looking down at her, the bright checks on his tank top instantly recognizable. His arms were pressed to his sides, that slightly too long haircut hanging down, the mud still making a dry pattern on his sleeves, even though his face shone with dampness. His eyes bore into hers as she stared at him and could see fear and terrible loneliness in them.

"What do you want from me?"

"You have to come in between. Into the storm. You have to come with me. While she's busy."

A flash of Ada Rose's face consumed by pain and panic filled Alex's head, and then she saw Mary— Mary in a bath gone cold with blood everywhere. Gasping, she clutched at the sink behind her. How was she seeing these things? Were they real?

"You're the only one that can come. We have to go now."

Gray reality attacked her so suddenly, the images of the women gone, that her legs buckled slightly under her.

"What if I don't want to go?"

She stared at the boy again, and his face contorted with the effort of lowering one arm to reach for her.

"You have to. The children are there. No one else can go there. Please come. Please come."

Looking up at the desperation in his young face, she knew she had no choice. Her heart thumped loudly inside her. Whatever the in between was, that's where she was going. She wondered for a moment if she were going insane as she contemplated what she was about to do.

"Who are you?" she whispered as she raised her hand to reach his.

"I'll show you."

Once again touching the cool damp of her fingers, she felt moisture spring out of every pore in her naked body, not sweat but rain, stale and musty, ripe with the scent of the earth as if it had fallen centuries before and yesterday. A rain from a time where no clocks ticked. Her breath hissed in, shocked, but the boy's fingers closed tightly around hers.

"It's always raining in between. Now shut your eyes."

There was so much sadness in his young voice that she followed his command and let her eyelids settle shut, sealing her in darkness, and she folded her other hand protectively around his. She felt her hair lift slightly with the hint of a breeze, and then they were gone.

CHAPTER TWENTY-SEVEN

The air shifted and she knew before she opened her eyes that the bathroom was gone, perhaps so far away that she wondered briefly if she'd ever find it again. Beneath her feet she could feel damp leaves and twigs pressing into the soles of her feet. *I'm not dressed, I didn't get dressed . . .* Her lids flicked upward and the thought stopped. She may have been naked when she took the boy's hand, but she was clothed now. Above her bare feet there was the hem of a dress, almost ankle-length, bright even in the weird green glow that filled everything, a gypsy-white cotton dress flowing out from her slim waist. Without even looking at the bodice she knew there would be a small embroidered pattern of blue flowers there, and lifting her free hand she ran her fingers over it, proving its existence. It was her mother's dress. Alicia's dress. The one she was wearing in the old photograph on Mary's dresser. *The one she was buried in.* Alex's dark hair hung over her shoulders and she touched it, needing a sense of her own reality.

Maybe this is a dream after all. Or maybe, like Alice in the book that had terrified her as a child, she'd just tumbled down the rabbit hole to a world of surreal insanity. Perhaps that was closer to the truth. Under the dry fabric of the dress she could still feel dampness coming from within her skin and soaking the inside of her lungs as she breathed in and out. *It's always raining in between.*

She looked down at the child holding her hand, her eyes squinting to see. There was no darkness or sunlight, instead only the sickly green glow lighting everything as if she were wearing night vision goggles or watching a surreal effect in a movie.

"Is this real?" Even her voice sounded watery. The little boy shrugged.

"It is for me. It is for us. There is nothing else."

Seeing the tiredness and age in his young eyes, Alex thought about her cancer. There was always something else. There was always death. Although here, wherever this place was, maybe death wasn't so closeby. Her body felt odd, almost numb, the pain and discomfort she was so used to living with no longer there, as if along with time her cancer had stopped. Just for a while. Was that what happened in the in between? Did the clocks stop?

"How did you get here? Where is here?" She asked the question and then shook her head, distracted. She could hear sounds and laughter in the rustle of the trees and for the first time, she really looked around her, past the green hue and the dress and the madness. "We're in the woods. I know these woods!" Her excitement lit her eyes. "Is this where Laura and Peter are? Are they lost in the woods? We've got to find them. Can you help me find them?" These were the woods she had played in as a child, the woods Melanie and Paul had played in all those years ago, and although the place the boy had brought her to might exist above or below her normal perception, the landscape would surely be the same. If anyone could find the children here, it was her.

"Laura? Laura? Can you hear me?" Alex called out into the trees and for a moment everything fell silent, the trees and the children who played hidden within them. And then a yelp came from somewhere deeper in the wood. It was Laura, she was sure of it.

The little boy tugged at her hand, pulling her against the bark of a nearby tree. "Not yet. Not yet. I need you to see first. I need you to see how I was taken."

Alex stroked his hair. "But Laura and Peter need me. I have to help them. They . . . they're not like you."

He shook his head vehemently. "You can't help them if you don't understand. You can't help any of us. I have to make you understand."

Setting aside her frustration, Alex took in the anxiety of the boy, his young desperation to make her do what he wanted. Who was she to dictate how it should be? This was his place, not hers, and he'd led her this far. It was time to trust him. She peered into the still green trees. If time were different here, then maybe a few more minutes would do no harm. Crouching down so that she was at eye level, Alex nodded. "Tell me what it is I have to understand. Tell me what happened."

"I need to show you. You need to see."

"Okay. Show me."

"Close your eyes."

She did so and the little boy came around behind Alex and put his hands over her eyes, the cool skin making her flinch slightly.

"Are you ready?"

She nodded.

"Now open them."

Once again, the world turned, nauseating giddiness spinning Alex out of control. When it finally settled, she was in blackness. No, it wasn't entirely dark. As her eyes adjusted she could make out shapes in the gloom, gray and fuzzy. Where was she? *I'm looking down. I'm looking down on things as if I'm on the ceiling. Just like he was in the bathroom.* With the room in perspective she tried to piece it together. Below, she could see stairs, wooden stairs, old and untreated, and at the top of them, a door. From the small gap under it, bright yellow light crept out. The air was musty and cool, leaving a taste of splinters and staleness in her mouth, as if no one had let any fresh air in for too long a time. Along the far side she could make out a high bench, maybe attached to the wall, she couldn't tell in the dark, but the objects on it reflected slightly in the light. A workbench maybe? The pieces dropped into place. It was a cellar. She was in a cellar.

A sniffling sound caught her attention and she focused on the dark shadow in the far corner. Was there someone there? The shape moved and let out a tiny, terrified, muffled sob. Straining to see, her consciousness shifted, launching part of her across the room and downward. With a silent scream, the part of her left on the ceiling tried to pull back, but it was too late, and suddenly she was *inside. Inside, looking out.*

The boy's body froze for just a fraction of a second as she slipped into him, and then continued its shivering, his whole form shaking with fear. *He doesn't know I'm here,* Alex thought with wonder. *He doesn't know I'm right inside him.* She could feel the heat of his panicked skin that was hers but not hers, and seeing through his wide eyes every shape in the cellar seemed to be a snarling monster waiting, just waiting for him to move or try to shift his numb legs to a new position where the rope didn't cut into them quite so hard.

He slowly twisted his head and wiped the stream of snot coming from his nose onto the shoulder of his tank top, the gag tied tight around his head cutting into the edges of his lips. And all the while, he kept one eye fixed on the small glint of light under the door. Because that's where the real monster would come from. That's where he lived. The man monster. Alex could see the red and yellow of the sweater even in this darkness and her heart squeezed tight. *What happened to you? Who's made you so frightened?*

The part of her left on the ceiling looked down and thought of the boy's words. This boy's words spoken in a place so far away from here. *You need to see. You need to understand.* She pushed her remote consciousness forward, digging deeper into his mind so that she was truly inside him, so that she *was* him.

Callum. His name was Callum Parker and he was nine years old and all he wanted was to go home and he was so very, very scared. She pushed backward into his memory. *Sunday afternoon. Walking home. Bethnal Green. Scared, but not scared like now. Nothing like now. He'd been to church with Mum and Gran while*

Dad stayed home to mow the grass, and he'd really wanted to stay and help because that would be so much more fun than sitting on the hard bench in the church that was never warm, not even on summer days like today, but knew better than to ask, especially when Gran was visiting.

She'd knitted him the new tank top he was wearing so that he'd have something like all the big boys at school wore, and although he hadn't known how to say so, he really liked it. When she'd unpacked it the previous day his mum had gone out and bought him a new shirt to wear underneath, a shirt he knew she couldn't really afford because he never even got brand-new shirts for school and he'd worn them both for church. Billy had been there too, squirming in the old-fashioned, uncomfortable suit his mum made him wear every Sunday, which surely must have been getting too small for him now, and afterwards he had asked Callum to come back to his house to play. His mum had wanted him to go home and change first, but that just seemed like too much time to waste, and there would only be two hours before lunch and he promised he wouldn't get messy and eventually his mum had agreed.

And that's where it had gone wrong. He had got dirty. He'd tried not to, but Billy caught a frog down at the pond and Callum had to go and see it, he just had to. He'd crept so carefully down to the water and stroked the back of the cold slimy creature before Billy let it jump away, and as they turned to get back to the safe dry grass, Callum had slipped, his Sunday shoes not made for gripping the mud, not like his sneakers that were at home in the kitchen, and as he fell one sleeve of *that new crisp white shirt got covered with mud. And that wasn't the worst of it. There was also a tiny hole in the sleeve where it must have caught on a twig or where it tugged when he landed.*

Tears had sparked in the back of his eyes, and although Billy's mum had told him it was going to be all right, Callum knew differently. Callum knew that his mum would be upset in the worst way, not in the angry way, but in the sad way like she was when she argued with his dad. And Callum hated that. He'd drunk his Panda Pop with a sick feeling in the pit of his stomach and then said it was time to go home. He didn't have any play left in him, and slowly he began to drag his feet along the quiet Sunday roads toward home.

He was two streets away from his house, his face hot with tears, when the car pulled up alongside him.

"Callum? Callum Parker?"

Stopping, Callum looked into the car. A man smiled at him from the driver's seat. He was wearing dark sunglasses and his curly hair hung over the collar of his blue denim shirt.

"What are you crying for? Are you okay?"

Callum stared at the man for a moment. "How do you know my name?"

"Easy. I work with your dad. Me and my wife Peg came to your house for New Year. And your dad's birthday party. Don't you remember?"

Digging deep in his memory, Callum searched for a name and then one came to him. "Mr. Wentworth?" he asked hesitantly.

"That's right." The man took off his sunglasses, revealing dark brown eyes, so dark that the pupil and iris blurred. "Come over here, son."

Feeling slightly awkward, but not nervous—after all, Mr. Wentworth wasn't a stranger, he knew his name and he'd been to his house—Callum moved to the open car window.

"Why are you crying?"

The sweet stink of slightly stale whiskey came with the man's words, and Callum slightly cringed, but it didn't unduly disturb him. It was Sunday lunchtime and all the men he knew drove to the pub and didn't go home till dinner was on the table. Even his dad.

Sniffing, he pulled his shirt around, tugging the sleeve into view. "My mum bought this new. I wasn't supposed to get dirty, but I fell and now there's a hole in it." With just the telling of it to an adult more tears sprung to life in his eyes and his nose began to run.

"Now that's a shame. That's a real shame." Mr. Went-worth looked up at him. "You're mum's going to be mad about that, ain't she?"

Callum nodded, his bottom lip trembling, and it seemed Mr. Wentworth stared at him for a long time, those slightly glazed, slightly drunk dark eyes looking into his, then down to his ruined shirt, and then up again. Eventually he spoke, his conspiratorial whisper forcing Callum to step closer.

"You know, I reckon we could get that sorted out without your mum ever knowing about it."

Callum's eyes widened. "How?"

"Well, we could go back to my house. My Peggy's pretty good with a needle and thread. She could stitch it up and wash out that dirt in no time at all. Iron it dry and bob's your uncle." He winked. "What do you say?"

Hope raised its head in Callum's heart. "Really?"

"Yep. Us men have got to stick together, ain't we?

Now come on! You'd better hop in if we're going to get you sorted and back home in time for lunch."

Callum didn't hesitate. His heart thumping with excitement and tears drying on his face, he ran to the passenger side and climbed into the car, grinning. It was going to be okay! It was really going to be okay and he wasn't going to make Mum mad or sad or disappointed.

Mr. Wentworth pulled the car away quite fast, and taking in the smell of leather and stale cigarettes, Callum was too elated to notice how he checked in the mirrors just a little too often and how when he turned to smile at Callum and squeezed his knee how his hand rested there just a little bit too long.

When they got inside the cool of the Wentworth's house, Mrs. Wentworth wasn't home. Standing awkwardly in the hallway and staring at the unfamiliar surroundings, Callum felt his heart sink. "Maybe you'd better just take me home, Mr. Wentworth." He didn't want to be late on top of everything else, and for the first time he got a trickle of the feeling that his parents might not be happy with him for getting in Mr. Wentworth's car. It was different when he'd thought that Mrs. Wentworth would be home. Women were different. Here alone with just the grownup man he suddenly felt weird. Maybe it was the intensity of the way he kept looking at him that uneased Callum.

"Don't be silly. She'll be home in five minutes. Probably just popped up to her mum's for something." He grinned again, and Callum could see his nicotine-stained teeth, some of them blackening at the edges. "Here you go. I made you a squash."

He held out a glass of juice and Callum didn't know what else to do but take it. Feeling the man watching him, he took a sip and flinched, his nose wrinkling. "It tastes funny." Something tingled on his tongue and it seemed that some of the sweetness was missing from the drink.

"Nonsense. Anyway, it's rude to complain." Mr. Wentworth held up his own glass and drank some. "See? It's fine. Must just be a different brand. Now drink it."

Something in the man's tone of voice made Callum not want to drink it at all; in fact, he wanted to put the glass down, make his excuses and go, but he was nine years old and he didn't know how. Instead, he stood rooted to the spot and downed the drink. Maybe if he finished it Mr. Wentworth would let him go home. Feeling it burn all the way down to his stomach, he put the glass down.

"Good boy. Good boy." Mr. Wentworth took a step closer, and out of nowhere Callum felt tears stinging in the corner of his eyes again as his head began to swim. He vaguely realized that there might be worse trouble in the world than a ripped shirt and maybe he should have just gone home and maybe just because someone knew your name it didn't make them any less of a stranger.

"When's Mrs. Wentworth coming home?" Those were the words he tried to get out, but his stomach was feeling sick and the world was swimming at the edges and when he heard himself it seemed that all his words had run into one. His legs started to shake and he knew he wasn't going to be able to stand for much longer. The tears were flowing freely as the man scooped up his unresisting body and walked deeper into the house.

"She's not coming home, son. She didn't understand me."

Callum tried to make sense of it, but the room was spinning. "Feel sick . . . ," he mumbled, trying to quell the panic that was rising somewhere deep inside him.

"That's just the vodka." They were at a doorway under the stairs, and Wentworth grunted as he shifted Callum's weight in order to undo the latch. Cool, musty, dark air rushed out at them. "And I popped half of one of her downers in there too. Don't worry, you'll be right as rain in a couple of hours."

Callum wasn't sure which came first, the awful dark of the cellar or unconsciousness, but as he slipped into it he wasn't sure that he would ever be right as rain again.

The first thing he noticed when he came around, other than the darkness, was the thick, musty smell of the cellar. His head thumped and his mouth was dry and sore. Something was in it, a cloth tied tightly behind the base of his skull. He moaned from behind the gag as more tears came. It wasn't a dream, it hadn't been a bad dream at all, and why had Mr. Wentworth taken him and why hadn't he just gone straight home? The panicked thoughts filled him and he wriggled and thrashed in vain against the cord tied around his wrists and ankles until eventually the panic could no longer sustain itself.

Panting and sweating, he lay back down on the thin sleeping bag that was all there was between him and the freezing concrete floor. He stared at the thin strip of light that came from the bottom of the door. It was too yellow to be daylight. More like the light from a bulb. How long had be been down there? Twenty minutes? An hour? Maybe even longer.

There was animal hair of some kind on his bedding and it tickled at his nose, but he didn't have the energy to move. What was his mum doing now? And his gran? Were they out looking for him? Were they angry?

Squeezing his eyes shut he tried not to cry again. He needed to be a big boy. He needed to be less scared. But it was hard, so hard down in the dark. His fingers were starting to feel numb and he really needed a drink of water, his lips and tongue crying out for moisture.

The pain in his head seemed to originate behind his eyes, and despite not wanting to relax his vigil against the shadows and the strip of light, he found them slipping shut. Maybe he could sleep it all away and when he woke up he'd be back at home in his own bed and his gran and mum and dad would all be there keeping him safe. Maybe if he went to sleep Mr. Wentworth would realize he'd made a terrible mistake and just come and take Callum home and pretend it had all been a joke. And Callum would happily go along with it. He'd pretend it was a joke. He wouldn't tell. He wouldn't tell anyone.

Somehow though, to the part of Callum that had stopped believing in Father Christmas back when he was six, that option seemed less likely than waking up and finding it was all a dream. It was the eyes. The look in Mr. Wentworth's eyes when he'd picked him up. He wasn't going to change his mind. He wasn't going to change his mind at all.

For a while he lay there behind his shut eyes drifting somewhere just above sleep but not quite conscious, his head filled with monsters in denim shirts with rotten teeth, all trying to ruin his new shirt. He twitched and shook slightly, even in his daze his hands tingling sharply from the tight bindings around them, and it was only when light finally flooded in that he squinted his eyes open, blinking against the sudden brightness. Mr. Wentworth's shape filled the doorway and Callum's heart thumped into his throat. Without speaking, the man came down the stairs and with each thud of his feet against the stairs Callum shrunk back against the wall as if he could somehow push his body through it to the safety behind the bricks.

When he reached the bottom, Wentworth paused and tugged on a cord, filling the room with a dirty yellow glow. Callum glanced up to see the unshaded bulb hanging above him, dust and dead bugs covering it and dulling whatever power the globe was giving out, sending shadows into the cracks and crevices of the approaching man's face. He whimpered quietly as Mr. Wentworth hunkered down next to him and grinned. "I've brought you some water. Thought you might be thirsty." His dry mouth raging, Callum's eyes darted to the glass in the man's hand.

"Now I'm going to take the gag off, but if you make any noise I'll put it right back on. And I'll hurt you. Do you understand?"

Callum nodded. There were ice cubes floating in the liquid. He could hear them clinking gently against the side of the glass. It looked so good and sweet and he didn't think he'd ever wanted a plain glass of water so much in all his life.

Mr. Wentworth stroked his hand through Callum's sweaty hair. "I don't want to hurt you, Callum. I want to be your friend. You've got to understand that." He leaned in closer to undo the knot at the back of Callum's head and when he pulled away he didn't come right back, but for a moment let his lips brush against Callum's, filling the boy's mouth with the smell of alcohol and stale breath. Terror clenched in the pit of his stomach and he sobbed ever so slightly. He could feel Mr. Wentworth's breath dampening his cheek as he started to pant, one *hand tightly gripping the back of Callum's hair. And then he heard the man's zipper coming down.*

That was the beginning. The beginning of the end, and from inside the little boy's head Alex could see the blur of images and acts that he didn't really understand, that moment of terror rushing toward this present one. She thought that maybe he had been in the cellar about three days now. It was hard to tell; time was all confused in his mind, but she had images of broken sleep, probably induced by pills, sparse meals and time spent bruised and sore and shamed, staring at the strip of light under the door.

But the worst part, the part that made her own heart feel as if it were bleeding, was that under his pain and his fear she felt the sheer desolation and despair that was an oil slick creeping across his soul.

She pulled back, making her consciousness whole on the ceiling, wishing there was something she could do to comfort the shivering child, broken and distraught below her, bringing some of his horror back with her, unable to shake it off entirely. But there was nothing. What she was watching was done. The past. Over.

The next time the cellar door opened it was the last time. Alex wasn't sure if it was worse watching from above or within, but she screamed silently for Callum as the man pulled at his own clothes and then at the boy's, the dirty glow of the bulb illuminating the depravity of his actions. But this time Callum didn't struggle or cry, the fight gone out of him, as if he finally knew that he was never getting out of the cellar, or maybe he didn't want to get out any more, to have to face the world and tell what had happened, and from the ceiling Alex could see the expression on Wentworth's face change, his lust mixing with anger, wanting *more* from the boy, wanting his fear to show. Pinning Callum down with just the weight of his body, the man moved his hands up to the boy's throat, squeezing just enough to force Callum's survival instinct to kick in. The boy's breath became hoarse, and as he twisted and squirmed, Wentworth began to mutter under his breath, lost in the moment, the words hot and angry and indecipherable.

Her own breath caught in her throat. *This is it. Whatever happens, it must happen now.* Callum was choking now, the man's grip tightening as his excitement grew.

A breeze rushed past her, the wind coming from nowhere and bringing with it the dampness of that musty rain, rain from no time and every time. For a moment, as she caught her breath, Alex shut her eyes, letting the mist settle on her skin. When she opened them again, the scene below her had changed. Wentworth was still grunting, destroying the child, his big workman's hands releasing the bruised throat to allow Callum to desperately suck in air and then gripping again. But despite his fight to breathe, Callum wasn't focused on Wentworth or his pain. And neither was Alex.

The tall man's leather coat creaked as he crouched down close to the man and the child. From above Alex could see the smooth ridges on his pale blue naked scalp, a scalp that had never grown hair rather than been shaved bald, and under the darkness of his coat and trousers the steel-capped toes of his heavy boots were visible. Callum had twisted his head around and his bulging eyes stared in disbelief.

"You know he'll kill you, don't you? Maybe not this

time. But soon. Later today." The stranger's voice pierced Alex's ears and she thought that if she were really here and real it would deafen her, its depth resonating so far inside that her insides shook.

"Who . . . who . . ." Callum was rasping the words out, words that Wentworth was oblivious to, and although he never got the full sentence out, Alex knew what his question was, and so did the stranger. *Who are you?*

"I'm the Catcher Man." He paused and sniffed. *"Do you know what death is, Callum?"* It seemed to Alex that Wentworth was now moving in slow motion, unaware of the presence in the room, but still obliging the stranger, the Catcher Man—*but the Catcher Man doesn't exist, wasn't that what Paul had said?*—by giving him more time. Callum just stared, bewildered, his pain almost forgotten for a second, as if like Alex, his mind and body were temporarily separated, and the Catcher Man leaned in. *"Death makes you nothing. As if you were never here."*

He sighed, and as he did Wentworth's face crumpled slightly for a moment in disgust, as if he'd caught a glimpse of how terrible what he was doing really was.

"I can change that. I can take you somewhere else. Somewhere you can be forever. It's called the in between. But if you want to come you have to choose now. Death, pain, and nothing here, or come with me."

Callum mewled slightly, tears creeping out of his eyes, and Alex didn't have to go back inside to know the fear and longing the child was feeling. He was afraid of the nothing. He was afraid of the pain. Just like everyone was. And all he really wanted to do was go home. To his mum and his gran. And all this was over a damaged shirt; it was so unfair and he wished he could just take it back.

"He'll bury you under these floorboards and you'll rot there. And no one will ever find you. I can see it. What will be, will be." The leather creaking again, the Catcher Man stood tall. *"I can keep you and I won't hurt you. But you have to choose. Will you come with me, Callum? You won't be alone. There are other children in between. Other children that I have given the choice to. Will you come with us?"*

Tears oozing down his cheeks, Callum nodded, a small movement, but definite. The air fell still and then wind and rain tore through the cellar, crackling with blue light, Alex's hair whipping against her face, causing her to twist her face away, protecting her eyes. The weather rushed in her ears and then fell to stillness. Her heart racing, she looked back down, knowing what she would see. Or actually, what she wouldn't see. Wentworth had twisted around, his undone trousers revealing his suddenly flaccid penis, his breath short and eyes wide. His head spun searching out the cellar, eyes darting into every corner like a panicked rabbit, his mind already unraveling.

Alex thought he might sit down there, staring at the old sleeping bag for a long, long time before he dared to move. It wouldn't change anything.

Callum and the Catcher Man were gone.

And then, so was she. Back to the green of the forest. Callum took his hands from her eyes and came back around to face her.

"Did you see?" He searched her face. "Did you understand?"

Her heart breaking, she shrugged. "I'm not sure. I saw him take you. I saw what happened. The Catcher Man is real, is that what you wanted me to see?"

Callum's forehead crumpled with frustration as he shook his head. "Come on." Taking her hand, he led her farther into the forest.

CHAPTER TWENTY-EIGHT

When Simon eventually opened his eyes, he didn't know whether he had drifted for a minute or a lifetime. There had been dreams, he was sure of that, but all that was left of them was a bad taste in his mouth and a sense of dread and unquantifiable unease. Although maybe that was just the truth of their reality slowly sinking in. Dead children sending messages. Missing children. Long missing children haunting them from the corner of their eyes. It was crazy, but lying there, surrounded by the history of the village, he knew he believed it. Sighing, he knew that despite his fatigue he wouldn't be going back to sleep, and he looked over at the clock. The red figures staring back at him from the bedside declared it was 5:45 in the morning.

Groaning, his muscles and soul screaming in exhaustion, he rubbed his face with his free hand and then turned to seek out the woman that had tumbled into sleep with him. The pillow next to him was empty.

He stared for a second, wondering if his eyes were playing tricks on him.

"Alex?" He barely spoke the word, staring at the room around him. The door to the bathroom was nearly shut and he couldn't see a light on, but that didn't mean she wasn't in there. Pushing the covers away, he sat up on the edge of the bed, shaking the last of his doziness away. In the gloom that seemed to be all that daylight had managed since he'd arrived in the village, he could make out Alex's clothes thrown carelessly on the chair in the corner. A minute of life clicked away on the digital clock and his brow furrowed. She must be in the bathroom.

"Alex?" He called her name a little louder this time. It was odd. He couldn't hear running water. And she didn't strike him as the kind of girl to leave the bathroom door ajar if she was using the toilet. He shook himself. It was stupid to be worried. Her clothes were here, for Christ's sake. She couldn't have gone far. She might even have gone downstairs in her dressing gown to get herself a coffee. He'd give it a couple of minutes and then go and check on her.

Thinking about her made him smile. There was something about her that was special, there was no doubt about that. When he thought about the way she had reacted with such grit to all the awfulness of the death they'd faced, it clashed with the ethereal quality of her nature, creating a fascination that struck his core. Maybe she was right to say that this wasn't the time to be thinking of the future, and if that's how she felt he wasn't going to argue with her, but he thought that maybe now was the perfect time to be planning for something good. And this could be good, he was sure of it. He hadn't felt the growing pains of love for a very long time, but if he wasn't mistaken he was feeling them now. More sharply and clearly than ever before.

There was still no sound from the bathroom and pulling his own crumpled clothes back on, cursing slightly to find them still damp, he padded over to the door, tapping on it gently. "Alex? Are you in there?" Again, there was only silence, and flicking the switch he pushed the door. The room was empty.

The unease that he'd woken with flared like acid in his gut and he tried to quell it. It was nothing. She'd gone downstairs, that was all. That was probably what had woken him. He splashed water on his face and tidied his hair before going back into the bedroom to get his glasses. Maybe she was on her way back up to him with a steaming mug of coffee, but he was awake now and he figured he may as well go and see how many others were up.

Pushing open the heavy door that led to the downstairs bar, Simon was struck by the surreal sight that greeted him. It seemed more like a scene from an apocalyptic nightmare film than what should have been, and what would have been only a couple of nights before, the stereotypical cozy English country pub. The natural warmth of the wood floor and pale yellow walls was dulled by the wash of the gray dawn light that filtered through the windows, cracking into tired shadows on contact with every surface. Some people were still dozing in chairs, others looking like they'd just woken up, hair and eyes blurred.

Paul was standing gazing out the window, his back ramrod straight, and Simon guessed that his friend hadn't so much as shut his eyes for more than a blink during the past few hours. What would he see in the darkness behind those veils if he did? His mother taunting a child to her death? Or Kay Chambers dying in front of him? Either way, it wasn't good.

The strange morning light seemed to caress Paul's face, inviting him to step outside if he were brave enough. Perhaps sensing Simon near him, he turned and gave him an imperceptible nod before looking back out at the new day. The storm may have stopped but the rain wasn't appeased, the road outside a ghostly blur through the water that ran down the glass.

"Have you seen Alex? She's not upstairs."

Paul glanced around the room. "No. I thought she was in bed. I went upstairs to try and get some sleep, but I'm not sure that I did. Maybe half an hour here and there. I was just going to get some coffee and go and see if Mum was awake."

Simon couldn't squash his disquiet so easily this time. "All her clothes are still upstairs. Where could she have gone?"

Paul looked at Simon for a second, then reconciled the unspoken and turned back to the window. Maybe a few days ago the idea of his friend sleeping with the cousin that was like a little sister to him may have upset him, but not anymore. Now, if anything, it seemed to give him a tiny shred of peace that at least two people had found some comfort in the night. His eyes had more focus in them at any rate.

"Maybe someone lent her some dry clothes?"

Alice Moore, her eyes hollow, silently drifted past them with a tray of white cups.

"Have you seen Alex?"

The old woman shook her head, barely pausing,

and Simon grabbed two mugs, handing one to Paul. His insides were itching, frustration building. Where could Alex be? And if she'd gone out, why hadn't she woken him? The coffee was tepid, but he drank it.

"Look mate, let's go and see if she's gone up to the Roses' place. They may even have got that radio working overnight. Why don't we do that and then go and wake your mum up? Surely if she's still sleeping that's a good thing." *And I need to know what's happened to Alex. I need to know where she is. Or where she isn't.*

His unspoken concern must have echoed loud, because Paul turned away from the window, really seeing his friend for the first time. "Why the hell would Alex have gone out without telling us?"

"That's what I want to know. She'll be up at the Roses'. She must be."

Paul nodded. "Yeah. Yeah, of course she is. But you're right. Let's go there before waking mum." His voice was slightly jittery and Simon knew he wasn't the only one suddenly concerned about Alex's whereabouts.

Downing their coffee, Simon sought out both their coats from the heap by the door while Paul signaled Crouch over.

"We're going to see if Daniel Rose has got the radio working. I think Alex might have gone up there already, so we want to catch up."

Crouch shrugged. "I haven't seen Alex come downstairs. I thought she was still sleeping. But then again, I'm so tired I don't think I could see my hand if it was waving in front of my face."

"If my mum wakes up, tell her I'll be back in ten minutes or so. Doesn't seem like anyone's sleeping for long."

Crouch's grin was worn but sympathetic. "Tell you what I'll do. I'll get some toast and fresh tea and take it up to her."

"Thanks, mate."

"Not a problem. All part of the service." He paused, a little awkward. "You know, she's been a good friend to me over the years, regardless of whatever she may have done in the past. She's a good woman, your mum. They don't make them like that anymore."

Paul's face tightened with many emotions, but Crouch turned away before he was forced to speak. Simon hoped that his happy-go-lucky friend of only days before hadn't gone forever, but looking at the man beside him it was hard to believe otherwise.

"You ready?"

Paul nodded, and they headed out into the rain.

The water was running in streams through the crevices and dips in the worn, steep road and Simon gazed at the purple sky as they carefully trudged up the slippery hill. "Just how long can this rain keep going?"

"I don't know. We'll probably have to build a fucking ark to get out of here." The bitterness had crept back into Paul's voice. "Maybe it'll be quicker than waiting for the police." He sighed, letting some of that rancidness ebb away. "I really picked the wrong weekend to bring someone down to meet the family." Raising an eyebrow, he almost smiled. "It's not always like this, you know."

Simon grinned back, relieved to know that somewhere deep inside his friend a tiny flash of humor still pulsed. "Glad to hear it. I don't know how my family will compete if I ever have you to visit."

Paul let out a snort, but as they approached the

house Simon wondered just how much Paul was laughing inside. He rang the doorbell. Nothing happened. He tried again.

"Try the knocker." Paul's voice was quiet, almost a whisper, all humor now gone. Simon banged the old metal hook down hard against the wood. The few seconds of silence seemed to last forever. *Shit. Oh shit.*

"Can we force it?"

Simon shrugged. "We can try. If it's just an old lock and key then we should get in without too much of a problem, but if there's a Chubb lock on, then we may have to find another way in." He appraised the solid wood in front of him.

Reaching forward, he grabbed the handle firmly and twisted it, pushing inward, expecting to feel the rattle of the locking mechanism holding him back. Instead the door swung smoothly open, inviting them in. Taking a hesitant step forward but staying on the street side of the entrance, he pulled the door back a little and peered at the locks, running his fingers over them.

"The lock's got the snib down to keep the latch off. They've got a chain here. Why haven't they used them?" *Maybe the Roses figured that a little thing like a locked door had no chance of keeping Melanie Parr out, so why bother? Or maybe like the rest of us they were too damn tired to remember a little thing like securing their home.*

Paul pushed past him and into the house. He stared down at something out of Simon's view for a second before signaling him in. "You'd better take a look at this."

The cozy warmth of the house made Simon's stomach turn as he looked down at the body of Ada Rose discarded in a heap by his feet. The sudden tightening in his heart surprised him with its ferocity. In the short time he'd known them, he'd formed a strong attachment to this elderly couple with their no-nonsense country ways. His breath caught in his throat.

Looking at the smallness of her form, his vision snagged on a nearby footprint. Following it backward, he saw several like it coming down from the stairs. *Small. Childlike. What a surprise.* What was it that had made the footprints, though? Water? It looked too dark. His brain wandered slowly through the possibilities, protecting him from the worst. "What is that? Mud?"

Paul knelt down and touched the mark, rubbing the substance between his fingers with distaste. "Blood."

Legs moving almost without his permission, Simon took the stairs two at a time, climbing through the house to the small radio room at the top, his thoughts in a whirl. *Maybe Daniel locked the door. Maybe he didn't know what had happened to his wife. Maybe he just hadn't heard them knocking. Maybe, maybe, maybe. And maybe you should grow up and face the truth. The old man's dead. You know it.*

Yeah, he did know it, but as he burst through the small door of the attic room, the twisted reality of Daniel Rose's death hit him in glorious Technicolor. There was blood everywhere. Nothing in the room was untouched. He could feel the heat pulsing out from Paul's body as he joined him, the two of them sharing the small space of the doorway, neither of them moving, just staring at the shrunken old body collapsed on the desk. Simon's stomach heaved as he realized that the sweet smell that filled the air was that of the old man's blood so richly spread about them.

Static blared out of the radio and both men jumped.

"Jesus." Simon stared at Paul as the roar turned to a crackle, then turned into distant words.

"Did you see? Did you understand?"

Paul shivered. "Who the hell is that? Are they talking to us?" Paul's voice was barely a whisper.

Stepping carefully toward the sticky pink machinery, it seemed to Simon that the walls of the tiny room were moving inward, forcing him to draw in deeper breaths of the blood-impregnated air. His stomach turned. Was he breathing in fine particles of Daniel Rose's cold lifeblood? Heat rushed to his face. *Get over it, Watley. You've seen worse than this. This is no time to develop claustrophobia. It's just one more death, no different from the vicar and sure as hell no worse than Kay Chambers. And so what if the tiny, tinny voice sounded too much like a child to be anything else? It wasn't as if that should be any great surprise after the past forty-eight hours.*

Still, his hand shook visibly as he gently lifted Daniel Rose's cooling wrist and moved it away from the Transmit button. *No. Maybe no different. But one more. And how many more are we supposed to be able to deal with before we all crack up?* He breathed deeply before pushing down the button. "Hello? Hello, is there someone there?"

Simon looked at the small knife embedded deep into the old man's neck, the blood congealing, threatening to glue it crustily into place before long. All that came back at him was static. Paul stepped up beside him. "Who was that?"

Simon shrugged, lifting his hand away from the microphone. "I'm not sure." They stared at the machinery, and then the words came again.

"Did you see? Did you understand?"

The words seemed more distant this time, and when the other voice came through it was so faint it seemed to be traveling across faraway universes. But despite its quiet, it was heart-stoppingly recognizable.

"I'm not sure. I saw him take you. I saw what happened. The Catcher Man is real, is that what you wanted me to see?"

Paul gripped at Simon's sleeve. "Alex. That's Alex."

His heart freezing and dripping cold into his guts, Simon knew he was right. That was her voice and it sounded like it was coming from far, far away. Alex was gone somewhere, and he had a feeling it was a place where he and Paul wouldn't be able to follow.

CHAPTER TWENTY-NINE

Holding Callum's hand, Alex was amazed at how strong her legs felt as they clambered through the trees up the steep bank. Not only her legs, but her whole body seemed changed. Healthy. Whole.

"Am I still dying? I feel different."

The little boy gripped her hand with his cold one. "There is no death here. No death and no life. Just in between. Like us."

Something in his words made her shiver. Limbo. They were in limbo. Despite her renewed health, the atmosphere around them seemed sickly, from the smell of the rain to the green hue. How long had Callum and the other children been here? Glancing down at his serious and desolate face, Alex wondered for the first time in months if perhaps there was something worse than death. To be stuck here, stagnating for years.

"Is it always like this? I mean, is the in between always in the woods?"

"No. Sometimes it's just the storm. It's always raining. Sometimes it's a place I can't even describe. An empty place." A dark shadow passed across his face and Alex hoped it was somewhere she wouldn't have to see.

From behind the trees ahead of them, two children stepped out. The small hand in hers tightened as Callum stopped suddenly. Alex recognized them immediately. They were the girl and boy that had been playing patty-cake in the street. The boy stared at her, his face hard and angry under his baseball cap. Raising one finger, he waggled it at Callum.

"She shouldn't be here. You shouldn't have brought her here."

Callum pulled into Alex's side, but didn't hide behind her, and Alex could feel his quiet determination. She was glad of it, because as much as she wanted to, she didn't understand what was happening. The girl in the old-fashioned tunic dress took a step toward them. "She doesn't belong here." She smiled. "Melanie won't be happy with you."

Callum stepped forward, his head at least a foot shorter than hers, but his chin held high. "She belongs here more than the ones Melanie brought. They're alive. Proper alive."

"She's going to be so mad with you. You'll be paying for this for a long time. Forever." She looked at the boy and they snickered. "Poor little Callum."

Alex stared at the two children, the blackness in their eyes that went right through their souls. What had happened to them to destroy their humanity? Was it this place? Was it whatever they'd gone through before they got here? Or was it just being so close to Melanie's poison that had done it?

Looking into their almost malevolent young faces, pale and sick-looking in the green light, Alex had a terrible moment of realization: most of the children in these woods, including these two and Callum, had been in between far longer than they had been in the real world. How much of their lives did they even remember? Probably only the final terrifying events. Jesus, and then they'd been trapped here. Even with their cruelty writ large on their faces, Alex felt sorry for them. Somewhere deep down in those twisted caricatures were lost children whose only fault had been that they were too scared to die. That thought gave her strength. Who cared if she didn't know what the hell was going on? One thing she did know was that Pete and Laura were in these woods somewhere and she didn't want them contaminated by it any longer than was necessary.

"Where are the children from the village? What's Melanie doing with them?" Her tone was authoritative. Whoever they were, she wasn't going to be intimidated by some lost children. There was nothing they could do to her compared to what Ian had done and the cards fate had dealt.

The boy snickered, the baseball cap keeping the constant rain off his glasses, but still Alex could see the slick water on the skin of his face. "Wouldn't you like to know."

"Yes, yes I would." Resisting the urge to slap him hard in the face, she reached forward and grabbed his shoulders, ready to shake it out of him. The minute she'd gripped him she felt the world sharply shift, and just before her surroundings slid away, transformed to bright sunshine, she heard Callum call out excitedly, "You've got to see!" Taking a deep breath, she let herself go, straight to the inside.

* * *

His legs were pumping hard as Alan pulled away from Archie's house, the bike roaring into life beneath him. He was going to be late for tea, but who cared? Archie's dad had brought home one of the new game machines from Sony, where he worked, and it was ace. They wouldn't even be in the shops for at least another year, and him and Archie had got to play on it for hours. It was going to be almost too cool talking about it in school.

His prized New York baseball cap kept off most of the glare from the low afternoon sunlight, but he still had to squint to make out the curves of the road, his mind still somewhere between the game and the here and now. Maybe Archie would invite him again tomorrow and they could get to the next level and see what the little hedgehog could do then. Archie's dad had said he could only have it at home for the one night, but you never knew, he might forget to take it back to work.

His glasses slipped slightly down his nose, blurring things for a moment before he took one hand casually away from the handlebars and pushed them back, the bike barely wobbling as it speeded up. He hated the glasses. Yes, they meant he could see the blackboard at school, and yes he could sit at the dining room end of the lounge and still see what was going on on the television, but what his mum and dad didn't realize was the sheer horror of becoming a four-eyes, a spec-head, when you weren't one of the geek squad. His mum said they looked nice. Made him look grown-up.

The thought of her made him smile, but she didn't get what school was all about. No grownup did. It was about football and friends and the playground. It definitely wasn't about seeing the blackboard. But as it turned out, he'd had the glasses a couple of weeks now and the teasing hadn't been too bad. He'd been made fun of a bit in the changing rooms, but then when he'd back talked old Mr. Stevens until he looked like his face was going to explode, all was well again. It had cost him an hour after school cleaning graffiti from all the desks and he'd been yelled at by his dad, but it was worth it. His status had been restored. No one would be calling him four-eyes again.

He turned into Mayberry Crescent and pedaled past three small children crouching by the gutter, staring into it at something that held them in wonder, chirruping quietly to each other. They didn't look up as Alan raced by, his head lost in his own thoughts. Maybe they'd have fish and chips for tea tonight. That would finish off what had turned out to be a pretty good day just about right. And since Mum had gone full time as the doctor's receptionist, what had been a once-a-month treat was getting to be more than once a week, and that was fine with him. His stomach rumbled with the thought.

Turning onto Queen Street, he stayed close to the curb as he rode. The sun was like a giant spotlight filling the end of the road, and he had to keep his head down because without sunglasses there was no way he could look into it. Even after one glance, sun spots danced in his vision. The wheels of parked cars loomed ahead and he pulled further into the road to ride alongside them.

Ahead he could hear a car engine traveling toward him, but he wasn't concerned. The sun was in front of him, not the car, and the road was easily wide enough for the both of them to travel through safely. It was only the sound of the engine, its roar, that made him ever look up at all. The car sounded like it was going fast, *too fast for this thirty mile an hour zone in which most people did more like twenty.*

Instinct raised Alan's head and the bike wobbled. Time turned into mud, sliding slowly around him. The car was much closer than he'd thought, too close to him, and it was too far over, far too far over on his side, and as he stared, the sunshine like a halo around the hulk of metal, he could see the man behind the wheel staring at the woman in the seat beside him, one hand raised as he shouted at her, oblivious to the road and to Alan.

The parked cars formed a barrier from the curb, and realizing there was nowhere for him to go, Alan felt his heartbeat pound to the rhythm of the sliding mud. The passenger who'd been staring out the window, trying to ignore the tirade coming at her, turned to snipe back, her gaze freezing as it fell on Alan, and as he stared into her eyes and saw the scream forming in the O of her mouth he knew what was going to happen, they were going to hit him and there was nothing he could do about it, and then time speeded right up again and he squeezed his eyes shut . . . .

It wasn't the impact of the car that forced Alex out of the boy and to her observer's position on the other side of the road. Nor was it the sickening series of crunches as his body hit the pavement, the bones shattering into his organs. That she was prepared for. It was the pain. The sheer awful pain. For a moment or two, she lay there inside his pulped body against the hard ground, neck twisted sideways, staring unmoving, incapable of moving, at the wreck of his bike that lay about twenty feet away—*only got it at Christmas, dad is going to kill me*—and his New York baseball cap that fell somewhere in the middle; then his brain registered the pain and she couldn't take that or the scream inside his head.

Suddenly, she was out. Across the street, barefoot in her mother's dress. Watching. The car, which had briefly paused, screeched away to its own future and somehow Alex knew that one day the woman in the passenger seat would take her own life because the boy had just disappeared. When the sound of the tires had faded, it seemed that everything was still and silent in the aftermath. From where Alan lay, she could make out wet slapping sounds, which she knew was the scream inside him trying to get out. He should be unconscious. He should be unconscious or dead.

Stretching herself, bracing against the pain, she dipped a little back into his thoughts. The mixture of pain and anger made her reel. Oh, he was still so awake in there, awake and in agony and knowing he was dying and *How could they have just driven off? how could they have just driven off?* and she pulled back again, knowing that he couldn't even feel her. He was beyond feeling her and there was nothing she could do for him but watch this play out. *To see.*

It wasn't long before she felt light rain on her face, the wind bringing it straight down the deserted street, and even though she kept her eyes open this time, she still didn't see him appear. One second there was only the broken boy on the pavement, and the next, the Catcher Man was standing next to him, his long leather coat blowing out behind him in the wind he carried. The sudden change in weather had made the baseball cap dance in the road, and the Catcher Man stooped to pick it up before turning back to the child and crouching beside him.

Even from the other side of the road, his words unclear, Alex felt the pain in her ears as he spoke quietly to Alan Harrison. She knew what he was saying. The words that were truth, but only part of the truth. He was dying. The agony was terrible and it would be for the next few hours. There would be no more games of football or computer games or fish and chips. Only death. Terrifying death. Cold and alone. And then came the choice. That she heard clearly enough. *You have to choose. Come with me to the in between with the other children.*

Her own anger whipped the wind into her hair, knowing already how the child would accept, knowing how he would become in the long years there and knowing how his family were destroyed in that instant because they would never know, would never know what happened to him, and that would be too much for them to bear. She let out a silent scream of frustration.

From the other side of the road, the Catcher Man looked up, looked straight at her, puzzled, and in his eyes she could see some of Alan Harrison. The boy on the pavement was gone. As was his hat. She wasn't sure who vanished first, the Catcher Man or her, but the world shifted again and she was back in the wood.

She was still gripping the boy's arms, and releasing him, she stepped backward. Her breath was coming fast. The boy was staring at her, and she wasn't sure if it was dread or awe she saw in his face, but there was less cruelty there, as if somehow a little bit more of his soul had found its way back to him.

"She's taken them to the clearing. The ravine. She's taken them to where the Catcher Man is. He said she could have her revenge." He sounded like an ordinary boy. He touched his cap almost tentatively. "You were there. I saw you." Alex would have smiled at him if he hadn't grabbed the girl's hand and dragged her running back through the woods, whatever had happened between them too much for him to deal with.

Callum was smiling as she stared thoughtfully after the disappearing children. "You see, don't you? You understand? You know how to stop her?"

This time Alex nodded, her voice almost a whisper. "Yes. Yes, I think I do."

CHAPTER THIRTY

He feels the ripple like a tug deep inside him, and with a gasp that makes the trees shake he lifts his head, eyes staring out into the clearing. He sees it all in front of him and inside him—the dry clearing, the hub of the storm with Melanie at the center smiling triumphantly as some of the others he's released from inside tie the girl and the boy who shouldn't be there to a large oak. The tree is hundreds of years old and has power of its own, as does everything here where once, in the old times, before such things got lost, magic took place.

It's not what he sees in front of him that sends the echo of disturbance through the vast spaces inside, but what he sees in the events of the past, in one of the choices he has made. Something has changed there. He tugs on each of the threads of time to see which one is vibrating out of tune and then he finds it. There is a street and a car and a broken boy, all making the moment. But things are not as they were. There is someone else present in the gateway to the in between when he is taking the dying boy, and he hears her silent scream threatening to shatter him. Her dark hair flies outward in a rage as they look at each other. He doesn't understand her anger. He doesn't understand her emotion or the children's or Melanie's. But his lack of understanding is irrelevant to him. Those things, the human things, hold no interest for him. What interests him is how she got there, and how it is that her presence doesn't jar the balance like the others do. He knows where she is heading, the way he knows so many things without ever wondering how. Wondering is a human trait and he has never been human. He knows she is coming and he knows she will try and stop Melanie, and if he understood human emotions he would know that the feeling running through him is relief.

The children tied to the tree are crying and he finds looking at them almost painful, their color, their life, too bright for him. But no matter. That would change. Melanie wants her revenge, to recreate the past and make him give them the choice, and when they are in between she can play with them forever. He hopes that after that her desire for revenge will stop and he will be able to gather them in and move the storm. He hopes that will be the case, but part of him is uncertain. Everything is changed, all is unbalanced, and perhaps she won't stop until all of the villagers are dead. And then? And then will come the battle between them. He reflects once again that maybe he shouldn't have allowed her power. Not in a place like this. A special place. Staring at it all, the past and the present, he feels himself ache with overwhelming exhaustion, the little girl a leech on all that is his essence, and again lowers his head into his hands.

CHAPTER THIRTY-ONE

"Do you think this rain is ever going to stop?" Paul's head was down as they made their way back to the pub, stepping carefully on the treacherous, wet road. His voice was hollow, any glimpse of humor that Simon had heard on their way to the Rose house now buried again in the depths of his soul, maybe forever.

Simon sniffed. "Yes, I do. I think it'll stop when all this shit stops. Although when the fuck that will be, who knows?" His language was slipping into the gutter as it always did when he was tired and frustrated, but this time, adding to it was a deep-seated fear. Not for himself, but for Alex. She had just vanished naked into thin air, gone somewhere or nowhere, and obviously thought that whatever it was she had to do, she could do it without him. Was that what bugged him most? That she didn't need him? Examining his feelings he knew that was partly right, but it wasn't everything. The main thing was just wanting her back in the relative safety of the crowd. The grit that had made her go off on her own was one of the traits that he liked most, but he was afraid for her and he knew Paul was too.

They strode on in silence for a few moments until the vague comfort of The Rock came into view at the curve of the road. Simon glanced over at the woods. They glared back at him, a wall of dark shadows and silence. Just what the hell was going on behind that serene bank of trees? After his and Paul's experience in there, he knew that the woods were hiding too much that was beyond his understanding, and he couldn't help but wonder if they were hiding Alex in there too. The other voice on the radio had been that of a child and he would bet everything he owned that it didn't belong to one of the local children. It seemed that although the strange children visited the village when it suited them, it was the woods they retreated to.

"What are we going to do, Paul?"

"We're going to get some recruits in the pub and then go back into the woods. That's where Melanie died. Somewhere in there. And that's where Alex, Laura, and Pete will be."

"Do you think we'll be able to find them?"

Paul laughed. "God only fucking knows. What do you think?"

Simon said nothing as they pulled open the door. *If whoever's got them wants them to be found, then maybe we've got a chance. Otherwise? Probably not a hope.*

It was good to be back under the warm glow of the old yellow lights that had stayed on all night, making the mahogany of the bar and wooden floor and tables shine as if just polished. And maybe they had been. Who knew what people had been doing to keep busy and sane? Even if it was just for a few minutes, Simon was pleased to shed his sodden jacket, and it was only when both he and Paul had hung them and got to the bar that he realized how silent everyone was. Crouch was pale behind the bar, his face trembling slightly. Paul didn't seem to notice and he sighed, letting his weight drop heavily onto a bar stool before looking up at the bartender.

"The Roses are both dead in their house." His mouth twisted slightly. "No message this time. I guess that little dead cow doesn't need to leave a signature anymore. God knows where Alex is, but somehow we heard her voice through the radio. Don't ask me how, because I haven't got a clue. She's with some kid. But not Laura or Pete."

It was only when Paul got no reaction from the silent villagers around them that he noticed that something seemed to be wrong here as well as in the Rose house. He stared at Crouch, then at the others around them.

"What? What is it?"

Crouch said nothing, just swallowed.

Simon felt his heart beating faster. *What now?* "Has something happened?"

"Yes. Yes, it has." Crouch's voice had none of its normal gruff confidence. "Look Paul, I'm really sorry. It's your mum."

Simon watched his friend's knuckles tighten on the edge of the bar. "What's happened to her?"

"I went up to take her some tea. Thought I'd wake her up while you were out, like I said. There was no answer and the door was locked. . . ."

"Get to the point." Paul's voice could have shattered glass.

"Well, when I got inside I found her in the bathroom." He leaned forward and gripped Paul's hand. "It wasn't the girl, Paul. The little girl didn't get her. It was . . . She . . . she was in the bath. She'd . . . she'd cut her wrists."

Paul stared. "She's dead?"

Crouch nodded. "I think she must have done it last night when she went up to bed. After what she'd said." He paused, his voice softer than someone his size should have been able to produce. "I think she wanted some peace."

"How do you know what the hell she wanted?" Paul pushed away from the bar, sending the stool tumbling backward. "She was up there dead all night?" Turning, he ran his hands through his hair, his eyes flicking to the ground, then the ceiling, and then back to the ground again. "Jesus. *Jesus*. I've got to see her."

"I don't think that would be such a good idea, Paul. I don't think—"

Crouch had come to the other side of the bar, but never got to finish his sentence as Paul stormed through the inner door.

Simon could hear his feet pounding against the ancient stairs and exhaustion flooded through his body. "I'll go up after him."

Simon had taken a couple of steps forward when a gentle hand stopped him. Alice Moore still looked somewhat like a wraith, her thin body frail and fragile, but her eyes had regained some strength. "No. No, I'll go. I've known him since he was just a boy. I can look after him better than you. You get a drink for now." She squeezed his hand lightly. "This isn't your fight, is it? I'm sorry you've had to meet us like this. This is a good community, really it is."

Simon smiled. "You're preaching to the converted, Alice."

Reaching up on her tiptoes, Alice brushed his cheek with a feathery kiss before tapping him gently on the arm as she moved away to go after Paul. Watching her go, Simon felt strangely abandoned, as if he had slowly been cut loose from everyone that he knew in this village. He may only have known Mary since the start of this insane few days, but the shock that she was dead, *that she had killed herself,* resonated inside him. Mary gone. Alex missing.

"Here you go, son. You look like you could use it." Crouch handed him a glass of what looked like brandy, and then clinked it against one of his own. "I know I need one." Both men had barely raised the drink to their lips before a soft voice cut through their thoughts.

"Um, someone better come and have a look at this."

Looking up from his glass, Simon didn't recognize the young woman who had spoken; she was just a tired and shell-shocked stranger, like the others that surrounded him. At the moment, though, he felt more closely bonded to these people than to any friends he had back in London.

Other people drifted toward the window, hauling their stiff joints out of their chairs, young and old moving slowly, stilted, bodies creaking from tense inactivity. Watching them as they approached the glass, Simon was reminded of zombies in some old 60s Hammer horror film.

Looking at the mix of old and young, all drained and pale with clothes untidy and crumpled, he couldn't see James Partridge and Tom Tucker. After being in the wood himself, Simon knew it was unlikely they'd made it out to another village, and he wondered what had happened to them. Maybe they'd headed to Tom's parents' farm like he and Paul had, and maybe after the discovery of their corpses Tom hadn't had the energy to head back to the pub. In some ways, he hoped that was the case. It seemed the better option than thinking of the two grown men stumbling around lost in the woods being taunted by strange ghosts of children. Surely if they were dead their bodies would have been presented to the rest in some way or another. It seemed to Simon that Melanie liked her work to have an audience.

Each person gasped as they reached the window, staring silently, faces reanimated, even if their bodies were still. Taking one more sip of the fiery liquid, Simon reluctantly put his glass down and followed Crouch over to where there was still a gap through which he could see out.

"Bloody hell." Crouch's mouth fell open. "What the hell is that?"

Simon stared out beyond the sheet of rain falling on the road that divided the pub and the wood to what was holding the attention of the village residents. Even though he had seen it before, he still felt his eyes widen as they were drawn in by the crackling blue light that danced across the tips of the trees, twisting through the branches like mad Christmas tree lights, chasing each other in a never ending loop.

"What is that?" Whoever had spoken didn't turn from the window, still caught in a moment of wonder.

"It is what Paul and I saw in the woods last night. It stopped us from getting out." When they'd returned the previous night, soaking and exhausted, Simon and Paul had shared the story of what they'd found at the Tucker farm and the events in the woods with the few people that were still awake, but some were dozing and some had focused only on the awful news of the deaths before retiring to grieve in quiet corners with their own families. The reality of the blue electricity sparkling in front of them was far more mesmerizing than when it had belonged in the ramblings of two men in shock.

"It looks like this time the point is to keep us from getting back into the woods. It seems that whatever's going on in there, we're not welcome."

"What do you think is happening?"

"I don't know. Some kind of showdown maybe. Alex is in there."

A little boy, his nose not much above the roughly painted ledge, pointed over to his left. "What's that, Mummy? What's that little boy doing over there in the rain?"

Following the boy's finger, Simon saw a very young child, maybe five or six, emerging from behind a tree lit up with the blue sparkling fire. He came into view but didn't move any further, instead just standing and staring at the pub. A few seconds later, another child appeared, this time a slightly older little girl, swinging out from around the sodden bark of an oak about ten yards farther on and coming to a halt when she too was facing the pub, still under the overhanging electrified branches above. Within seconds another came into view, then another, and then another, until there were thirteen children spread out along the edge of the wood opposite the pub, a mixture of girls and boys from about four to fifteen, their clothes running from the flares of the seventies to present-day fashions. None of them moved, simply staring in silence back at the tired and weary faces peering out from the pub's window.

"Yes," said Simon, thoughtfully. "I think we can definitely say we're not welcome in the woods today."

The woman whose son had pointed out the first child protectively gripped him by the shoulders and wheeled him around, leading him to a far table where he had been working on a crude drawing of a horse. It didn't take him long to settle back in and Simon was for a moment in awe of the child's capacity to adapt. Looking back at their new observers, he wondered how long it took for them to adapt to whatever existence they had now. A year? Ten? Twenty?

"Who are they?" Crouch's breathless question seemed to speak for them all.

Simon stared out, straining his tired eyes to make out significant features. "I think they're lost children." He wasn't sure what he felt more, fear of them or pity for them.

"What do you mean?"

"Look at them. Really look at them. I'm sure you'll recognize one or two from national papers and television appeals. Even twenty years ago that kind of news would have been big down here. Just look at them properly."

For a moment or two no one spoke and then a female voice gasped. "Oh, my god, but it can't be." Her hand raised up to the glass. "That boy . . . the third one along . . . He looks just like that Colin Brade that went missing . . . must be ten years ago." Her voice rose slightly. "That is him, that's what he was wearing, I'm sure it is. I remember 'cause he was the same age as my little sister. . . ." Her voice was a blend of awe and disbelief. Simon knew how she felt; he'd gone through the same when he realized he'd seen Alan Harrison playing in the village streets. It was that LSD moment again, and he wasn't sure he was ever going to shake it off.

A murmur of energy was running through the small crowd, some scoffing at the suggestion outright, despite the blue light, despite the deaths, and despite the evidence in front of their eyes, others pushing their faces closer to the glass, nodding as their breath steamed it up, blocking their view.

A different voice piped through above the general hubbub. "And that girl's Maggie Ray! That one there, near the end. Jesus . . . Jesus . . ."

For the next ten minutes the noise levels climbed high, the villagers reanimated as they argued and debated the identity of each of the silently watching children. Some remained anonymous, leaving Simon wondering sadly just who had lost them and why no one had fought harder to find them, but most were identified nearly positively from images consigned long ago to memory and now dredged up. Looking out the window, Crouch and he the only people not speaking, Simon thought he might feel more sorry for the children if they weren't smiling so unpleasantly. So inhumanely. Teeth glistening. Occasionally, he was sure they glanced sideways to each other as if confirming their part in a secret joke. An involuntary shiver slid down his spine. *What are you doing in there Alex? How can you possibly be able to do anything against this?* His heart clenched and he forced it to relax. *But she's still alive. She may be in there, but she's still alive.*

Around him the identity of another child was confirmed by majority decision and then one question dug into his ears, slicing through the excitement.

"But how can this be? How can they be here?"

The words silenced the room, and Simon thought about Paul upstairs, and poor dead Mary, and Melanie Parr and everything he'd seen since the madness had descended.

"That's easy." He spoke softly, to himself and to all of them. "The Catcher Man took them."

Silence fell so heavily that Simon could almost see it settling like dust across the old pub.

"What can we do?" Crouch's words were hollow, as if he knew the answer before it came.

"Nothing. Just wait. That's all we can do."

The huddle of people barely moved, just occasionally fetching a chair or barstool before continuing their vigil. After a while, Paul and Alice came downstairs, eyes red from crying but calmed, and joined them in the wait.

CHAPTER THIRTY-TWO

As she and Callum walked side by side through the wood, her stride steady, Alex could hear the rustle of movement in the trees around her, the sounds keeping up with them but maintaining a slight distance. The noise was tentative and hesitant, as if there had been a shift in the balance of power between her and the children.

"Why don't they just come out?"

"I think they're afraid of you. They're like me. They're not the ones gone bad. Melanie's sent those to the edge of the wood." He smiled. "I don't think she knows you're here."

"I wouldn't be so sure. Alan Harrison and that girl ran off pretty fast." The thought of the encounter with that little boy unsettled her. She hadn't felt the same since she'd grabbed him. It wasn't like the cancer pain, but deep in her core she could feel a cold space, as if someone had cut her open and then sewed her back up with a lump of ice left inside. And there was tingling in her hands like painless pins and needles. Maybe it had started when Callum had showed her what happened to him, but after the Alan incident she had felt the change. Something about it frightened her and she just wanted to find the children and get back to her own life, or at least what was left of it. While she still could.

A branch cracked loudly behind the trees to her left and she stopped walking. "Why don't you just come out?" She was surprised at how strong her voice sounded as she called out. Until now her words had seemed flat in the in between, as Callum's had in the bathroom. This time they were strong and resonant. "I'm not going to hurt you."

For a second nothing happened, and then, almost shyly, Alan Harrison was the first to emerge from behind a tree. The viciousness in his face was gone and he looked at her with a mixture of awe and trepidation. Following his lead came the girl in the tunic, her eyes still a little suspicious, and then five or six others emerged. A couple of the smaller ones quietly whispered to each other, their eyes fixed on Alex. She stared at Alan Harrison and the girl who held his hand. So that's why Melanie didn't know she was here yet. The children hadn't told her.

"Alan says you can help us." The girl in the tunic dress retained some of her defiance, and Alex wondered if it was some of that spirit that had led her to whatever situation had brought her there. "But you have to hurry. She's going to do it now. She's going to push one of them into the ravine."

Nodding at her, not needing to ask who *she* was, Alex turned, and with the children in tow like the pied piper, she moved up the bank, strong legs climbing. Her heart and head were pounding. How did they think she could help them? She couldn't, of that she was sure. Behind her, she could hear excited muttering. How disappointed would they be when they found out they were mistaken? That she was just like them, in limbo, somewhere between life and death, no real use to anyone? What would they do when they realized that? Still, she thought, glancing down at her mother's dress and taking a kind of comfort from it, she'd think about that later. For now, she had Melanie to deal with.

It could have been minutes or hours later when the strange group finally reached the high ground that led to the clearing. Alex had the strange feeling that it had been both, and her brain accepted that paradox. The whole of the in between was a paradox. Alive and dead. Real and unreal. All one and the same *in between*.

As the trees thinned, the children behind her fell back slightly, finding places to hide where they could peer round the safe bark and watch the clearing without having to cross into the arena. The rain pattered hard through the trees but at the edge the wind was barely a breeze. Not that it really mattered. Alex's skin was soaked from the inside out. It had been the whole time she'd been there, however long that was.

When Alex stepped into the open, only Callum, Alan, and the tunic girl came with her. For a moment, she just stared, feeling the rainwater falling from the leaves above and trickling down her skin. The air was still in the clearing, the storm paused, but it smelled rotten and sweet, like the breath of an old man who'd been dying for a long time. Around them she could almost hear the drip of the water held back in the woods, away from its maker. To her left, Peter was tied to a tree, his yellow coat in a heap by his feet, and she could see he had been crying, but now he was just staring at her as if he couldn't believe his eyes. Slowly, Alex raised one finger to her lips to keep him quiet.

On the other side of the clearing, next to the ledge by the river, lay a fallen log, gnarled, thick, and rotten, and on it, his head in his hands, sat the Catcher Man. Blue veins shone through the pale skin of his skull, and a thick network of crisscrosses ran up his neck where it emerged from the black collar of his coat. She was sure the veins hadn't been visible when she'd seen him crouching by Alan Harrison's broken body. The hands that held that huge head seemed too weak to do so. *You're dying.* The thought hit Alex like a punch in the face. *She's draining you.*

In the space between Alex and the Catcher Man, oblivious to her arrival, Melanie and two boys were dragging Laura toward the edge of the ravine. The crying girl was pulling back so hard that her bottom was almost on the ground, but still they dragged her forward. Melanie was laughing. "You can jump or we'll push you, it's up to you."

Laura shrieked as the edge came a foot closer. The two boys held onto her arms and Melanie grabbed a fistful of Laura's hair and tugged hard on it. "You're just like your mother, a scaredy-cat, scaredy-cat!"

It seemed to Alex that the madness shone out from the long-dead girl; what had been a seed of insanity in the child had grown out of all proportion in this strange place, fed by the power she'd drained from the creature on the log. This part of the wood was special;

Alex could feel the magical energy thrumming through the soles of her feet and this was the place where Melanie had been taken. Maybe that's what had given her the edge over the other children. Or maybe it was just her inherent insanity that gave her more manipulative strength.

Alex sighed, the small lump of cold in her core tugging at her, and despite the dead air she felt her hair lifting with the breeze, the tingle running from her hands all the way up her arms with some dread power.

The children had changed her and she wasn't sure it was a good thing, but for now, she just had to use whatever those changes had brought. And despite the cold and the tingling, she knew what had to be done.

"You need to stop this!" The trees around her shook as she shouted and even the three children with her stepped back slightly.

Nearly at the edge of the ravine, Melanie froze and looked up, her expression one of total madness and fury under the perfect blond curls. It was the face of someone much older than ten, staring out from smooth cherubic cheeks. "What are you doing here?" She stabbed a finger at Alex. "You can't be here! I didn't bring you here!" The words came out with a torrent of spit, her anger flying out of her.

The two boys holding Laura hesitated for a second, shocked by the combination of the new arrival and Melanie's outburst, and the girl took advantage of the moment, tearing herself free with a grunt and running to Alex's side.

"I said you have to stop this!" Alex called the words out again, louder this time, and Laura flinched, covering her ears.

Melanie laughed, running to the tree and tugging at the rope around Peter. "You can't make me! You don't belong here! You can't stop me!" Her eyes shone manically. "I don't know how you got here, but you'll never go back. I won't let you!" Her fingers pulled at the ropes around the little boy. "I was going to let him go. Not now!" Despite her protestations, there was a hot overeagerness in her voice and movement that hinted at desperation. Things were happening that were out of her control, that she didn't understand, and she didn't like it.

The two boys that had been helping Melanie stared at Alex and then slowly pulled back, away from the little girl with only one red shoe on. They'd realized something that Melanie hadn't. Alex wasn't talking to her. She was talking to the Catcher Man.

Slowly, he raised his head out of his hands. "I knew you were coming."

This time, although Alex felt the power of his words trembling her insides, her ears didn't hurt. She nodded to him. "You have to stop this."

He shrugged and for an instant the land underneath them rippled with his movement. "I don't know how."

Alex stepped forward, and in the one move she had crossed the clearing and was standing in front of him. Cupping his cold heavy head with her hands, she lifted his chin and gazed into his black eyes. For a moment she glimpsed the worlds beyond worlds within him, the faces of the children layered in his head, and the awful exhausting tiredness; then she pulled back, knowing that if she went all the way inside, she would never find her way out.

She smiled. "I do."

Behind her, Melanie was letting out a tirade of insults as she tried to grip the wriggling toddler, feeling her plans slip through her fingers with him, and Alex turned to face her. Across the clearing, watching with the others, her life-brightness standing out, Laura gasped. "Alex, your eyes . . . your eyes are black . . . ," but Alex raised her hand to silence her. Not now. No distractions now. *My eyes are black, how can my eyes be black? His eyes are black. . . .* She pushed the thought away and looked down at the Catcher Man.

"You have to take the choice back."

From behind the trees, Alex could hear the hushed breath of whispers running through the children. *Take the choice back. He can take the choice back.*

The Catcher Man was staring at her, and inside she felt another small part of core turn into nothing and freeze. In her peripheral vision, she could make out Melanie pulling little Peter toward the edge. Time ticked loudly, buzzing in her head. In the forest around them the storm fiercely howled as the Catcher Man tried to reconcile what she had said with his acceptance of how things should be, *that the choice was given, not taken back*, all those time lines playing out against the dark backdrop of his eyes, Alex watching them like a silent movie.

Reaching down, she took one of his hands, ignoring the electricity as his tingling skin met hers, and pulled him to his feet. "You have to take the choice back. And you have to do it now. While you still can." She wasn't even sure she'd spoken the words out loud or whether they'd run down through her fingertips and into his. "The choice is yours. Not hers. Take it back."

His fingers squeezed hers for a moment and she felt

it in the muscles of her ribs, contracting them, forcing all the breath out of her, until he let go of her hand and pulled himself up tall. He turned to face the clearing.

"Melanie." The word was nothing more than a whisper, but as it spilled out of him, everything around them stopped. Peter froze, his body twisted in its struggle, half upright, half tumbling to the floor. Looking at the edge of the clearing behind her, Alex could make out tiny drops of rain, paused in their journey from the leaves to the sodden forest floor. Across from her, Laura's face was still pulled wide in an expression of shocked concern, staring back at Alex, unblinking. Behind the trees, small pale faces peered out like statues, stuck in a moment they were leaving behind.

Nothing moved, nothing was sentient except for her, the Catcher Man, and the girl still struggling to move Peter from his stuck position. Giving up, she let go of his arm and stamped her foot. "You bitch! You fucking bitch!" Her shriek cut through the silence. "You shouldn't even fucking be here! This is my place! My place!" Howling, she launched herself full pelt across the clearing, small hands raised to attack Alex.

"No, Melanie. This is my place." The Catcher Man's words were only a whisper, but they dug into Alex's head, making her cry out and cover her ears, crouching onto the ground. When she took her hands away, there was blood on her fingers. *What is this place doing to me? What is it doing to me?* Looking upward, trying to ignore the throb of her burst eardrum, she watched the pale hand rise sharply, its palm facing toward the running girl, blue fire running up and down the sleeve of that long leather coat.

Everything changed all at once. Melanie was thrown

up in the air, the scream knocked out of her with the shock, falling awkwardly backwards, and her out-stretched arms could do nothing to stop her landing in a ghostly version of herself, sitting on the clearing and putting on her shoes. Peter's whole form shimmered and paled, as if he were there and not there, as Alex guessed was the case for them all as past and present collided. The little boy unfroze, first looking as if he would run toward Alex, and then turning to run to Laura and the other pale, awoken children on the far side. *Do I look that frightening? My eyes are black and my ears are bleeding. What else has changed?*

Focusing on the buckle of her first red sandal, Melanie was oblivious to them, locked back in the past, when she was still alive and breathing, the in-between having not yet happened to her. She must have heard something, because her head raised and tilted slightly, the second shoe forgotten.

Only hearing the roar of damage from inside her ear, Alex watched the edge of the clearing, knowing what was coming next. A few seconds later, the women emerged, transluscent. Alex gazed at their ghostly forms in wonder. They were the women she knew and yet not. Even in the green gloom, looking at their flick-ering outlines she could see the differences. Enid Tucker's waist was still slim, her shape almost hour-glass rather than thick-waisted and matronly as she had been in all the time Alex had known her. Leaving the second shoe on the ground, Melanie pulled herself to her feet, smug smile faltering.

Another woman, tall and willowy—*Kay's mum, that's Kay's mum standing next to Aunt Mary, Aunt Mary with no gray hair*—bent to the ground, her eyes firmly focused on the child, and picked up a solid twig. Rain had started to fall in the past, fall heavily, and the clothes of the women were sticking to their skin as they moved toward the little girl. They were speaking but Alex couldn't hear the words. The pain in her ears was receding, but the deafness remained. Not that she needed to hear what they were saying. She'd heard it before, back in the real world, poured out of Mary's soul.

The first branch slapped against Melanie's leg and she jumped slightly, backing away, as the other women circled. The women were glowing now, almost radiant in their attack, their vengeance all they could see, all they wanted. They couldn't see that with every taunt, every jab of the stick, Melanie stepped one foot closer to the ravine, which only seconds ago and thirty years in the future, the little girl would be dragging Laura and then Peter toward. Alex's heart ached for the strong and vital women reenacting the past in front of her. Every poke of their twigs was leading them to their own destruction and the destruction of those they were doing this to protect. Staring at the scene, Alex wondered who was most insane, the pack of women, mad pagans in the rain, or the girl, her own composure gone, her face terrified as she slowly backed away.

And then she took that final step backward, the fear on her face changing to confusion, and then terror as she realized that there was no solid ground behind her, just crumbling mud and then empty space. Her arms flailed forward, desperately trying to regain some balance as she tipped backwards, and then she fell. Disappeared down the ravine.

The temporary insanity dropped away from the

women as if washed off by the rain. They stared aghast, hands raised to mouths and hair, as the moment sank in. Without thinking, as one, they released their twigs and branches.

Mary was the first to kneel carefully at the edge and call down. Kay's mum joined her, their faces intent as they shouted things Alex couldn't hear down to the little girl. Enid Tucker was pacing the clearing, wringing her hands and muttering to herself. Mary and Charlotte Keeler pulled themselves to their feet, their eyes shaking with desperation as they shouted at each other. Eventually, something was agreed—*we need to go and get a rope, we'll be back soon, everything will be fine, we'll be no time at all*—and with Edith dragging Mary, they disappeared offstage, swallowed into the woods of the past. Mary's one look back confirmed what she had told them in the pub; what had haunted her all her life: That she knew they weren't going to get back in time. And that she'd be hearing that desperate plea for the rest of her life.

The clearing empty, Alex stared at the edge of the ravine. What now? Did they just have to wait for her to die? Thoughts of Callum in that cellar, and Alan Harrison lying broken on the pavement filled her head. All their fear. How afraid was Melanie now? She glanced up at the Catcher Man beside her, his face impassive, and wondered how this was affecting him, or if it was affecting him at all. Unsure of whether she was doing it for herself or for him, she slipped her hand into his. This time the electricity seemed warm, not shocking, but she gasped as the sounds flooded her head. She could hear, she could hear Melanie's screams—*I can't move my legs, I can't feel them! Don't leave me, please don't leave me!*—bursting into her very core. The terror in them was awful. How could the women have left her there? How could Mary have left her there?

The Catcher Man must have felt her thoughts, because he turned to her. His mouth didn't move. "I can make it stop. I can give her the choice."

Alex stared at him. He was in her head and she in his. "Is this how it is for you? Every time? Is this what you feel?"

He shrugged, "Only until they make the choice. And then it stops."

The idea of this filling his head constantly made her stomach turn. "Surely that would be too much to bear. Surely it must drive you insane." Alex stared at him, uncomprehending of his existence, and she felt his confusion at her words.

"I don't understand insane. This is what is." He turned to the ravine. "I can make it stop. I can give her the choice."

Alex stared at him and then at the ravine. She thought of the girl's terror and pain, and she thought of the children stuck in between. She thought of her own cancer eating away at her. All of these things were worse than death. It was only fear that held them back.

"No," she whispered, and this time she saw the Catcher Man flinch beside her. "No more choices."

She squeezed his hand tight before releasing it, sucking his electric power into herself, adding to that which she knew had seeped into her already, changing her, and then shut her eyes.

When she opened them again, she was on the small ledge far below the clearing, sitting on the edge, her legs dangling over the side into the torrent of the rising river. She was almost level with the rocky outcrop now, Alex's dress floating on the surface. It was icy cold, but somehow, although she could feel it on her skin, it didn't make her shiver. She looked down at the twisted girl next to her. Her back was broken, her legs sticking out at nauseating angles. Melanie gazed up at Alex. "I can't move my legs. I can't feel them." Water lapped across the surface of the rock, and the little girl mewled. "They left me. They left me. I don't want to be here. I don't want to be here. I don't want to die. I *can't* die. . . ."

Alex smiled at her, gently stroking the golden hair that had been muddied in the rain. "Shhh. Everyone can die. Everyone has to. It's not so very terrible a thing."

Melanie's lips were turning blue as the water rose. "I'm scared." The words were barely audible, but they cut into Alex.

"I know." Reaching down, she took Melanie's cold hand and squeezed it. "But you don't have to be scared on your own. I'm here. I'm with you." Allowing the power to do its work, she slipped right inside Melanie, filling her form.

The girl's fear almost overwhelmed her, almost pushed her out, but she absorbed it, caressing the child from the inside. *See? I'm here with you. Give me your fear. Give me your pain.* For a moment the girl stiffened against the presence in her mind and then relaxed, letting the other take from her, taking comfort in Alex's grip. For a while, the child and the woman were one and Alex saw her past and her present, all her badness and some good, and all the time she absorbed the awful blackness of that fear.

She could feel the water against her cheek and her chin, Melanie's cheek and chin, and when the little girl struggled and panicked she soothed her.

We're going together. Trust me. Don't fight it.

But I'm so scared, I can't breathe.

I'm here, right here with you. I'm coming with you, can you feel me? Right in here with you?

Yes. Yes . . .

Alex could feel the water pouring into her lungs and she breathed it in for both of them. She was dominant here now, Melanie just the passenger, safe and warm inside.

Are you an angel?

The voice was soft and sweet and everything a child should be. Alex smiled. She could feel something happening to them, a lightheadedness, a distance between them and the water that filled them up. The clock was stopping.

Maybe something like that. Maybe I'm the angel of death. She smiled a little at the thought and Melanie giggled, the blackness that swallowed them almost comforting as Alex led them into it.

Suddenly the water was gone. Alex felt heat, a good heat pour through them and a strange popping sensation inside. They weren't breathing anymore. Opening her eyes, their eyes, she gazed into the bright white light. The ledge was gone. The ravine was gone. There was nothing but warmth and light surrounding them like a blanket made from love, pure love, uninterrupted by human greed and jealousy. Eager and excited, Melanie moved, wriggled away inside, and suddenly they were separate, somewhere and nowhere, in a different kind of in between.

What do we do now?

Alex smiled at the girl, her hair bright, one shoe on, one shoe off. *Well, if you believe the stories, then I think we're supposed to walk into the light.*

It's beautiful.

Beside her, the little girl glowed.

And so are you.

She watched as Melanie ran into whatever was causing the radiance ahead, and still smiling, she took a step to follow her.

It was like hitting a brick wall, and as the light turned to blackness, the blackness of rushing water, Alex felt herself being pulled back.

What is happening, what is happening? She tried to call out to Melanie to wait, for someone to help her, but the water was filling her lungs as she lay on the ledge, choking her, and she couldn't move her legs, and the blackness and the panic and the fear were filling her up and all she wanted was to breathe but she was choking, drowning, and it was so terrible and she was so terrified. Panicked, she fought and fought, clutching at life until the cold blackness, no comfort in it, overwhelmed her.

When she opened her eyes, she was back in the clearing, gasping for lungfuls of the stagnant in between air, the children and the Catcher Man all staring at her. She looked at him, her lungs raw, but the pain fading fast. *The in between. Things are different here.* In seconds, her breathing was normal. "What the fuck happened there?"

The Catcher Man seemed slightly diminished, *thinner* in the gloom. He was looking at her with interest. "You took her death. You took her death for her."

"But why didn't I die too? I was there, I saw the light. . . ."

He tilted his head slightly, bemused at her reaction. "But you're in between. You *are* the in between now. Look." Reaching forward, he lifted her hand so that their palms were touching, then tilted them toward him and then her, making both sides visible. She stared. His hand was smooth and soft, and thick blue lines, like the veins that covered his skull, were rippling under the surface of hers, fading at the wrist where the skin returned to normal, and his became patterned. *Oh Jesus, Jesus Christ.* "What is it? What's happening to me?"

"Things are changing." His black eyes were expressionless. "I'm ending. You're beginning."

"I don't understand."

He looked at the children, who were edging toward them and sighed. This time the trees barely trembled. "You will."

The girl with the tunic reached them first, and behind her Alan Harrison and then the two boys who had been helping Melanie. They all stared at her, their eyes full of wonder.

"My name's Annie." The girl with the tunic was almost shy, one hand twisting into the other. "We saw . . . we saw what happened when you were with Melanie. We saw the light. We heard her laughing."

Alan Harrison slipped his hand into the girl's. Alex wondered how long had they been there together. A marriage-length of time spent in this purgatory. No growing up. Nothing but stagnating in a storm.

"It was a good laugh. She didn't sound like that before. We want you to do it for us." The boy's baseball cap made him look so young as his eyes flitted from Alex to the Catcher Man and back again. "We want you to put us back. Take the choice back."

Alex stared, the memory of Melanie's drowning too raw and real and terrible. How could she face the beauty of that light again, knowing that she was going to be pulled back to relive the death she saved them from? Didn't they realize what they were asking of her? How many of them were there? Twenty? Thirty?

Across the clearing she could see Laura and Peter waiting for her to take them home, to end this nightmare, little Callum standing alongside, pale and faded beside their bright colors. Her heart ached and she looked back at the pleading children in front of her. Of course they didn't realize what they were asking of her. They were just children. Children who'd been afraid for a long, long time.

Looking back up at the Catcher Man, she let out a sigh of her own and watched his skin ripple with it.

"We have to do this together. You have to take the choice back before I can do anything."

He nodded and turned to face the girl in the tunic. "Annie."

And then the world froze again.

CHAPTER THIRTY-THREE

Something was happening in the storm. They could all see it, peering out of the pub windows and into the mist that was settling in waves across the cobbled road. Thunder and rain still raged in the sky, but flashes of light broke through, the heat from the brightness turning the rain around it into clouds of steam.

"What is that?" Simon could feel Paul's warm, stale breath brush against his cheek as he spoke. They'd all gathered in closely, bodies touching gently. It had been a subconscious movement, strangers seeking comfort from the heat and proximity of others, the windows and old door seeming little protection against the strangeness outside.

"I don't know." Another burst of brightness filled a patch of sky above some distant trees. Even from where they stood the purity of it hurt the back of Simon's eyes, leaving pink and purple spots behind when he shut them. "But I do know that it's coming up from the ground rather than down from the sky."

Paul paused, and watched. "Are you sure? Look again."

Simon tried, but had to turn away. "It's hurting my eyes."

"It's not coming from the ground or the sky. It's coming from both at once. Or somewhere in the middle. Whatever it is, it's not natural."

"I don't know about that." Alice Moore's voice was like a butterfly's wings. "It's beautiful. So beautiful. I think something that beautiful must be natural."

"Look! Look at the woods." Crouch's voice made them jump.

"We are looking at them." Simon turned. "What's the matter?"

"Don't look at the sky. Look at the woods. Look. The children are going."

The older man was right. Where the children had been evenly spaced, regimented in their surly observation of the living, there were now gaps, gaps that were getting bigger as each of the watchers turned and slid into the trees, some taking others hands and arms, just like normal children. Just like *living* children.

"Where are they going?" Paul squeezed Simon's arm.

"I don't know. It must have something to do with those lights."

"Do you think it has something to do with Alex?"

Thinking of her, Simon paused, his breath hitching against his heart. "I don't know, but it wouldn't surprise me. Nothing about your cousin would surprise me."

"Shall we go after them?"

The children had all gone within the space of a minute or two, but staring out at the storm, Simon shook his head. "We can't. That blue electricity is still all over the trees. We won't get past it."

Another flash of light burst through the sky.

"Do you think that maybe the storm is passing? Maybe it's nearly over?" Paul sounded like a child himself.

"I hope so, mate. I hope so." It was what would be left of them at the end of the storm that worried him.

CHAPTER THIRTY-FOUR

There was a time, she wasn't sure when, time having lost all meaning to her, when she thought that the deaths were going to drive her mad. She was sure they would. She hoped they would; anything for some relief. Going into the children was bearable, she could live with it, or *exist* with it; it was a good feeling and it stopped the screaming and the fear in her head and the Catcher Man's. The real agony came from facing that beautiful light and feeling its potential touching her soul, oh so briefly, before she was sucked back to take each death isolated and alone.

Her soul aged each time the Catcher Man called a child's name, sending her back into their pasts to soothe them in their departure. It was ironic how much she had feared death. She could see it now all too clearly. Death was beautiful. Purifying. Comforting. It was the dying that was terrible. Terrible beyond her comprehension. Perhaps that was the cost for the beauty of death. The yin and the yang. Perhaps it was in the dying that hell existed, the awfulness of it cleansing sins and reducing each person to the essence of everything they could be. She thought she had felt pain and fear with her cancer, but it was nothing compared to this, coming out of each child's terror curled up on the ground, gasping for breath, for life, and all the time aching for the light, to follow the children into its comfort.

It had been an eon or maybe a second or maybe a length of time not quantifiable by normal measures, *in between* time, a paradox only understood without words, but when she finally opened her disoriented, panicking eyes, her mouth sucking at the filthy air, her whole body desperately shaking off the previous torment, the in between was almost empty of inhabitants. Pulling her body upright, readjusting to its proportions, she could feel its void reflected inside her. The cold that had filled a tiny part of her such a short time ago now ran from the pit of her belly up to the back of her throat, creating a hollowness in her, filled with the memories of the deaths.

She turned her head slowly, expecting to see the looming bulk of the Catcher Man, impassive at her side, ready to call the next child, the only in between child left, little Callum, who was staring at her, one hand in Laura's, one in Peter's. She didn't like the way they were looking at her. As if she were a stranger. And she didn't like the way that looking at Laura and Peter made her eyes hurt, their brightness too much to bear. Her eyes sought out the Catcher Man and they found him curled up on the clearing ground, his coat now way too large for his form, his presence fragile like a jarring hologram, as if he was almost not in between. He was almost nowhere. She stared at him with the same horror with which the children were looking at her.

Her mouth felt as if she had been sucking on dry ice, and she wondered if it would ever feel moist again. Looking down at her arms, at the blue veins which ran all the way along them now, the nails at her fingertips translucent black as if gateways to the emptiness inside and around, sorrow overwhelmed her as the reality of what had happened sunk in. What was it he had said, so calmly, so devoid of emotion? *I'm ending. You're beginning.* Why hadn't she thought harder about it?

The children were coming toward them, and she knew there wasn't much time. Sitting beside him, her mother's dress spreading out around them on the damp ground, she leaned forward and held his now delicate hand once again. His existence fluttered inside her in its death throes.

I think I understand now. She said the words without speaking, and his eyes flickered open, the blackness of his matching hers as they locked gazes.

I don't get to go into the light, do I?

His lids slipped down for a second, then opened again.

I don't get to go home and I don't get to die.

Her heart crumbled with the memory of the light. So much understanding tore at her soul that she screamed inside, making them both flinch. *I have to stay here alone, don't I? Stay here alone and take the deaths.* Already, in the distance of her mind she could hear terrified voices calling out to her. And she had a feeling that when he had gone it would get worse. Much worse.

He didn't answer; not silent from any sense of pity, that was an emotion he didn't understand—she knew that he was saving the last of his strength for Callum. For what they had to do for him. Three pairs of children's feet appeared cautiously in her range of vision and she looked up, smiling.

"Can we go home now, Alex?" Laura's voice was a whisper, her disbelief that Alex was still the same person clear in her voice, and Peter barely peered out from behind the girl's legs. *I must look like a monster to him now. The stuff of myths and legends. The bogeyman.* She tried to smile, but the expression felt uncomfortable on her tightened skin, the blue veins there not having the give in them for humanity.

"In a minute, sweetheart. We have to send Callum after the others first."

The little boy shook his head vehemently. "I don't want to go. I don't want to go back there. And I don't want to leave you here."

Inside her, Alex could feel the Catcher Man slipping out of existence. There were only minutes left, ticking away. His clock was almost unwound. Staring at the children, the ocean of sorrow inside her roared out her grief. Oh, how easy it would be to let the boy stay with her. To keep her company in the lonely forever that stretched out ahead. She looked into his young face and lied.

"But you're the last, Callum. And you know what that means, don't you?"

He shook his head, and she was pleased to see that he didn't look at her differently. Not like Laura and Peter. To him she was just the same as she had been when he'd took her hand in the bathroom, or held his finger across her lips in her bedroom.

"This time I get to come with you. We'll go into the light together and forever. Won't that be wonderful?" Tears that she was no longer able to cry flooded her insides as he smiled.

"Really? That's really what happens?" She nodded, and then his expression darkened. "But Mr. Wentworth will bury me in the cellar and leave me there. . . ."

Reaching out one of her alien hands, she stroked his soft cheeks. "Trust me, Callum. None of that matters. Only getting to the light. That's where you should be. Where you belong." Her voice was all wrong, high- and low-pitched at the same time. The boy didn't notice.

"And you'll come with me? You promise?"

The universe shook inside, cracking her heart. "I promise."

For a moment he paused, looking at the empty storm that had held him for so long. He smiled, happily. "I think I'm ready."

Summoning the very last of his strength, the Catcher Man whispered the boy's name, and for the last time, the in between froze.

When she finally came to on the forest floor, her head resting on the empty coat that was all that was left of the Catcher Man, Alex knew she had left the worst behind her. Mr. Wentworth had not strangled Callum, but killed him slowly and brutally, and despite the receding pain, she knew in the cold core that was what was left of her soul a part of her would always be screaming from the death and humiliation she took for the boy.

But that wasn't the worst part. In all its awful glory the dying wasn't what had broken her heart. No, her heart broke before she was dragged back from the edge of death. It shattered when he ran into the light. Ran into the light and left her without looking back. Not once.

Looking up at the live children, she sighed, causing the forest to tremble, and the incessant rain slithered down the trees.

"You have to go home now." Taking them by the hand, she wondered if her voice sounded as empty as her heart felt.

CHAPTER THIRTY-FIVE

At the edge of the woods she releases them, pulling the blue fire back into herself, and it seems to her that they step through the walls of a bubble, out of the gloom of the in between and into the cobbled road of the village where the rain has finally stopped. Watching through the overhanging branches, she sees so many things, drinking it all in. The lights in the windows of the pub are bright, almost too bright for her black eyes to look at, and through them she can see figures moving, rushing out to greet the two children running toward the building.

She knows that the two missing men will soon come down from the Tucker's farm and they will have stories of their own to tell of children in the woods. They will sit by the comfort of their fires and tell their tales, tales of ghosts traveling in the storm and a night of murder and madness. One day, a blink of an eye in time away, Peter will be an old man, the only one left to remember, and after he is gone it will all become folklore, more country stories and secrets whispered at bedtime.

Staring at it all, all the bright light and life, she won-ders if it was like this for the Catcher Man when he be-gan. Did he carry this sadness? Or was he saved from it by never being human? She wonders how long it will take for her humanity to fade. A century? A millennium?

Although it is still wet and cold in the wood, over the village the clouds are breaking, a burst of sunshine flooding through, highlighting the small crowd gather-ing the children to them. She sees Emma Granville hold-ing the small boy up, smothering him with kisses, raising him above her head and laughing, as if he were a sacrifice to an ancient god.

Two men move away from the group, staring out toward the wood, and she drinks their image in as they call her name. Paul looks thinner and tired, and she knows that Mary is dead, and she knows that Simon will go back to London and slowly recover, maybe haunted by dreams of the past and of her, and of the tales Laura and Peter will tell of their adventure in the forest, but he'll be able to live with them. In the comfort of the concrete and glass city, he'll persuade himself that she is dead and gone, and he will learn to live with it.

Simon is starting to jog toward the bank of trees, and for a moment she just watches him and allows herself to think of what could have been, if only for the few months she had left when time was still important. The trees shake and above her thunder screams for her. She doesn't want to see how in the future, when he has re-covered and married and had children of his own, and a storm breaks overhead, he will pause in what he is doing and allow himself to recall the bittersweet mem-ory of her and their one night together.

She takes one long last look at life and love before

turning her back on it, bare feet walking strongly on the forest floor, the long leather coat almost reaching the hem of her dead mother's dress. In her head the screams of the lost and dying children are becoming too painful to ignore, and accepting the legacy left to her, she gathers the storm and moves it on toward them, to their deaths and to their journeys into the light.

SARAH PINBOROUGH

BREEDING GROUND

Life was good for Matt and Chloe. They were in love and looking forward to their new baby. But what Chloe gives birth to isn't a baby. It isn't even human. It's an entirely new species that uses humans only for food—and as hosts for their young.

As Matt soon learns, though, he is not alone in his terror. Women all over town have begun to give birth to these hideous creatures, spidery nightmares that live to kill—and feed. As the infestation spreads and the countryside is reduced to a series of web-shrouded ghost towns, will the survivors find a way to fight back? Or is it only a matter of time before all of mankind is reduced to a…BREEDING GROUND

THE
FREAKSHOW
BRYAN SMITH

Once the Flaherty Brothers Traveling Carnivale and Freakshow rolls into Pleasant Hills, Tennessee, the quiet little town will never be the same. In fact, much of the town won't survive. At first glance the freakshow looks like so many others—lurid, run-down, decrepit. But this freakshow is definitely one of a kind....

The townspeople can't resist the lure of the tawdry spectacle. The main attractions are living nightmares, the acts center on torture and slaughter…and the stars of the show are the unsuspecting customers themselves.